Rivka's War

"Thoughtful and inspiring."   —Susan Isaacs

"Outstanding."   —Just Reviews

"A must-read."   —*Baltimore Jewish Times*

"A compelling heroine."   —*Publisher's Weekly*

Even You

"A gripping novel."   —*Manhattan Book Review*

"Solidly entertaining."   —*Midwest Book Review*

"You will stay riveted."   —AuthorsReading.com

November to July

"A healthy dose of adventure."   —Kiwi Book Advisor

"Entertaining."

"Beautifully written."

"A gift."

     —Amazon Reader Reviews

This Storied Land

a novel

Marilyn Oser

for Mark, with my thanks

Grateful acknowledgement is made for permission to print the excerpt from "Each of Us Has a Name" by Marcia Falk (adapted from a poem by the Hebrew poet Zelda) from *The Spectacular Difference* (Cincinnati: 2004). Copyright © by Marcia Lee Falk.

Also by Marilyn Oser

Rivka's War

Even You

November to July

Palestine: In the fifth century BCE, the ancient Greeks learned of a district of Syria called Palaestine located between Phoenicia and Egypt. The place name was widely used by later Greeks and Romans, though the land's exact location and boundaries remained indistinct. (Earlier references, to "Peleset" by the Egyptians, or "Palastu" by the Assyrians, or "Philistia" by earlier Greeks are equally geographically elastic and may or may not be related.) Jump to 135 CE, when the Romans crushed the Hebrews' Bar Kokhba revolt, exiled the Jews and leveled Jerusalem. The province, merging Roman Syria and Roman Judaea, was officially renamed Syria Palaestina.

Eretz Yisrael: Hebrew for the Land of Israel, referenced many times in scripture, with varying boundaries. Eretz Israel is an English variant.

1920

Here is a man on another man's back. They appear to be the same height, maybe five-foot-eight if they stretched their necks. The one up to his knees in turquoise seawater is darker complected. He wears short, loose breeches that once were a color but now have faded to drab. There's barely a surf, a matter of indifference to his sinewy legs. The rocks might defeat him, except for the mental map he follows as he weaves his way around and through their eddies and backwaters. It's not a great distance, and he's done this trudge ten thousand times before.

The blunt, pudgy fingers of the man on his back are biting into his shoulders. He (Abdul is his name) has made the natural assumption, based on the uncallused paleness of the hands, that this is a man who does no work. Abdul is wrong there, not having reckoned the strength of those digits. The man on his back is a pioneer in the young field of plastic surgery; his seemingly unpromising hands have saved war-ravaged lives both literally and figuratively. Dr. Morris Toby is in the business of making new faces.

Morris makes one now, a wry face so stretched between bafflement and buffoonery that his bride, already ashore, doubles over in laughter. At least he hopes it's laughter that's cantilevering her out from her hips. He hopes she's not going to puke again. He'd dearly like to leap from this porter's bony shoulders and slosh his way to her; but he'd make worse progress through the scum and spray than his surefooted carrier—and ruin his leather shoes and woolen trousers into the bargain.

"This is how it's done," he'd been assured by the French merchant riding the sea with him and Nellie in the battered rowboat that brought them and their luggage from the ship to the breakwater. "There are plans for a proper port to be built, but until then, this is how it's always been done." As a newcomer, Morris oughtn't to thumb his nose at the custom of the country, even when it prescribes riding piggyback like an overstuffed suitcase from the breakwater to the beach. But there was a boy in the boat bailing water. The boatman's son, presumably. Just a lad of ten or so, who should be in school or at play, who could get hurt out here. Morris thinks some customs are better off jettisoned.

-2-

It had been a leisurely honeymoon. The captain had married them aboard ship between Le Havre and the sea, and Morris had wired ahead to say he'd be delayed some months. They'd made land in La Rochelle, taking their time, getting to know each other as husband and wife. They'd visited the cathedral, the surrounding villages, the historical sites of Aquitaine, then crossed the Pyrenees by train and on foot— Morris proving a better hiker than Nellie had cause to hope. They'd meandered their way through Spain and Portugal, buying up what they'd need to make a home and shipping it on ahead to Jerusalem. Each of them had worked so long and so hard through the Great War and its immediate aftermath— in their early adulthood—that neither rightly knew what to do with all these hours at their disposal.

Evidently, though, they figured it out, Nellie being three months pregnant when they boarded ship in Gibraltar for the rough sail through the Mediterranean. Morris wasn't her first lover, nor even her second, but still she'd had few expectations of him in bed. It suited her that he proved tender and thoughtful and rather like her breakfast porridge: warm, satisfying, never surprising. He was a good man, and she'd been right to follow her aunt's counsel and marry him.

The sea was stormy, the crossing difficult, she endlessly at the rail. Then the landing in Jaffa, he watching her hilarity and his face suffusing with joy. Ah, if she could learn to love him with that same profound and rooted depth of love!

And now here they were in their new home, this Palestine, "this wilderness with its medieval health care system"—so Freddie Williamson had written Morris.

-3-

Hats! From the carriage such a riot of colors and styles in what covered the heads criss-crossing the crowded streets. Tasseled red tarbushes, black fur-trimmed shtreimels, checkered keffiyehs, khaki helmets, flower-strewn straw bonnets, silken skullcaps, embroidered cotton kerchiefs, peaked laborers' caps, businessmen's bowlers, nun's hoods, a turban or two, dry bunches of twigs balanced upon a woman's head. Nellie was accustomed to Parisian men forever in black top hats or homburgs, with the occasional pale straw boater in high summer; and on every Parisian woman's head, an up-to-the-minute frothy sameness. This jumble here was a revelation to her— and a puzzle.

-4-

Tarbush: a kind of fez, brimless, close-fitting, flat-topped and silk-tasseled, made of felt and customarily reddish in color.

Keffiyeh: a head covering fashioned from a square scarf of cotton or mixed cotton and wool, commonly used as protection from dust, sand and sun. In Palestine, in the tumultuous years ahead, the black-and-white-checked keffiyeh worn by peasants was to become a symbol of Arab nationalism.

Shtreimel: a circular-shaped fur hat, usually black and generally worn by Hasidic (ultra-orthodox) married men on Shabbat, Jewish holidays and special occasions. It being an ordinary weekday, the shtreimels Nellie saw must have been on their way to a *bris*.

-5-

The notion that clothes make the man dates back in Latin (*"vestis virum facit"*) to Erasmus citing Quintilian in his *Adagia*. It enters English in 1445, appearing in *Peter Idley's Instructions to His Son*, an otherwise obscure manual that advises "For clothing oft maketh man." Shakespeare lifted the idea for Polonius's advice to his son in *Hamlet*, "The apparel oft proclaims the man." Mark Twain outdid them all when he quipped, "Clothes make the man. Naked people have little or no influence on society"—an opinion that ignores the notorious influence of pillow talk.

-6-

Rivka Ben-Yohanan was out inspecting the groves when the horse-drawn diligence brought them. She'd been keeping an eye out for them since they'd written ahead saying they'd stop by. Stop by? Rehovot was miles out of their way, but here they stood as if becalmed, an awkward couple, Nellie a head taller than Morris, dressed in a traveling suit much too heavy for the season. Rivka sat them down to a nice glass of tea.

The one Russian custom Rivka clung to was to keep purest water bubbling at all times in a brass samovar. She'd picked up the samovar in Jaffa from an Arab junk dealer who'd got it from a Jew who needed money for passage back to Odessa. Avram, her husband, liked to grumble that the tiny flickering flame made the room hot. But Avram never felt comfortable indoors, and besides, having water ready at the boil made the place feel homelike to Rivka. "Care for a glass of tea?" was the first question she asked any visitor.

"Rough crossing," Morris said.

"Almost always in the Mediterranean," said Rivka.

"We refused full breakfast, just had biscuit."

Nellie's lip curled. "The tea was brackish."

Already Rivka was taking a liking to Nellie, who seemed quiet and composed, yet had the appealing air of one who is, by long habit, ill at ease. She began loading up a plate with bread and olives. Nellie, looking queasy, said not to bother herself.

Their talk turned to the peculiar way they'd been brought ashore—the Arab porter approaching the dinghy through the surf and presenting his back to the gunwale to be mounted. "'Ladies first,' offered my gallant husband," said Nellie, with a strained smile.

"My dear, I could hardly go ahead and abandon you to that overloaded washtub," offered Morris, with a small bow.

Morris was harder for Rivka to warm to. Chubby, pasty, with pockmarked cheeks and dun-colored curls, he typified for her the very opposite of strong, tanned and capable manhood, which was the template of Jewish Palestine. Avram himself could have set the standard. She'd fallen for his bright white smile, his darkly playful brown eyes, the way worry gathered in the star-shaped crease at the bridge of his nose. Six months these two had been honeymooning, and still they behaved so formally with each other, Rivka had doubts they'd ever actually undressed. She and Avram, in their three-hour honeymoon, had rounded all thirty-two points of the compass. Then it was back to work for them both.

No, Morris was nothing like Avram. But neither was he like the hunched, lank Yeshiva boys commonly arriving from Eastern Europe on every immigrant boat—and just as commonly about-facing and leaving on succeeding boats without ever understanding this country or really wanting to try. Morris seemed more British than Jewish, and for that reason, too, Rivka held herself back.

"Tell me, how is Gena?" Rivka asked. He was, after all, the excuse for their coming by.

Gena Fillipov was a mutual friend. He'd once—in 1917, could that have been only three years ago?—proposed marriage to Rivka. By the war's end in 1918, he'd been a horribly wounded patient under Morris and Nellie's skillful care. Nellie grew animated now, telling Rivka of the paintings he'd been doing, his growing popularity in the Paris art scene. Avram paced through the room and right back out again, not scowling as Rivka feared he might, but keeping watch over this intrusion into their day. When he barged in again, Rivka shot him a beseeching glance, and he invited the doctor outside to have a look at their new well. She watched Morris adopt a posture of interest. A well was something he might never in his life have given a thought to, but who knew? The information could be needed here in Eretz Israel.

They'd been in the Land all of eighteen hours. Nellie was going on now about—of all things—the hats she'd seen, what they might be able to tell her about Palestine's people. Rivka thought: this woman has crossed the Atlantic from Canada to France, nursed wounded soldiers through the worst war in history, clerked at the Versailles Peace Conference, and braved the Mediterranean to get here. And what strikes her is Jaffa's headwear?

-7-

The Fourth Lateran Council of 1215 is known as the "Great Council" for its whopping attendance, including 71 patriarchs and metropolitan bishops, 412 bishops, 900 abbots and priors, and sundry representatives of Europe's monarchs. Among its seventy decrees came an order for Jews and Muslims to set themselves off by their dress. Commonly, this was done with a patch worn over the heart. Later, the compulsory *Judenhat,* a distinctive cone-shaped, pointed head covering, marked out medieval Jews for abuse and exclusion.

-8-

Nellie turned ashen. It was that sudden. One moment sun-touched, the next greenish. She asked to use the toilet, and by the time she returned, her entire manner had altered. She sank into a chair. Her lip quivered. Could Rivka please get her husband?

-9-

With red-rimmed eyes Nellie devoured Morris's worried face, then abruptly turned her gaze to Gena's framed artwork on the wall. One of the newer sketches—Rivka grew aware—was a portrait of Nellie, her mournful eyes, her wide mouth, her widow's peak. The poor thing, she'd been three months along, but the trip must have been too much for her. Right there and then, in Rivka's latrine, she'd lost the child. The way Morris kept hovering over his wife, Rivka thought he deserved to be slapped. She said, "You'll stay here for a day or two until it's safe for Nellie to travel. No, don't object, I insist." Rivka knew what it is to lose a child, though the one she'd lost back in Russia wasn't physically her own. She'd raised him for two years, from an infant, and then been forced to give him up.

He'd disappeared into the chaos of the Soviet Union. She'd likely never know what had, or would, become of him.

-10-

Morris asked to use their telephone, since his friend in Jerusalem was expecting them this very day. The little three-room cottage—bedroom, kitchen, main room, electric lights (seldom used because of the cost)—wasn't yet equipped with a phone. There was one in the office, Avram would show him where. Avram strode through the groves, tall, dark-curled and agile, the doctor trotting in his wake.

Morris reached Freddie Williamson, full to brimming with apologies for yet another delay in his arrival. Freddie cut him short. "Just as well—we've got a riot on our hands up here. A curfew you wouldn't make in time."

Back at the cottage, a girl of about fourteen in shorts and a cotton blouse had been waiting for Avram. He grinned at sight of her. "You're needed," she said. Avram disappeared into the bedroom; reappeared moments later, a rifle in his hand, a bandolier sashing his chest, and a dagger at his belt. That fast, he and the girl were gone.

"He's Hashomer," Rivka explained.

Morris pulled words up out of old memory. "Like *Shomer Shabbes*?" he said

-11-

Shomer: a Hebrew word deriving from the verb meaning to guard, watch or preserve. The Yiddish *shomer shabbes* refers to observing the laws of Shabbat, which runs from sundown Friday to sundown Saturday.

Hashomer: "the Watchman," was a volunteer organization that guarded Jewish settlements. It would disband later that year of 1920, subsumed into a new volunteer organization, the Haganah, "the defense."

-12-

April is a beautiful month in that land. Warm, dry and sunny, it invites people outdoors, it invigorates sluggish winter blood. It incites riots. Early in April of 1920, during the Nebi Musa festival, when thousands of Arabs rejoice and make pilgrimage to the shrine of Moses, tens of thousands were gathered in Jerusalem. According to one account, Haj Muhammad Amin al-Husseini emerged above the crowd on a balcony at the Arab Club. Raising a portrait of Faisal he intoned, "This is your king!" Not the Ottomans, you see; nor the British, who'd ousted the Ottomans; but the Arab Prince Faisal. Amin's words are said to have touched off the riot that Freddie spoke of. Other reports stressed Amin's anti-Zionist invective, his rapt crowd thundering back, "Palestine is our land, the Jews are our dogs!" Still others suggest that the Jews themselves sparked havoc by manhandling an Arab who carried a nationalist flag—or by trying to spit on that flag—or by some other provocation known or unknown. There even were some who blamed the British police or military for stirring up the trouble.

Whatever the instigation, knives were drawn, stones hurled, shops looted, homes ransacked, synagogues set afire, tombstones pulverized, women violated, men murdered. Frantic victims scrambled from street to street dribbling blood, howling in anger, pain, fear or grief. Over four strife-torn days, the Jewish quarter of the Old City was mauled to shambles.

-13-

They were embarrassed, befuddled, grateful. They'd been given their hosts' bed to sleep in, while Rivka spread pallets for herself and Avram on the kitchen floor.

"Are you very disappointed in me?" Nellie asked. Whined, actually. Not a welcome sound, nor one Morris was used to hearing from her.

Morris kissed his wife's forehead, her fingers, the tip of her nose. "I'm very worried about you, but not disappointed at all. Why should I be?"

"It might have been your son in the latrine."

"In which case he wasn't meant to be. Or she. Not this time." He shifted his weight so that he could peer into her eyes. "And you? Very disappointed?"

A faint peep, a pause, a sigh. "I can't say that I am."

"It wasn't a good time for a baby. We have a new life to make for ourselves, a new country, new jobs. A new baby would only have complicated things."

"You didn't say so. Before, I mean," she whispered.

"No."

"I'm sorry."

"For what?"

"I felt the same."

-14-

An hour or two before dawn, Avram removed his boots and tiptoed into the kitchen. An owl was hooting from the trees.

"I'll make you something? A glass of tea?"

He grunted in the negative as he lowered himself beside her. "Forgive me," he said.

"For what?"

"Leaving you alone with them."

"You had a choice?"

He was silent, scratching his bare chest.

"Anyway, they needed to be alone with one another."

"Did Leila come? I stopped by the village and asked for her."

Leila was their Arab laundress. She'd recently begun to teach Rivka Middle-Eastern-style cooking. Rivka considered herself a good Jewish cook, like her mother before her, but Avram didn't do well on Ashkenazi food. Borscht he despised, though in her opinion there was nothing on a wet winter day like hot borscht with a boiled potato and a little flanken. If you could find the meat, if you could afford it when you did. Cholent he liked, but it didn't like him. He quoted her from the Talmud: "'Before a man eats and drinks he has two hearts. After he eats and drinks, he has but one heart.'" To which he added, "After he eats cholent, he has but to fart." So Leila was teaching her to use tomatoes and cucumbers, to cook with olive oil and chick peas, with rice and lentils. Leila had, indeed, come by, bringing her two little ones with her.

"How do you feel about having children?" Rivka asked.

Avram, nearly a-snore, roused himself. "From where does this come?"

"We've been married over a year. I just wondered."

"A year is not so long."

"We're not getting any younger."

"You're eighteen. I'm twenty-eight. What's the hurry?"

Actually, she was twenty. She said, "Leila is barely eighteen and already has two children who go potty."

He got onto his elbows, gave her a little poke with the part that, according to him, spoke the most eloquently, and according to her, spoke the most plainly. "You want two children who go potty?"

"In truth? Not yet. I love working the orange groves." She'd been hired to manage the packing shed for the owner, her boss, who sometimes traveled for lengthy periods. No one knew where he went, or why, though she had her suspicions. Meanwhile, she'd been slowly gaining the trust of the Arab field workers, no easy task for any woman, much less one who was blond-haired, cornflower-eyed, taller and rangier than most of them. She had hopes of developing one of them as a contact, a source of information. At heart, she was a spy.

"The Land needs people," Avram said, stroking her.

"I applaud your nationalist fervor," she responded, moving underneath him.

-15-

Ashkenazi Jews are those whose ancestors settled in northern and eastern Europe. Their traditional language was Yiddish. Hebrew was reserved as a holy language used for sacred purposes. Ashkenazi Jews began returning to, and settling in, Palestine beginning in the 1880s.

Sephardi Jews are the descendants of those who settled long ago in Spain and North Africa and Western Asia—as well as those who never left Palestine. While they used many languages—Ladino, notably—Sephardic Hebrew was the language commonly spoken in Palestine.

Rivka, having been born and grown up in Russia, was Ashkenazi in her bones. Avram, having been born and grown up in Palestine, was Sephardic.

-16-

Picture your quintessential Arab.

Now picture an unimposingly short man with red hair and

blue eyes and a lisp. That was *Haj Muhammad Amin al-Husseini*. Nellie would witness him rallying the crowd one Friday in 1924, when in error she'd get caught up in a river of men, a river that would sail her almost within the precincts of their mosque. Nothing bad would happen to her then, other than utter terror. Despite his lisp, Amin was expert at inflaming his people.

-17-

Prince Faisal—"that dark-skinned replica of Christ," per Upton Sinclair—was, by all accounts, the leader of the Arab nationalist movement at the time of the Great War. He it was who rode with Lawrence of Arabia; or rather, Lawrence rode with him. By his British and French allies, he'd been promised a great nation for the Arabs, with him as its leader. He was mild mannered and willing to sit down together with the Zionists, to entertain their visions of a Jewish state somewhere in Palestine.

Wartime promises are made to be broken: the British and French, in a secret treaty, carved up the Middle East to suit their own interests. In due course, by asserting that not all parts of the old Ottoman Empire were ready for full independence, the League of Nations established European mandates for the Middle East. Each mandatory power was tasked with "rendering administrative advice and assistance until such time as [the countries] are able to stand alone." At the San Remo Conference in April of 1920, Britain received the mandate for Palestine, Transjordan and Iraq; France received the mandate for Syria and Lebanon.

Faisal was made King of Iraq in 1921. Still he dreamed of an Arab state, free of the Europeans, encompassing Iraq, Syria, the entire Fertile Crescent.

Herbert Samuel was Britain's first High Commissioner for Palestine. His arrival in June 1920 sent shivers of delight through the Jewish world. The appointment of one of their own struck them as another confirmation of Britain's intention to honor the Balfour Declaration. Initially published in 1917, this British statement of support for a Jewish homeland in Palestine had subsequently been written into the League of Nations covenant and then again into the San Remo agreement: a wartime promise being kept—or at the least, re-pledged twice over.

Immediately following the Nebi Musa riots, Amin al Husseini had been sentenced to ten years in prison, though by then it was *in absentia*, Amin having fled to Transjordan. Among Herbert Samuel's earliest acts was commuting Amin's sentence. He invited the Haj back, declared him the Grand Mufti, and—icing on the Arabs' cake—suspended Jewish immigration for a period of six months.

Why was Samuel bending over backward to please the Arabs? As recompense for his being a Jew? Because the Arabs were furious with the Balfour Declaration and its re-affirmation? Was he thinking he could in one stroke establish good relations with Transjordan and have a single Arab leader to deal with—one now very much in Samuel's debt? Amin's family, the Husseinis, were leaders in Jerusalem. Wealthy, powerful and numerous, they were usually at odds with the other influential families—chiefly the Nashashibis, who boasted lawyers, politicians and scholars among their kin.

To raise one family above the others: an act that sent ripples throughout Arab Palestine.

Within a year, the Grand Mufti would be made president of the Supreme Muslim Council. Money would flow in. In those early years, he'd use it to restore the Dome of the Rock and the Al-Aqsa Mosque, both of which were crumbling to pieces. However much these works cost, over the years a lot more of the money would go to buy arms and to secure Amin's position. How much went into his own pocket is a matter of debate to this day.

-19-

Rivka knew a Nashashibi cousin—or rather, Avram did. A fortyish, gentlemanly fellow, he adored music and played the violin, as well as several Middle Eastern instruments. In those early days, when it was still possible to socialize with Arabs, she was invited on occasion to hear him make music. She was much taken with the haunting sound of the lute-like oud, and was honored when he dedicated to her one of the melodies he played on it. Some years later, at the Palestine Symphony, they'd chance to come face to face, but by then it would be prudent only to nod at one another in passing.

-20-

Before taking leave of their hosts, Morris and Nellie gave Rivka and Avram a porcelain fruit basket they'd bought in Portugal as a gift intended for Freddie Williamson. Oval in shape, with a flared top and small pawed feet, it was pure white inside.

"This is our first nice thing," Avram said, running his fingers across the blue enameled sprigs and gilt highlights on its outside. "Anything will taste better served in this dish."

"Anything?" asked Rivka. "Even something Ashkenazi?"

He flashed her a grin that vaguely unsettled Nellie. "Especially Ashkenazi," he said.

-21-

Rivka took to balancing herself in the porcelain basket when Avram would come home late at night. Naked and on one wobbly foot, she beckoned him in the moonlight. Never at the new moon, though. At the new moon the room was dark, and she didn't want him tripping, the dish getting broken.

-22-

Jerusalem, in the poet Dante's cosmology, sits at the very center of the inhabited world, exactly as one would predict. It's directly opposite the Mountain of Purgatory, on the same line of longitude—and also on a line with the very bottom and center of Hell, which is Lucifer's bum-hole.

-23-

Their welcome in Jerusalem would have been more expansive without the "unrest." Yes, the city was quiet today, but no one knew how long that would last. These things tended to spread.

"Spread?" Nellie said. "How?"

Freddie Williamson peered at her as if a houseplant had spoken up. A half-dead begonia, say, which was exactly how she felt. They'd been on the road all day, and she was hot and dirty. A bath would be nice. A place to sit still, without any jouncing. To sit very still, without dust blowing in her face. So still, she'd have no compulsion to crane her neck, strain her eyes and throw herself open to every glimpse, every impression. The land had a stark, barren beauty, but she needed respite from it.

"Spread like influenza," Freddie said in an accent so glaringly posh, she suspected it came not from Eton and Oxford, but from a mediocre teacher of elocution. "It pops up here, pops up there," he went on. "Who knows how it gets from here to there? Faster, it seems, than butterflies can flit. Ideas among these people are an infection."

Her eyes sought Morris's. *These people?*

He'd have taken them out for a festive meal, Freddie added, but not tonight. Not until he felt safe doing it. Then they'd do it. "Meanwhile," turning to her, "use the time to settle in. I know you'll want to find the proper house to rent. I'd recommend you start in Talpiot—an up-and-coming Jewish neighborhood, quite safe."

Her thank you came out in a piddling murmur, veiling her exasperation.

To Morris he said, "Tomorrow I'll bring you around to the office, show you what we've done so far, introduce you to Storrs. I've no doubt you'll be impressed with our operations. We've come quite a way in the last year."

Morris was cordial, she noted, but far from effusive. The meeting of two old friends who'd been together at the front was altogether stiffer than she'd expected—even for one as staid as Morris. She hadn't foreseen back-slapping or long, beery reminiscences, but neither had she imagined this stand-offishness, as if they only slightly knew each other.

-24-

They were booked in a suite in the second-best hotel in Jerusalem—so Freddie described it. It was more than ade-quate. Too much luxury would have given them qualms in a land this sunken in poverty. "Storrs?" she asked, once the door was safely closed behind them, and she'd collapsed into the nearest chair. Morris bent, removed her shoes, began massaging her feet.

"British military, a high muckety-muck."

"That's one of those parliamentary terms? Muckety-muck?"

He smiled. "You're not in politics anymore, darling. You're back in health care, where you belong. And in a country where I suppose every Englishman is in some sense a muckety-muck."

"Freddie doesn't seem to understand I'm here to take my own part. He treats me like the little wife."

"Oh, well. I'll take care of that tomorrow. Or as soon as I can understand the situation here, and where we fit into it."

"You're a doctor. You're setting up a hospital. I'm a nurse. I'm working with you on getting things going. Isn't that what we came out here for?"

Morris removed his jacket and carefully hung it away. "That had been my understanding," he said finally. "I suppose everything is subject to change...."

-25-

Fair-crested, joy of all the earth....
Walk around Zion,
circle it;
count its towers,
take note of its ramparts
—Psalm 48

-26-

Nellie did find a lodging in Talpiot, a lovely house with three bedrooms and a garden. Palm trees sheltered the garden: so exotic, could she ever come to think of it as home? They'd sent their luggage on ahead, and by the time they arrived, their clothing was already laid neatly in drawers. The house, it turned out, came with servants, a man and wife of middle age, he to do the yard work and she the cooking and housework.

-27-

The wall that rings Jerusalem's Old City was built by Suleiman the Magnificent in the 1530s atop an older ruined fortification. Roughly twelve meters in height and two-and-a-half meters in thickness, its length of 4,018 meters is pierced through by seven main gates. In 1927, the San Remo Hotel would open its doors in the new city growing up outside of those Ottoman walls. Across the road from the San Remo would be the new Bikur Cholim Hospital, which was to be completed about two years before the hotel.

Bikur Cholim was half-built when Morris saw it, having gotten together with Freddie for a long walk. The cornerstone for the hospital had been laid in 1912, but war and then lack of funds had plagued its construction. When finally completed, the new hospital would have five floors. The first floor would house the kitchens, the sterilization room, a laundry, a mortuary and a garage. The second floor: waiting rooms, clinics, laboratories, and employee quarters. Third floor: administration, pharmacy, isolation rooms, wards, library, synagogue. Fourth floor: Internal Medicine, various wards. Fifth floor: Obstetrics and Surgery, operating rooms, neonatal room, various private rooms and wards. All this was pointed out to him before Freddie took Morris inside the walls of the Old City to visit the hospital's predecessor, dating back deep into the nineteenth century and still operating with one ward for men, one for women.

Then they went out for a drink and a long talk.

-28-

"Promises are like pie crust." Though common use of the expression probably dates from satirist Jonathan Swift's *Polite Conversations* of 1738, it dates back at least as far as August 1681, when essayist Heraclitus Ridens wrote, "He makes no more of breaking Acts of Parliament, than if they were like Promises and Piecrust, made to be broken."

-29-

"So it appears we're not to be building a hospital after all," said Morris later.

"Not?"

"Not."

"But that's what we're here for," said Nellie.

"We're here to build a health care system."

"Words, Morris. How can you have a health care system without a hospital?"

"The hospital, it appears, is taken care of."

"I thought you said—or rather Freddie said—that they had none."

"He did—and I did, too, relying on him—but it appears that wasn't exactly so."

She threw up her hands. "Then what is so?"

"There are some older hospitals, all of them lacking in one way or another."

"Ah, then they do need a new one."

"Well, it appears Hadassah has beat us to it."

"Why do you keep saying 'it appears?' And what is Hadassah?"

"A Zionist women's organization, American, well funded it appea—uh, I suppose. They've sent over a squad of medical people and are planning a large installation on Mount Scopus."

"Where the university is to be?"

"Cheek by jowl, it appears. Which I keep saying because I'm finding it hard to tease out what is from what ought to be or what once was."

"Welcome to Palestine, I guess. I guess we shouldn't expect Jerusalem to run like Paris or London—or even Lisbon, for that matter."

"Lisbon—" he echoed. She saw his eyes go tender, and she smiled.

"Lisbon was such fun," she said.

-30-

"But Morris, what does Freddie have in mind for us, if you're not to be heading up a hospital and me a nursing staff?"

"Clinics. Even more than a hospital, they need clinics throughout the area to serve the local population. You don't find many Arabs coming up to Jerusalem to use the hospital. In general, they go to the *mukhtar*—the village elder—if they go to anyone. In general, they suffer in silence."

"And the Jews?"

"Have a number of hospitals, and doctors."

"Even those who live on a *kibbutz*?" She was so proud to know the word.

"So it appears."

"Morris, we've been brought here under a pretense."

He nodded feelingly, though he only said, "Not so. Freddie is working for the British administration, just as he claimed."

"And you?"

"The same."

After a silence, she said, "And me?"

Again he nodded, and again his answer came discordantly. "Have patience. We'll find you a place."

-31-

USSR
November 15, 1920

My dearest sister Rivka,

So it has happened, just as I told you it would. Finally, finally the war is at an end and the masses have won. The streets of Moscow are filled with people who've come out in celebration of the glorious victory of our Red Army. Oh, to have you here with me to share in it!

You and I, we are not so different, you know. Eretz Israel, as I have come to understand, is being re-created by the Jews into a socialist land through cooperative farming. Jews there, where you are, have stood up for themselves, are fashioning their ethnic identity, and Rivka, it is the same here, believe me.

I will soon be leaving Moscow as a Commissar of Jewish Ethnicity. It's true! Jews are an official ethnic group in this new world we have labored to bring forth; and I, as a valuable member of the Yevsektsiya, as it is called, am to oversee not one, but two key projects. The first is to establish Jewish community centers throughout the old Pale of Settlement. Gone are the synagogues that kept our people in ignorance, in darkness. Those buildings are to be repurposed as schools, theaters, studios, where Yiddishkeit will be not simply tolerated, but encouraged.

In the Crimea, we're establishing a Jewish collective farm. I am charged with the responsibility of encouraging our Jewish families to travel there and join. Jewish farming right here, Rivka, in the Union of Soviet Socialist Republics! You see, you didn't have to go halfway around the world. Right here, you could live on a productive Jewish farm at the edge of the sea, where your Jewish identity is prized and encouraged. You can be here, Rivka, instead of there. Won't you come join me? We have important work for you to be part of.

Have you heard of *Der Emes*, the Truth? This is the official organ of the Central Bureau of Yevsektsiya. I work under the most impressive of activists, Esther Frumkin, who does the editing. I've submitted several stories to her, most of which have been published—and now she has taken to assigning me stories. Just little things, adaptations of old Yiddish folk tales. Simple romances between young people whose parents object to their match based on outworn criteria of *yiches*. I love the Yiddish language, which is so rich in characterizations, but so poor in words for modern items, such as armaments. Well, don't you know I've been making up words that are now accepted in official Russian-Yiddish translations? What a time to be alive, Rivka!

So, my dear sister. Perhaps you will give this some thought. Give up the cultivation of oranges, which are foreign to your blood, and come here to grow wheat to feed your people. Give up the use of Arabic, and a people who do not like you. Give up Hebrew, which was never intended to be used as an everyday tongue. Don't bother studying English. The English people will abandon you, mark my words.

With hope that we will be together again soon, you have—
Your brother's love,
Mischa

-32-

Yiches: a family's history and social standing, its reputation.

Yiddishkeit: Jewishness, a Jewish way of life, though not necessarily a religiously observant way of life, Jewishness being also a culture, and the Jews a people.

1924

-33-

From the US Immigration Act of 1924: "The annual quota of any nationality shall be 2 per centum of the number of foreign born individuals of such nationality resident in the continental United States as determined by the United States census of 1890...." This quota system placed a severe restriction on southern and eastern Europeans seeking entrance into the country, while it favored those from northern and western Europe. The same law excluded Asians specifically and entirely. There was no such exclusion against Jewish persons in particular, but since the total immigration by quota was capped at less than 165,000, and immigration from the lands where they lived was painfully limited, the same end was achieved. America in 1924 effectively stopped admitting Jews. Which was good for the Jews of Palestine, who sorely needed more of their own coming to the Land. Arabs outnumbered them by a factor of eight.

-34-

Avram and Rivka were poor, but poor didn't mean much as long as you were young and strong and eager to work on the Land. They weren't socialists. If you asked them, they'd have said they believed in labor, in building the Land, and in the Jewish community. But primarily they believed that individual enterprise would build the Land. By early 1924, they'd achieved their first goal, of saving up a small pot of money to purchase a tract of farmland of their own.

Rivka had a good head for numbers. She liked keeping track of things, and she was honest. So when Ezra, her boss, started doing a lot of work for the Jewish Agency, he relied on her to manage first the packing, then the fields as well, then the workers, and finally—when Ezra was sent on a Zionist fundraising mission to New York—the business itself.

It had been the better part of two years by the time Ezra got back. Rivka, by learning on the job, had increased their yield by a stout percentage and without sacrificing fruit size or increasing the use of water. Ezra made contact with someone in the Jewish Agency who knew someone in the Arab world who wanted to sell a small parcel and wasn't particular to whom he sold. Finding such a person wasn't difficult. Finding one who could fill Ezra's additional specification was.

The land, a hundred dunams of good soil for growing oranges, came with a house that was larger and better equipped than the little cottage they'd been renting. It stood practically across the road from Ezra's land, his further requirement so that Rivka could continue in his employ as long as possible. How much over and above their nest egg Ezra paid under the table she only suspected. He never said a word one way or the other, not even when the property quadrupled in value over the next several years.

Nor ever a word of suspicion from him that she might be cutting him out with the fruit brokers, or worse, stealing his best workers. Not in a million years would she think to do either. Anyway, as to workers, he used only Hebrews in his fields, she used mostly fellaheen who'd been thrown off their land. Avram didn't like her employing Arabs, but Avram wasn't doing the farming. He was building new settlements, guarding them, training their pioneers.

-35-

Mischa wrote regularly, encouraging her to "return home." His letters called to her mind Papa's early warnings. Before he died, Papa used to tell how the lord of the manor would invite the neighboring Jews into his castle for their so-called protection. When he had them all inside—how easy to do whatever he wanted with them! "Doesn't Mischa think at all about this? To put all the Jews together to farm in the Crimea? Better everyone should come to Palestine."

Avram shrugged. "We'd be safer in the Crimea."

"We'd be safer anywhere, so long as you're not doing the guarding," she said tartly, but with a kiss.

He ran his hands across her burgeoning belly. "How is my little sabra doing today?"

Oy, the thought of another sabra in the house! "Active. As always."

-36-

Dunam: land measurement equal to about a quarter of an acre.

Fellaheen: (singular, *fellah*) peasants or agricultural workers, often share-croppers who lost their fields when the owner of the property sold it away.

Sabra: a Jew born in the Land of Israel—by extension from the word for an indigenous prickly-pear cactus said to be bristly outside, sweet inside.

Jewish Agency: organized in 1908 to foster Jewish immigration and settlement in Palestine. Originally called the Palestine Office, it served as the local executive branch of the World Zionist Organization and later became the liaison between the British government and Palestine's Jewish community.

-37-

Ahuva was born on the twenty-fourth of June—in travail, as God ordained in the time of Adam and Eve. Much as Rivka adored her daughter, she longed for Mama, who might be able to explain what the child was all about. Dark like Avram and full of his restless energy (no surprise after the tumult she'd commanded in Rivka's womb), when Rivka changed her diaper she pinwheeled her arms and legs, kicking and rolling and squealing as if her mother were trying to straitjacket her.

Avram, of course, was pleased as punch. "She hankers after freedom."

"Freedom from what? Her own shit?"

Rivka's orange trees were the same. If they could, she was sure they'd bolt for the fences. In the evening, just before sunset, she'd walk the neat rows of baby trees, some of them swaddled in burlap, and stop to utter small Hebrew endearments to this one, offer a mother's touch to that one. How could it hurt?

-38-

Mama had died in February 1923. For too long a time, Rivka didn't know this. The cousins Mama lived with in Russia got word to Mischa. They assumed Mischa would tell Rivka; Mischa assumed the cousins had done so. A blurred snapshot of her mother's headstone arrived in the mail ten months later: the first Rivka heard the news.

There's something peculiar, something provisional about a delayed report of death. Here you've been going about your daily routine with no sense at all that your world has changed forever. When finally you learn how completely it's been upended, you're bereft, you're undone. Rivka grieved for Mama with all her heart, knowing the hope of ever seeing her again or hearing her voice—always a slim hope at best—now was utterly lost. There yawned a hole in the world where her mother used to be—but that hole had opened up without her being aware of it, without her least niggling suspicion of it day after day, month after month. A hole that is only a hole when you come to know of it throws the most devastating of griefs into question.

Not until 1934 would physicist Erwin Shrödinger devise his thought experiment involving a sealed box, a flask of poison, a bit of radioactivity, and a cat that can be alive and dead simultaneously. Only one's observation of the cat's state in the box resolves the issue, collapsing into either alive or dead. For Rivka, Mama would always be both alive and dead. The ten-month delay made no real difference in that. But still, the delay was bitter.

-39-

Lacking her own womenfolk, Rivka came to rely on Leila. In exchange for Leila's tips on child behavior and cooking lessons and the hours of toil laundering their clothing, Rivka plied Leila with ideas about the rights of women in places like England. Also, Rivka taught her how to read Hebrew. Of course Hebrew. They spoke together in Arabic, but Rivka couldn't read Arabic. She trusted Leila would pick up that alphabet herself, once shown how a written language works. For Leila it was all up to Allah. What Allah wishes, will happen. Allah might grant her the skill to read Arabic—or not, since her husband assured her Allah saw no point in teaching women to read. Reading could only distract good wives from their duties.

-40-

Three favorite ways to prepare eggplant:

1. Peel, cut into flat round slices, set out in the sun to remove the bitterness. Fry and serve on bread. This was Leila's favorite.

2. Grill whole, spoon out the insides discarding the seeds, mash with a hard-boiled egg, dress with lemon juice, oil, salt and garlic, serve with a sliced tomato. This was Rivka's favorite.

3. Pickle with dill, using the small hard ones at the beginning of summer. This was Avram's favorite.

-41-

A few of Rivka's trees grasped the spirit of her attentions, grew straight and tall, greened out, started new branches. The rest, my God, she'd go out in the morning and find them bent, tattered, spindly and unmindful of their roots—as if they'd spent the whole night whoring. Avram suspected the Arab workers of poisoning them. He worked most nights protecting Jewish settlements from Arab marauders, so what else would he think? He had good friends who were Arabs, friends from childhood. A blood brother, one of them. But none of those worked in Rivka's fields.

-42-

Morris and Nellie were invited to garden parties at Ronald Storrs' house, at Government House, at Herbert Samuel's and so forth. All the upper-crust muckety-mucks went, not only British, but Jewish and Arab, too. Nellie had herself a closet full of elegant dresses with the hats and shoes to match, and the right cologne to wear. Did Rivka envy her? Not for the clothing. The parties were an awful bore, Nellie confided, and Rivka was persuaded of it. But the assurance Nellie acquired, the suppleness of mind and body to be able to sail through a room, wafting a scent of lilacs in one's wake, that Rivka envied. No woman wants to feel she couldn't be attractive in such a way if she chose, even if she wouldn't so choose. You want to think you'd be comfortable wherever life conspires to put you, whether a Siberian wasteland, or an Arab village or a muckety-muck's rose garden.

-43-

By this time, Nellie had suffered another miscarriage.

-44-

At one of those parties, between pulls at his third gin and tonic, Freddie remarked, "Why learn Hebrew or Arabic? These people must learn our language. A civilization that can't read Shakespeare in its original? No culture at all."

Nellie suppressed a cough.

"You Jews—" he went on. "You've learned English, in addition to God-knows-how-many other languages. Let the Arabs do the same."

Morris said, "We must get along with the Arabs."

"Once you've gotten established, they'll go away, won't they? Basically, they're a nomadic people. They'll fold up their tents and sally off. Lord knows there's plenty of desert to go around. Let them get off their tails and make it green, like you folks have."

-45-

"Sometimes I think," whispered Morris, his lips at Nellie's ear, "that British philo-Semites are more dangerous to us than British anti-Semites."

-46-

At yet another of what had, to her, become wearisome affairs, Nellie was introduced to Dr. Chaim Yassin, "the distinguished ophthalmologist," a distinction he waved off matter-of-factly. "I'm the trachoma hound," he said with a smile that crinkled the lines around his eyes. Nellie broached a question, and they spent the next hour on a bench in a corner of the garden, deep in conversation.

Hours later, Nellie lay wide awake in a buzz of thought. For too long she'd been downhearted and dull, her days fogged with the gray drizzle of loss, with the pain of her impotence and the old familiar fear that her existence could make no difference in the world. Ah, to Morris, surely. But to the wider world? Tonight, though, she'd learned of break-through work in the diseases of the eye. Tonight she'd found something of importance she felt cut out to do. Improving sight was a tangible good, especially for children whose whole lives could be changed for the better by simple measures that she could teach their mothers.

-47-

Trachoma: a highly contagious disease of the eye caused by the bacterium *chlamydia trachomatis*. Signs and symptoms include eye discharge, swelling, sensitivity to light, and distortion of the eyelid that causes the lashes to rub against the cornea. If untreated, trachoma gradually and inexorably brings blindness.

-48-

June 1924

My dear sister,

I have been traveling all over the Byelorussian country-side, facilitating Jewish community theaters to stage mock trials. Audiences love them, sometimes returning every evening after work for the three or four days in a row it typically takes to put the trials on.

I arrange the room to look official, with a presidium, a defendant's dock, places for the prosecutor and the defendant's lawyer. The "judge" enters, everyone stands up, just as in a real court. My favorite defendant is...Shabbes. Believe me, the arguments we stage are philosophical, and of the highest merit. They have to be so, in order to probe how harmful are our religious traditions. Still, it is up to the jury— our audience—to decide for or against. I love working with young people, who are eager to change their ways. On Saturdays some are doing voluntary work for the community; others earn a regular day's work and give the income to charity. These are more useful customs for our ethnic group than nodding the day away over old books and outworn ideas, don't you agree?

I'm developing now a new kind of presentation to put literary characters on trial. Or I might try the authors themselves. (Pre-revolutionary, of course.) Can you imagine— Sholem Aleichem? I've presented the embryo of these ideas to the Moscow Central Bureau, who encourage me to flesh them out.

Do you remember me telling you of my travels as a "living newspaper," bringing current events to isolated communities, reading to them from *Der Emes*? Sometimes even now, if I can find willing volunteers at a local theatrical club, we still perform the news, especially the lighter pieces. I never think of this as just entertainment. Often our sketches and ditties will generate a discussion (as they are meant to do) about some problem—such as how to overcome lingering anti-Semitism by fostering integration of Jewish workers into agriculture.

Well, Rivka, after the performance last night, a shy boy approaches me—twelve or thirteen, with blushing cheeks and a few pinches of freckles strewn across his nose. He holds out a copy of the very paper I've just read from. He purchased it, he tells me, with his own money earned in the nearby factory. He points out my by-line, the story I've just read aloud, and asks me to sign my name across it. I don't know who was more thrilled as I applied my pen—he or I!

Please don't think me swell-headed. All of this is for the education of the masses, for inculcating the values of Soviet life. If one of my stories gets through to even one of our audience—why, that means that our socialist worldview is spreading.

Your loving brother,
Mischa

-49-

Lenin had died in January of 1924. Mischa made no mention of it.

-50-

Nellie had to shake out her shoes in the morning lest a scorpion be lurking inside. Every so often, one would fall to the floor with a *tic* and scuttle away, its stinger curved over its back. "The things one learns to do in this country!" For instance, time was of no consequence, especially not in an Arab village. Being a half-hour late to a meeting wasn't late at all. And even then one couldn't get down to business. First must come the dance of greetings. Foremost, we praise Allah for keeping us in good health and bringing us together. Then I ask about the health of each family member. Then we repeat our praises of the deity. Then a refreshment is offered me. I turn it down three times before accepting. And after more proper back-and-forths, finally comes the fit time for business.

All this before she could begin winning the mukhtar's approval to visit the women—sometimes she needed the husbands' consent, as well. All this before she could begin winning the trust of the women themselves, which was crucial. All this before the time came to etch into their minds the primacy of cleanliness in face and hands, the urgency of preventing flies. Before they'd let her inspect their wells, before they'd let her near their children's eyes.

Trachoma was a foe worth fighting, worth hating and exterminating. A foe worth all the time it took.

-51-

Even before the advent of female warriors in Palestine, Rivka had served in the tsar's infantry in Russia. Her commander, Maria Bochkareva (long dead now, the harridan) had taught Rivka to make her reports both succinct and accurate. Near the end of the Great War, when she'd made her way to the Land, espionage had brought Rivka and Avram together. They worked as a team spying for the semi-secret Jewish defense groups that became the Haganah. They knew well what to look for, what signified. The intelligence they gathered kept a good many operatives out of trouble.

Whenever immigration was halted—and even when it wasn't, the Mandate's immigration laws being narrow and hedged about with difficulties—Rivka joined Avram in bringing Jews clandestinely by boat onto the beaches north of Tel Aviv. She had to slow down once Ahuva was born, but she didn't see why she must stop altogether. If there was something she could do close to home, she'd take Ahuva with her. No one in those days suspected a woman with a baby carriage of anything unseemly.

-52-

Sometimes Nellie, out on visits to far-flung villages, would stop in Rehovot to see Rivka. Sometimes she'd stay overnight if the visits had run late. Her work on trachoma wasn't going as well as she'd hoped. Nowhere near as well. "It's my Arabic. It's in no way sufficient. I have trouble making myself understood."

Rivka offered to go along as translator.

"It came about quite naturally," Rivka told her contact at the Palestine Zionist Executive. "My friend believes I'm doing her a favor." Bringing the baby along made Nellie's job easier, for Ahuva charmed the Arab women, who cooed over her, sang to her, laughed over her. At some point after the children's eye exams began, Rivka was able to take the baby for a walk from one end of the village to the other. Noticing everything, tucking away mental notes.

-53-

On guard at an isolated settlement on a black, heavy, soundless night, Avram picked up the tobacco scent stealing in from behind him. He loafed as if unaware, an interminable wait. Interminable, his prickling back exposed like that, twenty-five seconds, twenty-six twenty-seven twenty-eight twenty-nine, and now wheeling, he plunges his fast-wheeling knife into the would-be assassin's gut. A reek of blood, the hot intimacy of killing.

-54-

Sometimes it goes another way, and Rivka has to cut a bullet out of his flesh. Avram sits grimly sweating, not a sound out of him as she digs around with a boiled blade.

-55-

Ahuva walked at fourteen months. The fruit bowl from Portugal went up on a higher shelf.

-56-

The village was near enough to Jaffa that they decided on a whim to head over there. Nellie's ministrations had gone more quickly than ever. The mukhtar had everything organized, and the place was a model of order and cleanliness. An old man wearing a skullcap and striped caftan led them from courtyard to courtyard. The women came out and stood in front of their pale-blue plastered houses holding babies wrapped in ragged but clean bunting hung with good-luck charms. Children of diverse sizes clung to their skirts. In each courtyard, Rivka and Nellie were greeted shyly but cordially, "Let your day be happy," to which they responded, "Let yours be blessed." The ground had been swept, and the children's faces cleaned, and they were shooed under the shade of a tamarisk or jujube or fig sycamore tree. Beyond the mud walls, beyond the cactus hedges, the men worked together in fields communally owned by the village.

In the café in Jaffa, where they ordered a lunch of fried onions and yogurt with pita, there were stares, but mostly the two women were ignored by the men sipping coffee and smoking their water pipes. It was a short walk after eating to the high point from which they could peer down on Neve Tzedek, which had filled with Jewish immigrants—and beyond to where the sand dunes had been hauled away to make room for the developing city of Tel Aviv. An expanse called Rothschild Boulevard had taken shape, and all creation looked scrubbed-shiny in the sun.

-57-

Neve Tzedek: literally, Abode of Justice; in Jewish tradition, one of the many names of God.

-58-

The rapid growth of the earlier 1920s was soon to stagnate, and economic depression would begin taking hold. In 1926, Belgium and France suffered financial crisis and devaluation of their currencies. In 1927, the German economic system collapsed. In 1928, Brazil's economy would fail, and by 1929, the crisis would spread world wide.

-59-

The Syrian-African fault line is part of the Great Rift Valley that runs up out of east Africa and through greater Syria into Lebanon. It's the longest series of connected rift valleys in the world, and on July 11, 1927, it made itself felt in Palestine.

A hot wind, the hamsin, was blowing from the east. At three in the afternoon, Rivka was squatting in front of Ahuva, wiping the grit from her daughter's sweaty face while Ahuva played at grabbing for the handkerchief. There came a rumbling, and the ground shook under Rivka's feet, and she lost her balance. The whole thing lasted only seconds, she a-tremble on the trembling ground, Ahuva caught underneath her, shrieking. She got up, brushed herself off, took Ahuva in her arms and sprinted for the house expecting another jolt from—was it a bomb? But no. It was an earthquake, and what tremors followed were mild. Everything in the house was fine, nothing broken, not so much as a saucer. She put Ahuva in for a nap, and when that didn't work, settled her down on the kitchen floor with a pot and wooden spoon.

Avram was in the north building a settlement. Leila was at home nursing a new baby. The following morning, Rivka confirmed with the Arab workers that Leila's village, Zarnuqua, had been unharmed. Somehow they'd learned that Lydda, Ramle and Nablus were all in bad shape, Nablus especially. Houses had crumbled, with hundreds of their people badly hurt. The death toll already had climbed into the hundreds, they said, and more were to be expected. She tried phoning Nellie. The servant there told her that Jerusalem had had wreckage, but all was well in Talpiot, that Nellie was assisting at the hospital.

One of the Arab villages Rivka had visited the year before with Nellie—the orderly village, in her mind—was located nearby Lydda. Pretty houses, but built of clay. She was tempted to take Ahuva and drive there on the instant. They must be in need of help.

She didn't go. There were a dozen good reasons not to go. A Jewish woman alone among Arabs. A child in tow. The possibility of another quake. The likelihood of damage along the road. Her "interesting" condition. But these weren't her reasons. Why she didn't go she couldn't begin to say, except that she felt it would be awkward, and her best intentions might well be misunderstood.

-60-

You're always warm when you're pregnant, and the long months of summer in Palestine are beastly hot enough without having to lug around two babies in your womb. Just after Succot, October in 1927, Rivka finally gave birth. The delivery was difficult, both boys having big heads and wide shoulders. She realized now how easy she'd had things with Ahuva. But they both got born, and she lived through it, and in fact felt a special connection with the babies because, like her and Mischa, they were twins.

She'd contemplated taking three or four days to lie about as the indisposed Ima; she'd earned it—but couldn't carry it off. She was out walking her groves the second morning afterward. Avram insisted on walking with her, taking her arm like she was made of glass. In a way she relished the attention, though she snapped at him for it. Something in her heart wouldn't let her rest easy in motherhood.

Besides, there was a *bris* to prepare for. Excuse her, the *brit milah*. Either way she said it, it meant a lot of work. For all the help that neighbors and friends could offer, Rivka had to be up and about seeing to the disposition of tables and chairs, to the marshaling of plates and cups, to the preparation of salads and breads. Tomatoes and cucumbers and onions to chop, hummus and pita to organize. Rugelach, because she was still Ashkenazi, and she had to make the pastries herself, because no one else here could do it right.

A set of twins and a three-year-old to take care of—thank God for Leila.

-61-

Avram got himself a camera and strutted around taking snapshots. Two boys, he had. Two sons to raise. Esau and Jacob, he wanted to call them. Rivka hoped to name them for her father, Menachem Mendel. In the spirit of compromise, Avram proposed they find names instead from among the ancient tribes of Israel.

"Agreed, so long as it's not Yissachar."

"You have something against Yissachar?"

"He sounds like a fingernail scraping a blackboard."

Avram made up a list of their options, including

annotations he wrenched out of Genesis and Deuteronomy. With a genial shrug, he presented it to Rivka.

-62-

Avram's list of names:

> Reuven—unstable as water
>
> Shimon—fierce in anger
>
> Levi—faithful, but landless
>
> Yehudah—a lion's whelp
>
> Zebulun—settler at the seashore
>
> Dan—also a lion's whelp
>
> Gad—he shall raid
>
> Asher—blessed of sons
>
> Naftali—favored
>
> Binyamin—beloved of the Lord
>
> Efraim—like a firstling bull
>
> Menasseh—has horns of an ox
>
> Yissachaaaaaaaarrr...

-63-

Bris is Yiddish for the Hebrew *Brit Milah*, the "covenant of circumcision." A *mohel* officiates at this ceremony, performed on the eighth day after a male infant's birth.

Hebrew, the holy tongue of the Jews, is the ancient language in which much of the Old Testament is written. Hebrew fell out of use—except for literary, liturgical and mercantile purposes—after the third century BCE. It was revived for daily use as a spoken language beginning in the late-nineteenth century, largely through the efforts of Eliezer Ben-Yehuda, who, in 1908, brought out the beginnings of the first modern Hebrew dictionary. In 1922, Hebrew was adopted as one of Palestine's three official languages, along with Arabic and English.

According to comedian Billy Crystal, **Yiddish** is a combination of German—and phlegm. Referred to as the mother tongue by Ashkenazi Jews, Yiddish is thought to have originated in tenth-century Germany, spreading from there throughout Central and Eastern Europe, and incorporating vocabulary and syntax from Hebrew, Aramaic and the Slavic languages.

Abba: Hebrew for Father.

Ima: Hebrew for Mother

Yidele: Yiddish for little Jewish boy

-64-

Rivka begged Morris to do it, but Morris said the mohel would be better practiced at it. How any mother could stand it was beyond her imagining. These tiny boys of yours. You'd claw to death anyone who hurts them. Yet you have to turn them over to some graybeard, some mohel, and what does he know? She studied the two tiny penises, like tender shoots newly risen out of soft ground. With flawless warm aim, one of them spritzed her right between the eyes. Which one was hard to identify. The boys had no names yet, it being before the bris. They were "the older" and "the younger."

-65-

Women know. They crowd around the mother to distract her while their men observe a great ritual exaltation of the mighty penis—so mighty you can even take a slice off, and still it rules the world. But the poor tyke puts up a caterwaul no mother can bear. It's a wonder Rivka didn't drop down dead right there. It's a wonder she let the mohel leave the house alive. Some of the men turned greenish, their hands groping for their pants. Not Avram: the louder the babies' cries the better he liked it. It showed his boys' moxie. It showed strength. It showed proper outrage against anyone who might dare to violate them. By Avram's standard, both Yehudah and Naftali came through with shining colors. Left to Rivka was the job of comforting the boys afterward. Because there were two, she'd hired a wet nurse. Another Arab jezebel in the house, Avram grumbled, though the nurse was hardly an apostate or a fallen woman, being thirty-six years old, with sagging skin and bulging eyes and a sincere obedience to the law of Allah. She had a sweet and tender way with the boys, but she'd be gone as soon as Rivka could get them weaned.

-66-

Nellie suffered two more miscarriages. With each loss, she withered.

-67-

A pestilence killed off cattle in 1926; a drought parched the crops in 1927. In 1928, with the fields still thirsty, an infestation of field mice ate up most of what managed to grow, and locusts descended to take what was left. The worldwide depression starting in 1929 made loans hard to procure. For fellaheen, especially, these were wretched years. It mattered little to them who owned the land they worked, since they'd always owed their livelihoods to absentee landlords and were used to being in debt to the moneylenders. One landlord or another, what difference could it make?

-68-

An opportunity arose, a land broker offering anonymously a parcel owned by one of Jerusalem's aristocratic Arab families. With Ezra's help and a Hebrew bank loan, Rivka was able to double the size of her farm. Immediately, she employed the fellaheen who'd worked there. They knew the land, and what else would they do? They couldn't read or write.

Avram pestered her to hire Jews instead.

"I'd have to pay Jews higher wages. I can't afford that," she argued. "And anyway, the Arabs are easier to handle."

"It's wrong, when Jews need work."

"They don't want to work here. They'd rather labor in Tel Aviv and stop at a soda fountain at lunchtime and go to the theater or a jazz club at night."

He shook his head. "It's wrong, when our people need work."

-69-

Morris was kept busy setting up clinics, but he wasn't happy. He wanted to practice medicine.

"You're awfully good, you know, at smoothing ruffled feathers," Freddie told him.

Managing a bureaucracy wasn't his idea of doctoring. "It's not the way I want to contribute," he said. He thought, too, that he'd like to teach.

"Contribute to what?"

"Well, to the success of the Mandate I suppose."

-70-

Rivka always spoke of them as the twins. The twins belly-laughed at the same little games; the twins cooed and drooled over the same simple toys. The twins adored each other—so comprehensively, in truth Rivka felt somewhat left out, though she wouldn't admit to it. Always, collectively, the twins, even though they were anything but interchangeable. Yehudah was the inquisitive one. His head swiveled back and forth on his stalk of a neck, his brown eyes perpetually in motion. He was skinny, wiry, always leaning out from her arms to peer down wells and up tree trunks. Naftali was of sturdier build, his eyes the same toasted brown but deeper and quieter. He took in less, yet what he took in he seemed to chew over for a time.

-71-

Teething afflicted Yudi. With each erupting tooth he fretted and whined, putting everyone in the household into a bad mood. When she could get him to stay still, she'd cradle him in her arms crooning *Yudele mein yidele, yidele mein Yudele.* Ahuva picked up the cadence, rocking her dolly with a high, wispy hum. Ahuva was quite the baby-sitter. She pulled her rubbery flesh into all manner of grotesque faces for the twins, jumped about and danced for them, eagerly coaxing a rise out of them. As soon as they crawled, she stalked them, lifting and consigning them wherever she chose, never letting them reach wherever they'd been headed. Rivka overheard her pretending to scold them and worried, do I sound like such a fishwife?

-72-

One evening, when she was sent to kiss her Abba goodnight, Ahuva wrapped her arms around Avram's neck and whispered in his ear, "*Abbale mein yidele, yidele mein abbale.*" Rivka watched him stiffen, not understanding why. Later, he grilled her: what other Yiddish words was she teaching the children? He thought they two had agreed to keep Yiddish between themselves. Wasn't it she who insisted that a new country demanded a new language—in this case, a new ancient language?

"What, you think my babies' lips are tainted from a baby word like *yidele*?"

Hebrew was for him the mother tongue. He'd been brought up on it. German he had no use for and would not speak, although he understood every word of it. Turkish, too. Arabic, yes, he spoke. His English was rudimentary, though improving. He didn't mind Yiddish, but if Rivka made the rule no Yiddish, then he was damned if she was going to fall back on it. Because she'd been right, it signified. People here fought over language like they were fighting over the life of the Jews —as indeed they were.

-73-

The real world is, to a large extent, unconsciously built upon the language habits of the group. No two languages are ever so similar that they represent the same social reality. The worlds in which different societies live are distinct, not merely the same with a different label attached.

—Edward Sapir, 1929

Speak a new language so that the world will be a new world.

—Jalal ad-Din Muhammad Rumi, 13th Century

-74-

Yudi's hair was dark and full. When he was small, it stood out all over his head, a nest of cowlicks, untamable. Tali's hair grew in lighter and finer and so rich in ringlets she resisted cutting it. Often Leila brought her youngsters to play, four of them now, four straight curtains of dark hair above black-olive eyes. The children got along like cousins scampering about, chasing butterflies in the sun. Rivka did nothing to discourage this bond they had. She was sure they'd learn their differences soon enough as they grew. She thought if every mother across the Land did the same, then the next generation would be able to work together and build one country.

Leila was cutting up a watermelon and setting the slices out on a tray. Rivka fanned herself, musing, my children are the world reborn: unafraid, unstooping, unapologetic, bold, sure of themselves. Her eyelids grew heavy, and she let her thoughts run on. My children are sabras: strong, willful, sure of themselves in a way I'll never be. Sometimes I can't bear sabras....

"No, no," cried Leila, jumping to her feet, upending the tray. There was an odd interstice in which Rivka imagined herself scolded. Then seven shrieks went up together, and for some minutes bedlam held sway. Too far away to prevent him, Tali had poked his nose into a wasp nest.

In addition to the stings swelling his face and neck, just imagine the mess tangled within Tali's curls. The poor guy suffered in silence all the while Rivka cleaned him up and applied a salve. He was stoic like that: he'd fall down, scrape himself raw and never say a word. Never again, though, would he permit his mother to grow his hair longer than half an inch.

Tender sweetness of glossy ringlets—no more.

-75-

Leila and Rivka had learned to speak plainly with each other, as best friends do, as Rivka had not been able to do since the death of her friend Tsipi, of malaria late in 1919. On another day outdoors with the children, Leila asked Rivka,

"How do the Jews think this land can be yours?" Much as she'd pondered this point of view, she couldn't understand it. She'd never had occasion to make a like story for herself and her children.

Rivka sighed. "Listen, it's not easy, married to a sabra. He thinks his every action is important by nature. He thinks he's the center of the universe. The world revolves around him."

Leila giggled. "This is the way with every man."

"No, the sabra is different, is special, is—how to say it? He's a Jew born on Jewish soil, he's the hope of all Israel. Nothing he does can be strictly personal, nothing, you understand? Everything involves the future of the Land and its promised people."

Dismay wrinkled up Leila's slender, bow-shaped nose. Was this the answer to her question?

-76-

The twins had their own way of communicating. Some subtle lift of an eyebrow or a finger, some twitch of lip or flare of nostril. Rivka never could catch it, if there was such a sign. They'd be at lunch, say, finishing off a pitcher of lemonade. And suddenly they'd be gone, each rising at the same time and banging off in the same direction with every indication that they had the very same goal in mind. How did they do it? she asked Avram.

He shrugged. "They just do, I suppose."

Even Ahuva thought it was spooky.

-77-

"Spooky action at a distance" is the term Einstein attached to the phenomenon he himself would soon propose, called "quantum entanglement." In the realm of quantum mechanics, when two particles become entangled, if a change is measured in a property of one of the particles, then an *instantaneous* and *opposite* change will occur in the same property of the other particle—and when measured at *whatever distance apart the two particles may be*. Entangled particles can be said to have lost their individuality, behaving as a single entity. Spooky, but true.

1929

-78-

From the Churchill White Paper of 1922, a legacy:
"During the last two or three generations the Jews have recreated in Palestine a community, now numbering 80,000, of whom about one fourth are farmers or workers upon the land. This community has its own political organs; an elected assembly for the direction of its domestic concerns; elected councils in the towns; and an organization for the control of its schools. It has its elected Chief Rabbinate and Rabbinical Council for the direction of its religious affairs. Its business is conducted in Hebrew as a vernacular language, and a Hebrew press serves its needs. It has its distinctive intellectual life and displays considerable economic activity....But in order that this community should have the best prospect of free development and provide a full opportunity for the Jewish people to display its capacities, it is essential that it should know that it is in Palestine as of right and not on the sufferance."

-79-

She kept it to herself. Her body had told her almost immediately, but she'd been leery of saying the words aloud. Four months: her breasts tender, her belly swelling, her appetite skittish.

He'd known, too, for several weeks. Finally Morris said, "You're with child," a phrase Nellie embraced as both dear and quaint.

"I am, yes."

"And it's holding."

"So far."

He reached out his hand, gingerly touching the bulge at her midline. "Is it mine?"

Her eyes flared.

"I'm all right, you know, if it isn't."

"How can you say that?" She began pacing, triangulating their bedroom.

He caught her arm, stopping her. "Haven't you understood by now? Whatever makes you happy makes me happy—even if it's at my own expense."

Nellie had understood—and she hadn't. It shamed her, not to love Morris in the selfless way he loved her. "Of course it's yours," she told him.

-80-

The hard times they'd had in the mid-twenties were past, and now whatever they set their hands to seemed to prosper. Rivka's trees produced a fine crop of oranges in the '28 season. The children were growing fast, full of questions and explorations, with potential for everything, like the Land. Everything, everything seemed possible. At the end of the season, in December, she threw a party in the groves for the workers and their families: Jews and Arabs together dancing and singing half the night. Here, at least, it was possible to believe in a congenial, neighborly, frictionless and open-hearted future. Even Avram caught the spirit—a bit too heartily, in point of fact, specifically regarding a fetching Arab girl of sixteen, if that old, who'd come to the party with her father. It was harmless, Rivka told herself.

-81-

The following month, January of 1929, up north near the Jezreel Valley, workers at Kibbutz Heftzibah were digging irrigation canals when one of their shovels clanked against the mosaic floor of a sixth-century synagogue. Such excitement among the Jews, even those who'd never given a thought either to art or to religion! They pored over the photographs in the newspapers. This find mattered, and most especially to those who'd been holding on through the bad period, who hadn't gone back to Russia or wherever. The central figure rendered in small inlays looked every bit a Byzantine goddess —but was not. She was of Jewish heritage, one of theirs. Mutely she proclaimed their unbroken and continuing presence in the Land. She gave them strength against all those who questioned their right to be in Palestine. She, too, shone with potential.

-82-

The mosaic strengthened the Jewish hand, you see—one more confirmation of the position taken in the Churchill White Paper that their community belonged and was there by right, not by sufferance. Eight months later, when Arab riots erupted near the Western Wall, Morris would find himself blaming the mosaic.

-83-

One of the first places Rivka had gone when she'd entered the Land was the Western Wall. It was a treasured destination, akin to a pilgrimage. Jews have prayed there since the destruction of the Second Temple in the year 70 CE. The vicinity was cramped, dirty, nothing like the great plaza you can visit in Jerusalem today. Arabs' homes and businesses were piled up every which way all about. But the wall itself stood unchanging: the towering sight of it, the cool, dimpled feel of it under her hand, the essence of holiness. As was customary, she'd written out a note of supplication and tucked it into a crevice.

-84-

Islam knew it as the Buraq Wall, the site where Muhammad had tethered his flying steed on the sacred night he ascended into heaven and met God. To Muslims the wall was part of the Al-Aqsa Mosque. They nursed suspicions that the Jews were plotting to seize it all, with the goal of converting the mosque into a synagogue.

-85-

Long and long had Arabs protested against the stream of Jews incessantly bobbing and muttering at the wall. To no avail. Now, muezzins began chanting the Islamic call to prayer just there in their midst, drowning out praying Jews until they couldn't follow their own rhythms and words. Soon, the Grand Mufti was ordering new construction nearby, and pack mules were tracking through the narrow area, soiling the pavement and fouling the air with their droppings. Young David Ben-Gurion proposed "redeeming the Wall." Whatever he meant by that was mild compared to the designs of other community spokesmen. Many demanded an immediate takeover or an immediate legal transfer of the Wall to sole Jewish ownership. Rumors gave rise to counter-rumors; demonstrations to counter-demonstrations.

On Tisha B'Av—the Jewish summer observance commemorating the destruction of both the first and second temples—hundreds of hotheaded Jews took to the streets protesting, "The Wall is ours." In their turn, overzealous Muslims mobbed the Wall the following day, August 16, where they yanked out and burned up countless supplicatory notes, along with any Hebrew prayer books they stumbled upon. A week later, on Friday, August 23, Muslims from Jerusalem's surrounding villages rose in their thousands to pray at—and defend—Al-Aqsa Mosque.

-86-

The riot started with knots of Arabs attacking lone, unarmed Jews in the Old City. Quickly it spread to the Jewish Quarter, where shops were looted and destroyed, and over sixty Jews killed, including women and children. To avoid trouble, four thousand Jews abandoned their homes in the Jerusalem suburbs. Morris and Nellie would not leave. On that they were in full agreement. How could they go, when they were needed for long hours at the hospital? The injured were presenting with all manner of trauma—Jews with broken heads, broken bones; Arabs with wounds from British guns; and British policemen with lesions they made stiff-lipped light of.

-87-

While Morris and Nellie worked to heal the wounded, their house in Talpiot was looted. They got home late to find that their Arab Christian caretakers had fled, possibly in fear of Muslim hooligans. The furniture had been overturned, silver and jewelry taken, their crockery smashed, and—what froze them speechless—every pillow was slashed. Their bedroom resembled an ill-kept poultry house, feathers strewn all over everything, stray fluffs floating on the breeze from wide-open windows. Nellie sank down on the ransacked bed and wept.

-88-

Slashed pillows: a signature gesture of European pogroms against the Jews.

-89-

In the end, they had to stay with Rivka for a few days, their house in such a state and Nellie seven months pregnant.

"You shouldn't be working at all," Rivka chided.

"You're one to talk."

"Me, I live beside my fields. When I was pregnant I could run home if I needed to. Also, I deal with trees, not with malaria, cattle fever, leprosy, who-knows-what."

"I only deal with eyes."

Rivka snorted.

"Except in the middle of a riot."

"I know what you deal with. I've been there with you. You go into their homes. You inspect their wells. God knows what you expose yourself to, along with your unborn child."

"I've already promised Morris I'll stop circulating to the villages. I'll work from the regional clinics. Afula, maybe."

"Afula. That's grand. A Jewish woman traveling alone."

"I'm Canadian. Who's going to bother me?"

-90-

The rioting spread, condensing in viciousness: to Hebron, where Yeshiva scholars were stabbed and stoned and mutilated; to Safed, where Jewish homes were burned down with their residents locked inside, and where children were trampled. To Migdal Eder, Beer Tuva, Neve Yaakov and Atarot. To Ramat Rachel, Motza, Hartuv, Kfar Uria, Hulda and Mazkeret Batya. To Tel Aviv, Nablus, Tulkarem, Jenin, Beit She'an, Beit Alfa, Heftzibah, Mishmar HaEmek, Haifa, Acre, Kfar Hittim, Ein Zaitim and Yesud HaMa'ala.

-91-

In a few spots, including Kibbutzim Beit Alfa and Heftzibah —where the mosaic had been uncovered—the attacks were beaten off.

-92-

God on their lips and swords in their hands....
—Psalm 149

-93-

The reports in the newspaper were terrible. Rivka begged —and failed—to keep Morris and Nellie with her a few days longer. Where Avram was, she knew not—only that wherever he was, he was protecting Jews. He'd been away almost a week when her guests went back to Jerusalem. She shuddered in the night, alone with the children, Arabs all around. Her workers assured her they didn't believe the Mufti's propaganda. But the reports were terrible, the rumors worse, and the nights with her rifle at her side—interminable.

-94-

The Qu'ran on the Jews:

The example of those who were entrusted with observing the Torah but failed to do so is that of a donkey carrying books. (62:5) They are not true believers. (5:42)

-95-

Unemployment in Britain that autumn was topping 12.2 percent.

-96-

...on this land of mine
Conquerors never lasted.

—Tawfiq Zayyad

-97-

In December, Rivka hosted another party to celebrate the end of the season and an abundant harvest. What a difference from last year! Awkwardness and hesitation hobbled Arabs and Jews alike, the one group standing off from the other. By midnight the festivity, such as it was, had worn itself out. The summer's riots had shocked everyone and changed everything. It was the last such party she'd make. In subsequent years, she'd use the money to hand out small bonuses instead.

-98-

British policy must change, warned the Arab leadership. They offered a kind of choice: in Palestine, there could be peace, or there could be a Jewish national home; there couldn't be both. Not to be outdone, the Jewish leadership shot back that a mere fragment of Arabic peoples lived in Palestine, whereas this was the single only country connecting the Jewish fate and future. Rivka grew more convinced with every word—only in Palestine, she parroted, could independent Jewish life be renewed and a special Hebrew culture be revived. With a quizzical smile, Avram said, "And still you trust in a peaceable country? Arabs and Jews striding forth into the sunrise together?"

She chose to ignore the sarcasm. "I do, yes."

"You're stubborn, Rivka!"

"I hope so."

-99-

In those days, the term "Palestinian" had no special reference to the families and clans who'd lived for so long in the selfsame place and felt identity with the selfsame land. The people of Palestine were known as Arabs, pure and simple. Even by most of their own, they were seen as having no nationhood separate from their Pan-Arab identity.

-100-

One night Morris treated one Avraham Stern. Only a flesh wound that didn't require a skilled plastic surgeon, but Morris was the doctor on call. The patient was twenty-two years old, a self-described scholar of classical languages, and a poet.

"What sort of poetry?" Morris idly asked.

"Of dedication, of self-sacrifice, of longing for a sovereign land."

Ardent words, though he spoke them mildly. He seemed to Morris a polite young man, probably not much of a poet. Though Morris was hardly qualified to judge. The only stanzas he knew in Hebrew were the two sung in "Hatikvah."

-101-

עוֹד לֹא אָבְדָה
תִּקְוָתֵנוּ,
הַתִּקְוָה בַּת שְׁנוֹת
אַלְפַּיִם,
לִהְיוֹת עַם חָפְשִׁי
בְּאַרְצֵנוּ,
אֶרֶץ צִיּוֹן וִירוּשָׁלַיִם.

כֹּל עוֹד בַּלֵּבָב
פְּנִימָה
נֶפֶשׁ יְהוּדִי הוֹמִיָּה,
וּלְפַאֲתֵי מִזְרָח,
קָדִימָה,
עַיִן לְצִיּוֹן צוֹפִיָּה,

As long as in the heart within
The Jewish soul yearns,
And toward the eastern edges, onward
An eye gazes toward Zion...

Our hope is not yet lost,
The hope that is two thousand years old,
To be a free nation in our land,
The land of Zion, Jerusalem.
                    —"Hatikvah," Naftali Herz Imber

-102-

Avraham Stern had, indeed, been a gifted student of ancient languages and literatures before he picked up a gun. A follower of the hawkish Ze'ev (formerly Vladimir) Jabotinsky, he would become leader of the most violent of Palestine's Jewish resistance fighters.

-103-

The British government's response to the 1929 riots and the continuing Arab threats was typical, one might even say habitual. Jewish settlement had not taken into account the livelihoods of Arabs, so Jewish immigration must therefore be curtailed.

-104-

But where else were Jews to go? All over the world, immigration was being closed to them, even in places where they'd been accustomed to finding refuge: America, South Africa, Mexico, Canada. Meanwhile, Poland and Romania had been adopting new anti-Semitic policies. It used to be that almost all the immigrants coming up to the Land were

Russian. Now they became almost all Polish. And after 1933, when Hitler came to power, all German.

-105-

"Abba, are you old?"

"Yes, Ahuva, I am."

"No, like really old, like—"

"Like what?"

"Like Ima."

Avram suppressed a laugh. "I'm older than Ima."

"You can't be."

"Why not?"

"Because you talk like us."

"Hmmm?"

"You talk like me and my friends. Not like the other parents, or the teachers."

"You mean without a foreign accent?"

Ahuva nodded.

"That's because, like you, I was born here in this country."

"Oh," she said, and went skipping off as if there was nothing of moment in the fact that most of the Hebrew-speaking adults she knew were immigrants.

-106-

In 1929, the population of Palestine neared a million people. A little over 712,000 of them were Arab Muslims, a little over 81,500 of them Christian Arabs, and about 156,600 of them Jews. The total Arabic population grew in the seven-year period from 1922 to 1929 by about 133,000: in part due to natural increase, in part to better health care under the British Mandate, in part to immigration of Arab workers from Egypt, Transjordan and Syria. The Jewish population in the same period grew by about 73,000, a little over half the increase of the Arabs. But the relative number of Jews in the population as a whole grew from about eleven percent in the 1922 census to over sixteen percent in 1929. The coming seven years would give the Arabs fresh cause for concern.

-107-

Nellie gave birth to a baby girl. Morris, over the moon, presented Nellie with a blue velvet box, inside of which twinkled a diamond ring. Privately, she was of the opinion that the money would better be spent on one of those new refrigerators her Aunt Faye had written about from Paris. A diamond merely sparkled, but think what a refrigerator could do for the little one's health, for the safekeeping of her food. Ah, she was pure miracle, this infant who nestled her downy head against her mother's cheek. Nothing in Nellie's life had ever been so warm and sweet-smelling and lovely.

Now they were a real family, and in the wake of the riots, they agreed on the need to take a side now as Jews. Morris changed his name to Moshe Tobi; Nellie to Elli Tobi. Being cautious parents, they left room for the baby to decide her own national fate. They named her Marian Ellen Tobi.

-108-

Each of us has a name
given by our stature and our smile
and given by what we wear…

Each of us has a name
given by the stars
and given by our neighbors
　　　　—Zelda, translated from the Hebrew
　　　　by Marcia Falk

-109-

Sooner or later, most of them did change their names. David Gruen became David Ben-Gurion...Eliezer Yitzhak Perlman became Eliezer Ben-Yehuda...Szymon Perski became Shimon Peres...Golda Meyerson became Golda Meir...Iccak Jaziernicki became Yitzhak Shamir...Mieczyslaw Biegun became Menachem Begin...Moshe Klaynbaym became Moshe Sneh....

-110-

March, 1930

Dear Aunt Faye,

Yes, I know how eager you are to hug and kiss the baby. In the entire world nothing is as satisfying and joyful. So you must know how sad it makes me to ask you to put off your trip for a little while. The riots have done a bit of damage to Jerusalem, and it will take some time for things to return to normal.

Much love to you, to Jorg, and to Paris—
Nellie

-111-

With each wave of immigration, the Yishuv was forced to adjust to new sorts of people harboring more-or-less oddball manners, habits and certainties. Every group of foreign Jews had to be taken in and made part of the Yishuv—by embracing what was found favorable in their ways and by trying to quell what was not. As the thirties ripened, German immigrants grew to a multitude. Their Hebrew was preposterous. They pronounced their words gutturally with monstrous accents, and they constructed their sentences with grammars that were staggeringly gymnastic. Their ways, too, were singular. If you had any sort of appointment with them, they showed up on time, fastidiously so, and sometimes ten minutes early. Worse, they expected the same fault in you! Every other minute they yammered please or thank you, please or thank you, please or thank you, until you wanted to scream. One newly arrived Berliner, when introduced to Avram, briskly clicked the heels of his highly polished shoes. With a horselaugh, Avram pointed to his own sandals.

-112-

Yishuv: the community of Jews living in Palestine in the years before 1948.

-113-

Telegram from Paris, January 1931:
CARELESS ME STOP BROKEN RIGHT ANKLE STOP DR SAYS NO TRAVEL NEAR FUTURE STOP KISSES TO BABY AND PARENTS STOP FAYE

-114-

After 1929, the violence never really ceased, but nor did the building. Somewhere, always, a settlement was going up. Somewhere, always, a Jew was being attacked, or his store, or his home.

After 1933, when Hitler came to power in Germany, it only got more so.

-115-

September 1933

Dearest Nellie,

Once again, we find ourselves forced to put off our visit. This time it isn't infirmity that keeps us away. This time it's the enabling of Mr. Hitler in Berlin. Jorg is receiving frantic calls for help, and we're off to Germany, our pockets stuffed with money, to do what we can for the Jewish artists he represents.

Next time, no excuses.

Hugs and more,

Aunt Faye

-116-

The children would ask him what the bandage was for, and Avram would tell them that he'd had a bullet—as if it were a splinter—which he'd bitten out of his flesh with his strong, white teeth. He'd grin fiendishly, and they'd shriek, running to and fro while he caught them one by one, covered them with kisses and brought them to Rivka. This feint succeeded until the day Ahuva, with knitted brow, soberly inquired how he'd managed to chew a bullet out of the back of his shoulder. Avram, reddening, stammered out some garbled pretext that put her off. He'd been ashamed of taking a shot in the back and sought to make nothing of it. Rivka's unease about shattered bone and the possibility of infection had overmastered him. She'd called Morris/Moshe, who walked her through the extraction by phone and "looked in" a few days later to check the wound, traveling hours each way to do it.

-117-

Millions of farmed dunams of Arab land were damaged or lost in the early 1930s. An infection carried off eighty percent of the dairy herds. Then a massive migration of starlings wreaked havoc on germinating crops. The olive crop failed, too, in the years 1932-5. Arab peasants, rarely out of debt, went deeper into it.

-118-

Ahuva arrived home from school wriggling with excitement. "We're going to have a Queen Esther contest, and I signed up to compete!"

"A beauty contest?"

She nodded, suddenly solemn, having picked up a hint of something—some spasm of alarm or derision in her mother's tone. "Am I not pretty enough?"

"Am I?" Rivka said, wagging her hips. "Maybe I'll compete in the pageant."

Oh, the poor thing looked stricken! Oh, how to explain?

In Tel Aviv, in the late twenties, the Jewish festival of Purim had ballooned into the city's major holiday. In advance, houses, balconies, automobiles and carriages were decked out with flowers and festoons. Tourists in their thousands streamed from far and wide to take in the dancing, the parade, and above all, the election and crowning of the year's Queen Esther. Editorials were written and arguments touched off over the comeliness of one contestant as against another. Debates were joined over the merits of European features (read Ashkenazi) versus Oriental (read Sephardic), and these had a disagreeably racialist tang.

For once religious leaders found themselves on the same side as Zionists in their paired clamor against a cheap "carnavale" atmosphere. They agreed the wrong values were being glorified, whether by violating the spirit of Judaism in cheap secular entertainments, or by cheapening Jewish women by failing to highlight their strength and valor as pioneers. Rivka steadfastly boycotted the spectacle, and she did a private little jig when the Queen Esther contest was abandoned in 1931. Now—even if it was only in a children's classroom—here was her own daughter, flesh of her flesh, pursuing the same sham of fame.

At Rivka's blithe threat of a rivalry, Ahuva had flushed, her eyes filling. *What on earth has come over me*, Rivka scolded herself, as without another word her daughter slunk off to a corner, where now she slumped, twisting a hank of her hair. Still only a girl, after all, and if Rivka were to be scrupulously honest, not a particularly beautiful girl—except in the way all children are beautiful. But if Ahuva couldn't be beautiful to Rivka, even with a too-low forehead and too-wide mouth, then to whom else could she be?

Instantly contrite, Rivka flew to the cupboard and fetched her choicest table linen, with its soft and creamy touch of lace along the hem. Her first penance was to fashion out of it a costume of pure white majesty; her second, to teach Ahuva how to pace regally within it. By the appointed day, Rivka was able to send her daughter off to school to dominate the pageant in triumph.

-119-

In 1932, Stavit the cow was dropped by her dam Esther, a Damascene, on Kibbutz Kfar Giladi in the Galilee. Her sire was a Dutch breeding bull. The little hybrid grew hardy even in Palestine's rough conditions. Resistant to infection, she went on to produce lavish quantities of milk. Records were made of every aspect of Stavit's handling, for she was key in the Zionists' project to revive, literally, the land of milk and honey. Over her lifetime, she'd complete fifteen pregnancies, and one of her daughters would win a place in the dairy cows' hall of fame with a lifetime production of 53,000 liters. Stavit's own fame would be such that twenty years further on, the newspapers would report her death.

-120-

On September 8, 1933, King Faisal of Iraq died of heart failure, age 50. His brother Abdullah of Transjordan stepped up to wave high the banner of Arab unity, an ideal that had been gathering followers since the Great War.

-121-

Birobizhdan, USSR
October 1933

My dear sister,

I beg to differ with you. How can you call Yiddish "jargon"? How can you so demean your mother tongue, your mother's tongue, in which I write you today? Yiddish is the carrier of all the hopes and dreams, all the fears and aspirations, all the history of us Ashkenazim and all our future as well. And you can abandon it so lightly? Mark my words, Rivka, when you are old and frail, when your teeth have fallen out of your head and your eyes have fallen dim, it is to this "jargon" you will return, for it lives within you and is the very light within your soul.

Yes, I speak of a soul, for though I do not believe in God, I do believe in the people, in the soul of the people, which is amassed from each individual soul, which speaks to you in Yiddish. I say this to you as the scholar I once was. I still remember how you envied my ability to study and how you badgered me until I taught you to read.

Someday soon you must come to visit me at Birobizhdan. We have our own land here, and it is bigger and more fertile than the meager land of Palestine. Neither flat nor mountainous, it is a sea of rolling hills and dales with wheat fields as far as the eye can see. Yes, life is hard here, but it will become easier as the years go by. I live in a small wooden house of Russian design with a neat little yard, a garden, a fence to keep in the chickens. My next door neighbor is from America. Word of our venture has spread even as far as that, wherever Yiddish is spoken—and where, other than among the Jews of Palestine, is it not spoken?

You have called this Jewish land of Birobidzhan "just another Pale of Settlement, another way to corral the Jews and keep them separate." But Stalin is not like that, Rivka, I assure you. How do I know? I sat with the great man himself for three hours attending a play in Moscow. And what play was that? Why, one written by Peretz Markish and directed by Solomon Mikhoels at the Moscow Yiddish Theatre. The great man smiled and applauded as enthusiastically as I— confirmation that one can be Jewish and Soviet.

You write to me about the Hebrew culture that you are inculcating in your children. We have a full cultural calendar here. A newspaper, an amateur theater, our own community orchestra. Even, we have a movie theater!

-122-

Birobidzhan, located at the eastern end of Siberia close to the Chinese border, was established as a Jewish autonomous region in 1931. Yiddish was its official language.

Peretz Markish: Jewish poet and playwright. He would be arrested in 1949 as a "Jewish nationalist" and put to death along with thirteen other writers on the "Night of the Murdered Poets," August 1952.

Solomon Mikhoels: Gifted actor and artistic director of the Moscow State Jewish Theater, which was founded in 1920.

He would be found dead on a road in Minsk in 1948, purportedly the victim of a hit-and-run, more likely murdered at Stalin's behest.

-123-

Yudi was his mother's joy: always cracking jokes, singing as he went about his chores, skipping down lanes in front of her. A happy-go-lucky child, he willingly started school. Tali, not so willingly.

-124-

Leila's husband worked a farm share of forty dunams alongside Lydda's narrow airstrip. The British went into negotiations for purchase of the undivided property, and its owner evicted his ten fellaheen in hopes of speeding the sale along. For this, Leila's husband blamed the Jews. If they would only stop immigrating here, he told Leila, the British wouldn't need to buy up land to build a bigger airfield to bring in more Englishmen to control them.

Rivka had her hands full and refused to hear a word about it. All three kids had come down with chicken pox. Poor Yudi was suffering the worst case. He could be comfortable only in a tin bath of cool water mixed with oatmeal, roosting naked in there making patty cakes by the hour.

-125-

June 1935
Dearest Nellie,
    Never fear. I understand how busy you both are with your work, but that won't bother us in the least. Jorg and I will travel the country, do our sightseeing and our shopping, and spend such time with you as you can allow.

I understand, too, that the upsets in Palestine haven't died down as you'd hoped after 1929—not the way all went quiet after 1921. But Nellie, how long would you have us wait? I think we've been patient long enough. Suppose things get worse, rather than better? Suppose—God forbid—Jorg proves prophetical, and a new European war breaks out?

My dear, I don't want to meet and be introduced to Marian on her wedding day!!! Already she's five. At the rate we're going....

Hugs and more,

Aunt Faye

1936-39

-126-

Rivka went out in preparation and bought herself an Austrian radio set in a handsome two-tone mahogany and walnut cabinet. Although she was assured it could bring in the European frequencies when the weather was right, she didn't even try for them. She bided her time. And just before 4:15 in the afternoon of March 30, 1936, she sat herself beside the radio with the children gathered on the floor around her chair, and she clicked the dial. "This is the Voice of Jerusalem"—and the children went berserk, leaping and cheering and racing in circles. "Shhhh," she said. "I want to listen." The first broadcast of Palestine's very first radio station, but hearing it was hopeless—so she joined her gazelles in their rowdiness until the Queen's Cameron Highlanders band played a march, and with that she paraded them in high struts straight out the front door.

In addition to broadcasts in English, there were times set aside for the Arabic broadcasts of *Hoona Al Koods*, and the Hebrew broadcasts of *Kol Yerushalayim*. Every night at 7:55, Rivka turned on the main Hebrew news bulletin of the day. Afterward, she'd enjoy whatever music was sent out over the air—Beethoven, Mozart, Haydn, Wagner, and other composers she'd never heard of. Who was Pursel—or was it Purcell?— and where had he come from? Sometimes she'd hear Middle Eastern music. The thrumming of the oud still touched her heart.

-127-

The scene: a bright April afternoon along the road between Tulkarem and Nablus. A clutch of Arab brigands sets up a barricade, stops a bus and goes about robbing its passengers, Jew and Arab alike. Somehow, a Jew gets murdered and two more injured, one of them mortally. By the time this news reaches Rivka in Rehovot, two irate Jews have assaulted and killed two Arabs outside of Petach Tikvah—and this reprisal then ignites the rioting that explodes in Jaffa. Stones are hurled, cars upended, buses torched. Broken glass and fresh, wet blood glitter across the pavement under the sun.

-128-

Whether the Arab Higher Committee already had a walk-out in the works or whether they turned the outbreak of violence to their quick advantage—whichever, now they called a general strike to protest Jewish immigration. A few days, Rivka thought, and everything will go back to normal.

-129-

A few days turned into a month.

-130-

Owing to the strike, some Arabs found time on their hands, time to make mischief. All over Palestine, they cut British telegraph wires and pitched homemade bombs into Jewish marketplaces. They buried explosives along the roads, and their ambushes could wreck a traveler's plans anywhere along his route. Many Arabs, lacking guns, made deadly use of whatever came to hand. Never underestimate what can be ravaged with an ably wielded plow handle.

Before the culprits could be caught, they'd melt back into what British soldiers called the "native population," behind market booths in the *suk*, or at *narguilas*—water pipes—on street corners, or over small cups of thick coffee in the cafés, or amid crop rows in village fields.

-131-

Most of the organized Arab attacks made trouble for the settlements, where Avram was patrolling. But even in Jerusalem, even in Rehovot, a mother couldn't feel sure that her children's school building wasn't booby trapped; or that she wouldn't be stabbed on her way to buy underwear for a youngster's growing body, or to have her shoes repaired, or to visit the dentist. She thought twice about taking a bus or a train. Then she took it. What else was there to do but go on with life?

-132-

Ahuva wouldn't be put off anymore with Avram's tales about eyes in the back of his head and incisors that could slide like trombones. The next time one of Avram's wounds required a phone consultation with Moshe, Ahuva held the receiver and acted as intermediary between the surgeon and her mother, whose both hands were busy. Ahuva liked the implied stature of her role and looked forward to the next time she could be almost-a-doctor. But Avram didn't seem to get home very often since the Arab strike.

-133-

My dear sister,

Have you seen the movie Seekers of Happiness, about a family who travel from Palestine to Birobidzhan to begin a new life? Everyone loves this story, from children to old folks. I myself have seen it three times. If you do not have this excellent film in Palestine, who, then, is the backward one?

Mischa

-134-

As a week of rioting had turned into a month, so a month turned into several months. All over the country, Jewish trees were savaged. Rivka had not a moment's respite all summer from worrying over her groves, whether they'd be lost to Arab vandals.

-135-

She charged Avram, when he finally showed up alive and unharmed, with avoiding her and abandoning the children. She was convinced it was his choice to fight up in the Galilee, or on the Lebanon border, rather than, say, the Jezreel Valley, from where he might hope to come home more often. He didn't deny it, much to her confusion. He said the fear of entanglement was driving him off.

"Entanglement," echoed Rivka, arms crossed, foot drumming the floor.

See, Avram knew the Arabs around here. He'd played with them as boys, had bought eggs from them and cheese. He'd helped them repair their wagons, their houses; had taught them modern farming techniques. Near to home, he might find himself battling face to face with the fellow who sold Rivka her yogurt, or his son or his cousin. Even at a day's distance from home, he recognized—thought he recognized— people he'd known since childhood. "It's not hard for me to shoot a complete stranger, especially one who's shooting at me. But when you've known a man since childhood, whose brother you know, whose mother you've watched hanging out the wash, whose father you've seen leading a laden donkey along the footpath to his village...."

-136-

Entanglement: We know their language, we pray to the same God: Allah, El, what difference? We eat the same food; we're rooted in the same land.

-137-

Entanglement: Each of us is a coproducer of a possible future.   —Antony Gormley

Entanglement: When the Arab is observed by a Briton doing X, the Jew will be observed to do the opposite of X.

-138-

Entanglement: (n.) quantum physics term for when the sheets wrap around two bodies in space.
                          — Sol Luckman, *The Angel's Dictionary*

-139-

Entanglement: If you think hate is a good reason for argument, try love.

Entanglement: Avram promised Rivka he would try his best to come home more often.

-140-

Leila ignored the strike—in fact, refuted it by coming to work faithfully, as usual. Rivka was surprised to see her, and grew more and more puzzled as the days and weeks wore on. Obliquely, she inquired how the rest of Leila's family was taking her—her what? Her resistance, was it? Leila gave out an amused little chuckle. "Oh no, nothing of the sort. It is the family's decision that I should keep working for you." By "family" Rivka assumed she meant her husband; though one didn't always know. Perhaps there'd been a council of all of her kinsmen, or even of all of their clan.

Avram offered his opinion that any Arab man would lose face if he ignored the strike—but since they thought a woman beneath contempt anyway, what Leila did mattered not at all. In this way, the family had a small income to rely on.

The country's volatile state of affairs made it impossible for the women's friendship to thrive. It became hard to talk at all without bumping into some incendiary subject, and they found themselves inwardly tiptoeing around one another.

-141-

On one thing the two women found they could agree, and heartily: on the British, who were a queer and fickle lot. Some of them deplored Rivka's people as money-grubbing, chicken-hearted scoundrels—and loved Leila's people as noble and daring knights of the desert. Some of them esteemed Rivka's people as God's chosen and the wellspring of Western culture —and despised Leila's people as backward, filthy, ignorant and primitive thieves. All this, while trying earnestly to do their duty to rule the country fairly. All this while brandishing guns to maintain order.

-142-

The Jewish Council kept urging *havlagah*. Jews kept being killed on buses in the streets. Killed in their own beds at home. Still they practiced *havlagah*. Most of them.

-143-

Havlagah: self-restraint. Defend yourselves when you have to, but never initiate a fight.

-144-

Arabs, too, became casualties of the strike. Hundreds of rioters were killed by the British police. More than a scattering of Arabs were murdered by their fellows: for failing to strike or for wearing the wrong head covering, Turkish tarbush rather than Arab keffiyeh; or as a matter of revenge against a rival clan.

-145-

Even so, the night was owned by the Arabs. No one else was free to move about after dark. Not the police. Not the soldiers. Not the Haganah. Not Avram, and how it grated on him!

-146-

One day late that summer, Avram seized the porcelain fruit basket from its high shelf and drew back his throwing arm. Rivka yelped, and he froze, the proto-missile clenched between his fingers. He gaped at what he'd been about to do on small provocation—a sharp word from her, hardly unexpected, certainly not warranting an act of war. With tender care he set the precious china down and went out to the tool shed he'd built behind the house, where he puttered about for several hours.

Up to the very highest shelf it went, and from then on she used their prized possession only for holiday candies. The children grew to believe there'd be no sweets at all without it. They knew better than to misbehave anywhere near it.

-147-

Overwhelmed and losing control of the country, the British established and trained a corps of Jewish police, equipping them with trucks, armored cars and weapons for use against the continuing Arab threat. Soon Jewish mobile patrols were scouting the Jewish areas of settlement, organized and overseen by the Haganah.

-148-

Telegram from Paris, September 1936:
RESERVATIONS FIRM STOP ARRIVE JAFFA DECEMBER ONE NINETEEN THIRTY SIX STOP

-149-

The strike ended after six months: in time for the citrus harvest, the Jews said; in time for Ramadan, said the Arabs. Whatever the reason, it stopped, and at once all the strikers sought to return to work. Life had become hard for them, with precious little money left to spend. Hard for the rest of the country, too, since the menial work ordinarily done by Arabs was essential.

-150-

In all that time, Rivka's trees weren't touched. She attributed Arab restraint in her case to the good treatment she'd always shown her workers. But really, Avram said, who knows? Sometimes luck is just plain luck.

Rivka hadn't been able to hold their jobs open for them. When her Arab workers were ready to come back, they found the jobs occupied by Jews. What choice did Rivka have? Should she turn around and fire the people who now worked for her, and worked loyally—in favor of those who'd left her in the lurch? It wasn't she who'd abandoned her workers, tricked them and left them flat; it was their own leadership. But try telling the Arabs that. It only heightened their hostility. Even Leila was angered.

-151-

The Qu'ran on patience and retaliation:

> You believers will surely be tested in your wealth and yourselves, and you will certainly hear many hurtful words from those who were given the Scripture before you....But if you are patient and mindful of God— surely this is a resolve to aspire to. (3:186) God is truly with those who are patient. (2:153)
>
> Whenever [the Jews] kindle the fire of war, God puts it out. And they strive to spread corruption in the land. And God does not like corrupters. (5:64) Permission to fight back is hereby granted to those being fought, for they have been wronged. (22:39) God does not forbid you from dealing kindly and fairly with those who have neither fought nor driven you out of your homes.... God only forbids you from befriending those who have fought you for your faith, driven you out of your homes, or supported others in doing so. (60:8-9)

-152-

> People of my country, our days of sacrifice
>   have arrived;
> they shine, radiant across the hills of this
>   holy land.
>
> —'Abd al-Raheem Mahmoud

-153-

After all these years, all these delays, could there be a worse time for Faye and Jorg to visit? The strike was said to be over. This didn't stop Elli from feeling how shaky the lull was, how unpredictable their peril from resentful Arabs. But the journey from Paris to Jerusalem had been in the works too long to be put off again. Marian was already six years old, and an aunt didn't get any younger either!

Elli was briefly rattled by how much Faye had indeed aged. Her hair had grayed and was now cut short in a cap of curls; the skin of her face had slackened; it wore the unmistakable faint gleam of anti-wrinkling creams diligently applied. Jorg had become—well—rotund, as if his midline advanced in the same daily progression as his hairline receded. All the same, they arrived broadcasting their familiar boundless zest, and Elli was eased by the childlike curiosity shining out of their still-unchanged bright eyes. With an insistent confidence in their own safety, Faye and Jorg planned to prowl the city and rummage into all its corners.

-154-

On the first Shabbat after their arrival, Jorg arranged a visit to the studio of a local sculptor. He invited Morris—"Do forgive me, that's Moshe—you don't seem to me a Moshe, you know,"—to come along and bring Marian. This left a leisurely couple of hours in the garden for Elli and her aunt. The garden was lush most times of year with cyclamen, lilies, roses, hyacinths and—Elli's favorite—scarlet poppies; with neat rows of vegetables and two pomegranate trees still now in winter fruit. The December sky was overcast, and the riot of green hues under the silvery gleam of the clouds was a lesson in greenness itself.

For a while the two women sketched companionably, an old familiar habit they'd started back in Canada—some twenty-five years ago, who would've thought it?—when Faye had presented Nellie a set of colors for her twelfth birthday. Aunt Faye was then a spinster with a pinched income and a bohemian outlook on life; several years into the future, she'd take it into her head to leave New Brunswick for Paris, with Nellie in her charge. They'd sailed in the lovely but inopportune month of June 1914. When war broke out soon after their arrival, both had elected to stay on. Faye, in fortunate consequence, met a Netherlandish widower, Jorgen de Jong, the wealthy art dealer who fell head over heels in love with her.

"You know what I've been wondering?" Elli said, looking up from her sketch pad.

"Tell me."

"I cannot think of a single time in my whole life when the world was perfectly at peace, when the newspaper didn't bring word of men somewhere shooting something at each other. What is it about human beings that makes us fight all the time —and about everything?"

"This is what bothers you?"

Elli nodded. "Doesn't it you?"

"Not as a rule. What bothers me is how you seem to have a special talent for putting yourself into places where the shooting is happening. And worse—"

"I don't put—"

"—and worse, to regard places where some sort of squabble is not ongoing as rather dull."

"So as usual, Aunt, you're asking not what's wrong with the human race, but what's wrong with me!"

"Of course, my dear. What do I care about the human race? That's an abstraction."

"An abstraction which shoots real bullets."

The uneasy silence that edged between them was

gradually smoothed by the balm of their quiet work. The sky was clearing, and a butterfly came to rest in the rays of sunlight streaming into the garden's center. Partially obscured amidst a patch of white crocus, it exercised its slow wings. Irregular thick stripes of olive green stood out against a creamy background. "Interesting markings," said Aunt Faye.

"Mm-hmm."

"What's the name of it?"

Elli moved to examine the creature more closely, and of course it flittered away. She said, "I don't know. Can't say I've seen one like it before." The truth was, she rarely sat out here in the yard, never had the time—but she wasn't about to admit that to her aunt, who'd be bound to admonish, "You've never made the time, Nellie."

-155-

In the early 1960s, MIT meteorologist Edward Norton Lorenz would observe that infinitesimal changes made at the starting point of his computer weather models had the potential to trigger unpredictable and profound consequences —anything from mild and sunny skies to titanic storms. Since the initial change might be as small and insignificant as the twitch of a butterfly's wing, this became known as "the butterfly effect." Its ramifications have made their way into fields of study far removed from weather: into mathematics, biology, physics, even the social sciences, politics and diplomacy.

The Middle East is, of course, a wonderland of ravishingly colored butterflies, where for ages the metaphorical twitch of a wing has impelled world-wide consequences. Just in Palestine alone, nothing ever seemed to happen in and of itself. Events there were generated from Arabia, from Europe and Asia, from the New World; events there radiated to Arabia, to India and China, to New York and London and Paris and Moscow and Buenos Aires.

Within the week, Edward VIII, King of the United Kingdom and the Dominions of the British Empire and Emperor of India, would address his subjects over the radio. He would announce to them and to the world his abdication of his throne for the woman he loved. Who knew, in these uncertain times, what effect, mild or titanic, might or might not be triggered by England's constitutional crisis and the coronation of an unprepared King George VI?

-156-

"And our little butterfly Marian?" said Faye. "Does she like fighting?"

Elli brightened. "No, like a true socialist, she shares everything she has. Though like a true sabra, she does seem to sift Arab children from Jewish children, and to be wary of the Arabs."

"Me, I haven't been able to tickle out the difference, not a bit. Except in the way a person is dressed or groomed…"

"If you mean to suggest, Aunt, that all Arabs look dirty and smell worse, it's not so—no more than the opposite is true of all Jews. Or Britons, come to that." Remarkably, trachoma made no distinction among the three populations, nor among rich and poor; nor even, it sometimes looked to Elli, between clean and dirty. Nor among blue eyes, hazel and brown. Nor by which of Palestine's three official languages you called the disease. It struck and, if not treated, blinded all equally.

But every day, when she'd go out to fight it, she'd kiss her husband and daughter goodbye as if she were never going to see them again. This she did not tell her aunt. Faye would misunderstand, take her literally. In point of fact, Elli knew her departing embraces to be overwrought and mawkish. Arab attacks mostly fell elsewhere—up in the Galilee or down in Hebron, on the kibbutzim and moshavim, or at the border. She'd hear of them on the radio, read of them in the news, or be told of them by neighbors. And yet. Even within the tranquil shelter of this garden, the obverse was also true. For who was not aware—going about each day working, shopping, taking a walk, riding a bus, sketching a butterfly—that there were people who hated you, didn't want you here and were determined to do something about it?

-157-

The biblical Bezalel was chosen to head up design and construction of the Tabernacle, the Israelites' portable desert sanctuary. In Exodus 35-6, we learn why:

> And Moses said to the Israelites: See, the Lord has singled out by name Bezalel, son of Uri, son of Hur, of the tribe of Judah. He has endowed him with a divine spirit of skill, ability and knowledge of every craft and has inspired him to make designs for work in gold, silver and copper, to cut stones for setting and to carve wood—to work in every kind of designer's craft—and to give directions.

Jump to modern times: in 1906, Jerusalem's first Bezalel Academy of Arts and Design was founded by Boris Schatz, an accomplished painter and sculptor. His dream was to blend Jewish artistic traditions of Europe and the Middle East into a new style fitting a new nation. Housed in a building provided by the Jewish National Fund, the school produced glazed decorative tiles of great beauty, well known in the art world. Faye and Jorg had stopped for a day in Tel Aviv just to wander the streets viewing the tiles, which were still something of a novelty, having gone up on new construction in the 1920s. On public buildings and private residences and even on street stanchions, Jorg spotted single plaques and Faye an entire tiled facade, the two of them halting heedless in the middle of the road to exclaim over scenes that depicted classic Hebrew narratives or new Zionist labors. To this day, many of those same original tiles stop Tel Aviv sightseers in their tracks.

The Bezalel Academy's product was enchanting—but its finances were a mess; it had limped along until 1929, when finally it had to close its doors.

-158-

Jorg and Moshe, with Marian in tow, found their way to the corner of Shmuel Hanagid and Rehov Bezalel, where two crenelated stone buildings stood in a small park behind a similarly crenelated wall. This was The New Bezalel School of Arts and Crafts, which had opened its doors just a year ago under the leadership of Josef Budko, the graphic designer renowned for reviving wood-cutting as an art. Budko had fled Germany after Hitler's takeover in 1933. Other German artists of the Bauhaus movement made up a good part of the school's faculty, and three of those (the best three, if you asked Faye) were represented in Paris by Jorg. Hence today's visit. No classes were in session, it being Shabbat, but the rooms were open, and wafting from them, the mingled smells of turpentine, wet clay, wood dust....

Moshe never did get the fellow's full name. Fritzl, Jorg called him. He offered them tea in chipped cups from a paint-spattered hot plate. His eyeglasses, too, were littered with specks of red, yellow and blue, and the grubby corners of his fingernails couldn't fail to disquiet a surgeon. The paintings, though, showed another side of the artist. They had sharp, clean lines and gave off an air of orderliness, with planes that neatly overlapped one another. At least, so it seemed to Moshe, though what the paintings were about he couldn't begin to hazard an opinion.

The visit seemed more in the nature of a friendly get-together than an opportunity to do business. Presumably, the nitty-gritty of dealing in art was transacted by letter and phone. Or else Moshe missed that part, his attention waylaid by Marian, by the fear that she'd trip over some paraphernalia and get hurt, or else cause damage to a masterwork. She'd become captivated by small clay-and-stone sculpted models that were grouped together on a table in the corner. One vaguely resembled an acrobat or dancer, its back and leg one smooth curve. Marian couldn't seem to stay her fingers from running along the curve over and over again, despite Moshe's warnings. Finally, he took her by the shoulders and led her away under her ear-splitting wail. The moment he released her, back she flew to the table. Fritzl, thus alerted, burst into laughter. If only he'd known she was coming, he told her, he could have saved himself a good day's polishing. "Stroke away there as much as you like." Which no doubt was nice of him. Moshe reminded his daughter to thank the nice man—and then sent up a silent plea that she wouldn't learn the wrong lesson about getting her way. Then he subsided into musings on the riddles of fatherhood.

-159-

Awake, O harp and lyre!

—Psalm 108

-160-

In 1933 in Germany, Hitler had ordered all music by Jewish composers to be silenced and all Jewish musicians to be dismissed. Bronislaw Huberman, the celebrated violinist, had swung into action. For the next three years he scoured Europe and America, scouting out topflight musicians, lining up enthusiastic funders, and grubbing acceptable visas, all the while arguing, "One has to build a fist against anti-Semitism."

Tel Aviv in late December of 1936 witnessed the launch of his prodigious fist. The inaugural concert of the brand new Palestine Orchestra was given under the baton of the world famous guest conductor and ardent anti-fascist, Arturo Toscanini. The maestro led a symphony orchestra of some eighty Jewish men plus a few women, outcasts mostly from Poland and Germany, but also Latvia, Estonia, Ukraine, Hungary, Czechoslovakia, Austria, Croatia, France, the Netherlands, Italy, Georgia and Russia, the United States and Argentina.

Although the hall held three thousand, tickets quickly sold out, and many people who wanted them couldn't get them for love or money. So many, in fact, that Toscanini graciously opened several rehearsals to the general public. Yet still, on opening night there were fanatics who climbed up to the roof to listen in.

True to form, Jorg contrived in his unassuming way to snag four tickets to the social event of the decade, December 26 being his and Faye's last night in Palestine. At the last moment, Moshe had to bow out, and Rivka was tapped to fill the seat next to Elli. The hall was electric with anticipation: men in starched collars and women in soft gowns; voices babbling and humid clouds of cologne; craning necks and once-overing glances. Everyone who was anyone was there. They spotted

British High Commissioner Arthur Wauchope, Chaim Weizmann, David Ben-Gurion, Golda Meyerson and Tel Aviv's founder and first mayor, Meir Dizengoff. It was a cultural moment for the ages; but also, for at least one in the human crush, a private moment for shivers. Rivka was able to chat lightly with Faye and amiably enough, though she was on edge all the while, speculating whether an Arab-made bomb might not be ticking inaudibly beneath one of their seats. Once the concert started, this made the music so much more poignant, to think each note might be the last she'd ever hear. Her heart filled with the strains of Rossini, Brahms, Schubert, Weber and—notably—Mendelssohn, a Jew. And then, sure enough, an explosion of sorts did erupt—a clamorous ovation at the close that rose unebbing for half an hour and more, the crowd on their feet, three thousand adoring new fans, not a one yet ready to leave the hall.

-161-

At the pier next morning, Elli blurted out, "Stay here with us in Palestine. Europe isn't safe."

A final hug, and Faye countered, "It's Palestine that's not safe, my dear. Come back with us to Paris, the three of you."

Straightaway, Moshe urged them, "Go back to Canada, Faye—you and Elli both and Marian with you. Just until the future becomes clear, you know."

-162-

The upshot was predictable from the first, Jorg said as he stood with Faye at the ship's rail, waving to the receding crowd on shore. Pick up and move? Why? Was anyplace safe?

-163-

Gradually, life in Palestine returned to a kind of normalcy The twins joined the scouts and went on hikes all over the country. Tali adored being outdoors. Rivka thought he might become a farmer someday, never mind his frank lack of interest in growing anything. He preferred to watch the weather and study the clouds. Like Avram, he had an affinity for the desert. On their rambles together, Avram reported, Tali chattered away and could not be shut up—though when he was with Rivka, he'd leave the schmoozing to Yudi. She could almost watch the boys shooting up day by day, growing tall and rugged, with long, loose limbs. In April of 1937, they climbed Masada and came home brimming with the romance of self-sacrifice.

-164-

The terrorism never wholly stopped, though. By now it had gained a name, the Arab Revolt, or Rebellion, and even her children had grown used to the sound of gunfire. Unless it crackled really close by, no one paid attention.

-165-

Then, too, the shots were as likely to come from Jews in the Irgun, who as a rule took their revenge within hours following an Arab attack. Rivka detested the Irgun. To her mind, every last one of them was a savage who put Jewish Palestine's future in jeopardy.

-166-

The Irgun had been formed in 1931, when a disgruntled cadre of officers split off from the Haganah. Unlike the Haganah, they were militaristic and opportunistic. They did not consider themselves solely defensive. In Jerusalem, the Irgun attracted numbers of Hebrew University students, Avraham Stern among them, but beyond that, they drew few members.

One June evening in 1933, Chaim (formerly Vitaly) Arlosoroff and his wife, Sima, were ambling along the beach in Tel Aviv when he was shot in the back. The well-liked Arlosoroff chaired the political department of the Jewish Agency. His brazen murder came as a shock and a quandary. To this day, the crime has not been solved. Three members of the right-wing Revisionist Party were charged, but in time were acquitted. Word got out that the Haganah had participated in gathering evidence against the three suspects. This was a taint to the Haganah's purity as a home guard, damaging its prestige. A tide of new volunteers rallied to the Irgun. It certainly didn't hurt when the warrior-politician Ze'ev (formerly Vladimir) Jabotinsky—a celebrated founder of the Haganah and the Betar youth movement—signed on. By 1937, the Irgun counted five hundred members.

-167-

A watch tower, a searchlight, a fence all around, a few huts, a water supply, and miracle of miracles: the genesis of a viable Jewish settlement. With enough people and trucks it could be done in a single afternoon. Near Beisan in April of 1937, Avram labored long, building one new tower-and-stockade settlement after another. The perimeter fences he organized with double walls of wood, the space between slowly filling with boulders and earth. Given enough hands, this, too, could be finished in the one day. If not, barbed wire made the perimeter whole until he could oversee the rest of the work. All that spring, overnight settlements sprang up like fresh seedlings out of the earth south of Tiberias, just west of the Jordan River.

-168-

Early one sweltering morning, Avram tiptoed in carrying a sleeping baby, maybe ten months old, and leading a small boy by the hand. The baby, he told Rivka, was said to have an aunt and uncle somewhere near Hadera, or possibly Zichron Yaakov. He'd already sent a fellow to track the family down.

The boy was a tougher proposition. His mother had died of typhus several months back; his father fell in last night's firefight against an Arab raid on a new settlement. When Rivka asked his age, the boy held up four dewy fingers. Avram went on to recount the shoot-out, not sparing any of its lurid particulars. Hearing him tell it, you'd be led to conclude he'd run off the whole band of attackers singlehandedly. Rivka might have called him on it had she been more than half-listening. She was way ahead of him. You have it in mind, man of mine, to lure me in. You're thinking to entice me to fight by your side. And leave the children with whom, I'd like to know?

Time was, she might gladly have joined him. Time was, she'd embraced such adventures. But she'd grown up since then. One can't be running around the countryside assailing people when there's a home to take care of and a business to run. He might believe he was the one building the Land, but in truth if not for her, what would he have? Certainly not a hot breakfast at three-thirty in the morning!

"This boy," she said.

Yes, this boy, now curled up like a puppy asleep on the pallet she'd laid for him on the floor.

"He has no one."

"There's the orphanage in Tel Aviv," she said.

"So there is."

"It's crowded there."

"Overcrowded, I hear."

"I could contact Elli Tobi for an appropriate placement."

"You could. Or…"

"Or we could keep him with us," Rivka said with a sigh.

He waited for her slow smile, an ember out of her old fire. Another son. So now we are six. "What's his name?"

"I suppose we can call him anything we'd like. He has nothing."

"He must own a name, Avram. He's not a pet, he's a child."

Avram pulled at his lower lip, grinning.

"What?"

"Shimshon."

"Who, that little runt?"

He nodded. "Well, I suppose it's a name to grow into, Shimshon."

"I'll have to teach him a thing or two about women," she said.

"You do that," said Avram lifting her up and carrying her off to bed, where he taught her a thing or two she didn't yet know about that man of hers.

-169-

Shimshon: Hebrew for Samson, a leader of the Israelites, the last of the prominent biblical judges. Dedicated before birth to the service of God, Shimshon matures into superhuman strength—until, lovestricken, he confides the secret of his strength to the Philistine temptress, Delilah. By cutting off his hair, she opens the way for his transformation into the blinded, weak and humiliated prisoner of the Philistines. At last, on display before a jeering multitude at their temple in Gaza, Shimshon receives a divinely granted burst of power that enables him to bring down the temple, annihilating the Philistines and himself.

-170-

A Snow of White Papers

Like day follows night, each major riot in Palestine was followed first by a flurry of Mandate inquiries, then by a special commission, and finally, months or even years later, by a hefty, official White Paper. In 1920, when the British reopened Palestine's Land Registry (which had been closed for two years) Jews began buying up land, first from the British government and then from Arab landowners. The underlying cause of Arab rioting in Jerusalem in 1920 and in Jaffa in 1921 was determined by a special commission to be resentment against Jewish immigration and fear of the loss of peasant livelihoods. Accordingly, the "Churchill" White Paper of 1922, though reaffirming once again Britain's commitment to the Balfour Declaration, introduced a provision that Jewish immigration was not to exceed "the economic absorptive capacity" of the country. What defined this "economic absorptive capacity?" Initially, the Jewish immigrants' ability to find employment.

Following the riots of 1929, the Passfield White Paper of 1930 redefined "economic absorptive capacity" to include Arab unemployment, as well. It called for a halt in Jewish immigration and advised that sales of government land be restricted solely to landless Arabs. Such a Jewish outcry ensued that the following year an explanatory letter nullified the findings.

After the strike in 1936, the 400-page Peel Commission Report of July 1937 proposed for the very first time that

Palestine be partitioned into two separate entities—a small Jewish state of some five thousand square kilometers, and a much larger Arab state to be merged with Abdullah's Transjordan. Britain was to retain control of Jerusalem. This trial balloon got shot down by everyone. The Arabs rejected it out of hand, and so ended the six-month brittle peace that had held since the strike's end. The Jewish Agency, although anything but pleased, did at length accept the proposal—with what was going on in Nazi Germany, what choice did they have? But now a true rift cracked open between those Jews who still favored standing with the British by following a strict strategy of self-defense, and those Jews who'd been aching to meet Arab attacks with deadly force.

-171-

"Partition, my posterior" scoffed Rivka, crumpling up the map that overspread the front page of her newspaper. Such a miserly little place for us Jews you never saw. What will Mischa write me when he sees this? And immigration to be restricted to twelve thousand a year? With all those Jews from Germany clamoring to come in? Twelve thousand cats better they should restrict!

-172-

"Arabs don't want Jews ruling over them, and who can blame them for that?" said Elli. "But why won't they even consider sharing the land with us?"

Moshe hadn't given much thought to the intricacies involved. "It could be shared, I suppose, either in one country or in two. Though if I were an Arab, why would I give over a single inch of Palestine? I suppose I'd fight to keep it all."

"I don't worry about them and their violence. I worry what the British might end up doing." She now feared a sovereign state where the Jews—where Marian—would form a permanent underclass. Cross-legged on the floor, Marian hunched over a sheet of newspaper, painstakingly sounding out the words syllable by syllable.

-173-

Lewis Andrews was the British district commissioner up in the north. One late-September Sunday he was walking home from the prayer service at the Anglican church, shadowed closely by his bodyguard. A burst of fire from several Arab gunmen murdered them both. Shot to death in Nazareth in broad daylight! Immediately, the British outlawed the Arab Higher Committee and arrested its leaders—most of them, anyway. The Mufti, slippery as always, dressed himself as a woman, and thus costumed, escaped Palestine. Three weeks later, he showed up in Lebanon.

-174-

One day Shimshon carried in a small, maimed toad cupped in his hands. He was so quiet, that boy. Never a fight with playmates, never a bloody nose from his brothers. Right from the first, he fit seamlessly into the household, running off by himself, exploring a wadi, bringing home insects or small rodents to study—or in this instance, a one-legged amphibian that had somehow escaped its hungry predator. Leila helped him fashion a cage from wayward bits of orchard waste.

"Do you have a name for this animal?"

"Toad," he pronounced.

-175-

Leila returned that night to beg some first-aid supplies for her brother-in-law. Land mines, presumably Arab-laid, were always a danger on the stretch of road along which he'd been walking. A passing British police convoy had stopped and picked him up to use as their "minesweeper." Forced onto the hood of the lead car, he was transported several miles up there without incident, Allah be praised. When they were through with him, they didn't bother to stop the convoy. Instead, the lead driver swerved the nose of the car side-to-side vertiginously until Leila's frenzied, scrabbling brother-in-law was pitched off. With a leg broken in two places, he was blessed to be able to crab-scramble out of the way. The practice is common, and they've heard of unluckier ones getting run over by the next vehicle in the line.

-176-

Often, for one village home harboring an Arab insurgent, the British dynamited, then bulldozed the entire village. Cruelly as they treated the Arab fellaheen in these years of revolt, it was a different story when it came to their dealings with Arabs who held power. There they temporized, going out of their way to placate the Arab leadership, especially by putting the brakes on Jewish immigration. Some sixty thousand Jews had entered the Land legally in 1936 and '37. In the six months between April and September 1938, the British clamped down hard, allowing in only three thousand. Their zigzagging tactics succeeded in antagonizing Arabs and Jews alike. Cumulatively, the British were growing to trust no one, finally not even their own.

-177-

On March 15, 1938, Hitler's forces made their Anschluss—their union—with Austria by marching in and taking over the country. Thunderheads of war roiled at Europe's bleak horizon. In the diplomatic crisis, gas masks were issued to civilians in Britain. When, in September, Neville Chamberlain came back from Munich trumpeting "peace for our time," nobody Rivka knew swallowed a word of it.

-178-

All over the globe, intake doors got slammed in Jewish faces.

-179-

Just like Adam, that's the way he named them: Toad, Snake, Rat, Spider, Locust, Lizard. He didn't kill or torture the animals. He kept them in tanks and cages and fed them and watered them until they died. Then he threw their carcasses away—or else cut them open and studied them, then threw them away. Rivka took this as a sign that he'd become a great scientist, a professor of biology. She started him in school. He went off each day, a solemn little boy with a pinched face. He did okay, never spoke a word in class.

-180-

In the same way, it seemed preordained that Ahuva would grow up to be a surgeon. Not a farmer, more's the pity: the only use she had for oranges was to practice her dissection techniques. Try downing your breakfast while your daughter sits across from you scalpeling her breakfast fruit, all the while scrupulously narrating the details of her progress.

-181-

At breakfast one morning came news from Russia that Mischa had been arrested early in 1938, along with his editor Esther Frumkin, of *Der Emes*. The anonymous letter had no word directly from him. Just his signature on a scrap of paper would have sufficed. Rivka grasped at straws. "He'll get word to Stalin. It's only just a little misunderstanding, that's all."

-182-

Orde Wingate was a little crazy. This reputation he'd earned for himself in the two years he'd served as a British intelligence officer in Palestine. He was known to have unexceptionable credentials, being the nephew of Britain's former high commissioner in Egypt. Even so, his appearance was a bit mad: long narrow face, long narrow body and long narrow nose—and especially those cold, bright, deep-set eyes that fixed on Avram as if zeroing in on his secrets.

Avram had been ordered to report to Wingate, who was looking for Arabic-speaking Jews, Jews who knew the terrain and could handle themselves with a knife or a gun. There was a pipeline that carried oil from Mosul, in Iraq, through Palestine's Jezreel Valley to the port in Haifa. Arab landowners whose property it crossed had never been compensated for the land it occupied. Since the outbreak of the strike two years back, Arab gangs had made the pipeline their nightly target. The British were resolved to secure it at any cost. Wingate now had permission to create three "night squads" to stop the raids. His ambitions ranged far wider than the Jezreel Valley, though. All over Palestine, Arab marauders commandeered the night, while British law enforcers kept to their stations and billets. Wingate was confident he could take back the dark. As he put it, "a single Jew is worth twenty, thirty, even a hundred

Arabs—and a single British soldier considerably more."

When Avram was brought into Wingate's tent, the man was sitting in a chair reading the Bible, and he was naked. Avram, feigning nonchalance, waited until, having finished the passage, Wingate turned his unsettling grayish-blue gaze on Avram. "You're from Hashomer?" A reek of raw onion wafted on the words.

Avram shrugged, identified himself, and reached for one of two fat round onions in a plate on the small table at Wingate's side. "May I?" his hand hovering.

"By all means."

Avram lifted the white orb, opened wide, and took a quarter of it into his mouth, chomping vigorously, staring into the eyes boring back into his.

"You're hired," said Wingate.

"Not until I hear what you have in mind."

That night, Avram went out on his first sortie. It was by way of a training: Wingate worked the squad hard in order to whip them into the shape he required. About a half hour after midnight, he ordered a man to shoot an Arab who'd come into view on a ridge, silhouetted astride his horse against the moonbright sky. The man balked, or didn't act fast enough— Avram was never sure which. Quick as an adder's fang, Wingate's swagger stick lacerated the man's cheek. A crack, a moan, a lesson to the whole squad.

He's mad all right, thought Avram, but only when he wants to be.

-183-

Hadassah Hospital would soon open its flagship on Mount Scopus. Moshe was recruited to practice and teach there. Elli would be there, too. She could finally stop gallivanting through the country—way too dangerous now—and would work some days at Mount Scopus, some at Hadassah's hospital in Tel Aviv. If Tel Aviv, she decided, she'd stay over with Rivka. Rivka needed her.

Mischa had been executed.

-184-

Night and day, Rivka flayed herself with useless questions and accusations. Why hadn't she insisted her brother come here? What was he doing in the Soviet Union? Making Jewish life, he'd claimed. With Shabbat destroyed, Hebrew destroyed, the connection to Eretz Yisrael destroyed?

Surrounded by people, Rivka felt intensely alone.

It became too hard to go outdoors.

Even in the heat, she wrapped herself in blankets.

Leila nursed her with exquisite kindness, which Rivka felt only as pain. Elli sat in silence with her. Elli's mournful eyes were no comfort. Rivka only wished her back in Jerusalem.

Avram came home. By turns, he tried to crawl into bed with her or to scold her, but either way she couldn't respond except to order him away.

She became haunted by the near-warfare going on outside. No one in Palestine was safe from gunfire anymore, from bombings, stonings, beatings, stabbings, arson, robbery. The Arabs rebelled; the Irgun sought revenge; the British brought in yet more reinforcements. Rivka wrung her hands, tears trickling onto her pillow. Avram mused aloud on the sticky situation the British were in, needing to protect themselves against harm, while at the same time protecting the moderate Arabs from the extremists, the Jews from the Arabs, and the Arabs from extremist Jews. She curled herself tighter and muttered something incoherent.

Avram stayed a week, tried his best, then went back to Wingate's night squads.

-185-

In Hanover, Germany, there lived a Polish Jew by the name of Sender Grynszpan. In August 1938, Poland stripped their citizenship from all Polish Jews residing in foreign lands. Two months later, on October 26, twelve thousand newly stateless Jews were arrested in Germany, milked of their property and herded aboard frontier-bound trains. Among those dumped stranded and penniless just inside Poland—no longer legitimate on either side of the border—was Sender Grynszpan.

At the German embassy in Paris ten days later, Sender's son Herschel made his protest against this perfidy by assassinating a mild-looking fellow who turned out to be one of the junior diplomats. The young Grynszpan had been gunning for someone higher up, but the five bullets he fired into the abdomen of Ernst Edward vom Rath did their work, and more. Vom Rath died on November 9. That night, all over Germany, the streets crunched with shattered glass and the air blurred with curtains of smoke as Jewish shops were looted, synagogues razed, homes ransacked and random Jews murdered at will. It was called Kristallnacht—the Night of Broken Glass.

-186-

One night Avram's squad rounded up four Arab gang members—teenagers, high-spirited and cocky. They were brought in, and on the spot Wingate singled out the brashest of them, whom he ordered bound to a chair. "Who is your leader?" he asked. No answer from the boy, just a roll of the eyes toward the other three, being held at Avram's gunpoint a few yards off among the shadows of the tent. The light from a single lantern shown upward, making a death's head of Wingate's bony face. Mildly enough, he untied the keffiyeh from the Arab's head and blindfolded the prisoner's eyes with it. "Where did you rendezvous?" he then demanded.

Klutzy questions, judged Avram—disappointing from Wingate, the man reputed to be a virtuoso of interrogation. Avram had hoped to learn by watching him how to dig out good intelligence.

It's said that Gertrude Stein, before her death, asked Alice B. Toklas, "What is the answer?" Toklas replied that there is no answer. "In that case," Stein murmured, "what is the question?" What Avram was missing about Wingate was that, for the moment, the answers were of no importance to him—only the prisoner's willingness to play ball with the questioner, or not. And again, no answer to the question, just a smirk. Wingate reached into a bucket close to his foot. He came up with a swift fistful of sand, which he forced down the boy's gullet. Coughing, spitting, the boy now tried to speak. But another scoop of the grit stopped his mouth, and a pistol shot to his chest stopped his heart.

In the utter horrified silence that followed the crack of the pistol, Wingate turned on the other boys and roared, "Now, speak!"

Yes, he's mad, thought Avram, and damn me, I like it.

-187-

Them that asks no questions isn't told a lie.
                    — Rudyard Kipling, "A Smuggler's Song"

-188-

She couldn't seem to carry it off, not like the long-drawn-out melancholic spells she'd endured when a young woman. Then, she'd been known to languish for months on end. Now, a week and five days after Avram went back to his posting, Rivka could no longer avoid feeling silly: with the children tiptoeing through the house, with Leila bringing her tea and sitting beside her, as if Leila had nothing else to do when Rivka knew full well how much laundry was waiting to be boiled, churned, beaten, rinsed, wrung and hung out—while at Leila's own home in Zarnuqua were dried linens still hanging on her line waiting to be taken down and ironed and folded. So Rivka pulled herself up out of bed, walked out into her orchards, and went on with her life, spoiled and tattered though her life now seemed.

-189-

Lizard had lived the longest of Shimshon's menagerie, flourishing for quite some months under the boy's care. Then one morning, he found Lizard belly up and stiff on the floor of the cage. He took the small corpse to Rivka. With a deep-felt hug, she offered Shimshon help in burying the animal. The finality of burial would help her, she sensed, as much as him.

At Shimshon's calm stare, a tremor ran the length of her spine. His eyes were a clear, clean aquamarine, reminding her of a swimming pool bordered all around by a margin of gray stone. They gave Rivka the impression she could dive right in, and it would feel cool in there, moist and depthless against her hot skin. This was only an illusion of openness, of having nothing whatever to hide. Rivka had dealt with blank eyes before—eyes that stared back at her without any acknowledgment of her existence. Eyes that said I'm all there is, and

I'll treat with you as long as you're in accord with me on that. She'd dealt with deadened eyes that had witnessed horror they could never unsee. Eyes that had filled with anguish too often, that refused to take in any more. She'd never before come across eyes like Shimshon's. Shimshon's actively slapped you in the face, actively refused to let you in, actively told you there was nothing therein to find, though you knew that couldn't be true.

"No thank you, Ima," he said. "But you can bury Lizard by yourself, if you want to."

-190-

You wouldn't label Shimshon sneaky. It wasn't something particular he kept hidden, it was himself. Whoever lived inside there, when you went looking for him you'd look in vain. You could only hope *someone* was there inside, and that he hadn't shriveled up from loneliness or concealed himself so cleverly that he couldn't anymore locate himself.

-191-

He caught a large beetle and held it up inside its cage for Rivka to admire. Rivka thought his love of beetles must have to do with their hard shell. Sometimes she'd call the boy "beetle," using the Hebrew word that could also mean book-worm. This time when she called him beetle, he put down the cage and asked her to stop. He said it was like calling him a cockroach.

Cockroach was an entirely different word. "And what if I did call you—" she began.

"They're dirty. Like the Arabs."

She slapped his face. He was just a youngster, had probably picked up this attitude in school, parroting what some other child had said, but she was too shocked to stop her hand. And then it was too late.

He stared through her. Then he turned and headed for the kitchen.

"Don't you want your beetle?"

He came back and with a quick fist squashed it inside its cage. A yellow substance shot out from the insect's belly, like pus, only thicker.

1939-43

-192-

By 1939, somewhat less than five hundred-thousand Jews lived in Palestine; Arabs numbered about three times that sum. In the early days of the Mandate, the British had found they could work with Palestine's Jews, who understood how to talk to them, knowing Western expectations of behavior. During the revolt, the British had lost confidence in their Arab-manned police force and had turned to the Jews, arming and training them to keep order. But now, as war became imminent, everything changed. Britain would need the Arabs—would need the good will of Muslim countries across the Middle East and Asia; and of course would need their oil. The Jews had money, some of them quite a lot of money; but the Jews were already in Britain's pocket. Where else could they go? They had to side with Britain and her allies, whereas Arabs could very well decide to back the enemy.

-193-

A new White Paper came out in the early spring of 1939. Avram renamed it the Black Paper because, by its dictates, the fate of the Jews was dire. Over the next five years, only seventy-five thousand Jews in total were to be admitted into Palestine. Also, sales to Jews of Arab lands were to be made only within tracts equivalent to a twentieth of the country's full size. Worse, after those five years, the Arabs would gain the sole right to legislate these matters for Palestine, meaning that all further Jewish immigration and land sales would depend upon Arab forbearance. What were the possibilities for Jewish life in such a future? Even now, despite all the pressure the Mandate could exert, the Arab leadership would not so much as sit down at any bargaining table where a single Jew had a place.

-194-

Bleak spring was followed by a bleaker summer. In July, Czechoslovakia was invaded by Nazi Germany. In August, Hitler signed a nonaggression pact with the USSR—or, as Rivka put it, with Stalin-may-his-name-be-blotted-out.

-195-

Jews were making their way illegally into Palestine any way they could, coming down the Danube or through the Adriatic and Aegean seas. Perhaps you've heard of the *Dora*. A leaky old coal ship, but this bucket of jumbled miseries managed to lumber all the way from Amsterdam, safely bringing hundreds of Jews to the shores north of Tel Aviv. Plus maybe a small herd of cattle: whether the cows on board were beached there, too, has been unclear ever since.

-196-

From *The New York Times*, September 1, 1939:

GERMAN ARMY ATTACKS POLAND; CITIES BOMBED, PORT BLOCKADED; DANZIG IS ACCEPTED INTO REICH;

-197-

As Shabbat fell over the Land on the first of September, the cargo ship *Tiger Hill*—having been fired on by the Royal Navy off Tel Aviv—ran aground on Frishman Beach. Its cargo was more than twelve hundred Eastern-European Jews. Huddled together on the sand, they sang "Hatikvah" as British searchlights raked them. Jews from the area raced to overtake the refugees and shepherd them into hiding. Too late: almost all of the "illegals" were bundled off to the Sarafand Detention Camp on the Tel Aviv-Jerusalem road.

-198-

From *The Palestine Post*, September 4, 1939:

ANGLO-FRENCH WAR ON HITLER
BRITAIN UNITED AGAINST NAZI TYRANNY

His Majesty the King broadcast a message to the people of the British Empire at 5 o'clock G.M.T. yesterday afternoon (7 o'clock Palestine time.) The message was relayed by the P.B.S. from Jerusalem.

-199-

Rivka was out among her trees when the first thundercrack tore the sky. Instinctively she hit the ground, nose in the dirt. Fifteen miles away, Italian planes were dropping bombs on Tel Aviv. One explosion now stepped on the next. With a start, Rivka humped to her hands and knees, then to feet that were already in motion. Her breath spasmed in sharp, harsh gasps.

Home. Tali and Shimshon rowdy at the kitchen table playing a hand of gin rummy. Leila slumped nearby, Yudi helpless by her side. Tears slid quietly down her cheeks and dripped from her lifting chin. One mother's panicked gaze met the other's.

"Boys, where's your sister?"

"Bedroom, I think."

Rivka found Ahuva under the bed, her trembling arms over her ears. The mother dissolved into whoops of relieved laughter and scuttled in beside her daughter, who curled herself into a tight ball.

As abruptly as it had appeared, the danger evaporated. In the deep silence that followed, Rivka walked Leila to the outskirts of Zarnuqua, a village of about 450 homes. All looked calm there.

-200-

Leila's husband's family had lived in Zarnuqua for as long as anyone could remember. Maybe not as long as its land had been populated, which went back to the Bronze Age or even earlier. When you dug in the ground you came up with Byzantine or early Ottoman shards. On a map of the area from the year 1799, the village was marked, though not named; and the mosque where Leila's sons went for Friday prayers dated as well to the late eighteenth century. Travelers' diaries from the nineteenth century describe tobacco fields, olive groves and vegetable gardens surrounded by cactus hedges. The gardens and cactus hedges still survived, though by the time Leila came there as a bride most of the farmland was in citriculture.

Jews from Europe began settling nearby late in the 1880s. The first village record of a run-in with a Jewish neighbor dates to 1892. Pasturing rights provoked it, and two years were needed to smooth it over.

A school for boys was established in 1924; one for girls would come in 1943. By then, Zarnuqua's population would top two thousand.

-201-

Ahuva was ashamed of herself. For as long as she could remember, she'd aspired to be a great heroine, a pioneer like her mother and father. They hadn't gone to university; they'd opted for adventure. They'd plunged right into the thick of war, bravely fighting and fearlessly winning: Ima a girl-soldier and spy who won the heart of Ahuva's dashing Abba the very moment he laid eyes on her.

Fifteen years ago, they'd chosen for their firstborn the name Ahuva, meaning Beloved. Why couldn't they have picked something fierce, like Arielle, which meant Lioness? A lioness—even one holed up underneath a bed—would still be scary-dangerous.

-202-

"We will fight with the British against Hitler as if there were no White Paper. And we will fight the White Paper as if there were no war."

Count on Ben-Gurion to come up with the rallying cry the Yishuv needed to move forward. There and then, the Haganah set about turning itself from a self-defense force into an army. With its own air force, even. A handful of crop dusters, but still....

-203-

Immediately, Jews volunteered in their hundreds for service with the British.

-204-

It was bitter to watch the strictures on immigration tightening yet again. For what was called security reasons, "Reich nationals" were now banned from Palestine, with the preposterous result that German and Austrian Jews who applied for asylum were turned away. But along the coast, refugees kept landing illegally. The fortunate were guided inland, where they blended into the settlements. Too many got caught while still aboard ship or as they waded onto the beaches. The seagoing British quickly became adept at intercepting refugee-laden boats and towing them to harbor at Haifa. Jewish passengers soon were sitting tight and refusing to disembark into British custody in Haifa. The British soon were going aboard with truncheons to force them off.

Supposing you got caught. You might still be lucky enough. You might end up in the internment camps at Sarafand or Athlit. At least you'd be in the Land. More likely, you'd get sent to camps in Mauritius, where conditions were terrible, just terrible. The British had the mistaken notion that if they made conditions terrible enough, the Jews would stop coming. Is it possible they failed so flawlessly to imagine what horrors the Jews were escaping from?

-205-

Wingate's night squads were disbanded that September after, among other snafus, they brutally attacked the wrong village. Avram had, by then, quit the squad. Earlier in the year, Wingate's Jewish fighters were informed they would only be permitted to serve in support operations. Avram flat-out refused to obey the order not to fight, and that was an end to it.

He'd never stopped building new settlements, and now with redoubled effort he worked on maximizing the secret hollows where refugees and weapons could be smuggled in and hidden. The British would show up at some settlement's gates at any hour of day or night to search for both sorts of illegals. Uncovered them sometimes, and tethered and carried them off. But sometimes not.

-206-

Scarcely had there ever been love lost between Britain and France, the Allies. With the war on, their mutual suspicion bristled in the Middle East. Each took for granted a plot by the other to appropriate the region, perhaps outright or perhaps through client states. Britain was romancing the Arabs with an eye to their oil. France, equally avid, plugged away at strangling the Arabs' national movement, which was barely out of its cradle but toddling along quite nicely. It's no wonder, then, that the Vichy government and the Free French were receptive when, in 1940, the Haganah offered the means to transmit "Radio Levant Libre." By then Vichy had firm control of Lebanon and Syria, and good reason to favor the Zionists. Over time, their cooperation would grow to encompass a retinue of intelligence operations. A honeymoon of France and the Zionists: Britain's two chief obstacles to hegemony in the Middle East.

-207-

An offshoot of the Irgun made its debut in 1940, and it was even more militant than the militant Irgun. Its name was Lehi, but it was commonly known as the Stern Gang after its leader, Avraham Stern. That wavy-haired, bookish fellow would have nothing to do with the British, even though it was wartime and even though the Jewish Agency urged cooperation. He and his fellows practiced a vicious "gun Zionism" against the Mandate's White Paper, organizing themselves into hard-to-infiltrate, three-member cells. Some of their guns came from the Vichy French, for the Stern Gang were never too dainty or squeamish to do business with Nazi sympathizers (even Nazis themselves would do, if they could serve a purpose). To raise money for more weapons, the Stern

Gang took to robbing banks—and not just British-run concerns, but Jewish branches run by the Histadrut. Soon they took to extorting money from Jewish shopkeepers. For them, it was a given that every Jew was honor-bound to support their work, since their work served to further a Jewish homeland.

-208-

Lehi: acronym for *Lohamei Herut Israel*, Fighters for the Freedom of Israel. The Lehi salute involved two raised fingers of the right hand—the pointer and the third finger—representing the passage from Psalm 137, "If I forget thee, O Jerusalem, let my right hand forget its cunning."

-209-

A fellow by the name of Peter Bergson showed up in New York in 1940. His background was a blank. Straight nose, light eyes—was he Jewish? America wasn't in the war, and yet he undertook a campaign to raise a Jewish legion to fight independently against the Axis powers. With his dark hair swept back in a pompadour and his pencil-thin mustache, he made a good appearance, speaking forcefully enough to gather support from countless celebrities, not all of them Jewish. But who was he?

-210-

His real name was Hillel Kook, and his "Bergson Group" was a front for the Irgun. Supporters would eventually include Frank Sinatra, Bob Hope, the Marx Brothers, Eleanor Roosevelt, Leonard Bernstein, Stella Adler, Thomas Mann, Langston Hughes, Moss Hart....

-211-

Not a single immigration certificate was issued in all of 1941. Even the measly quota had been suspended.

-212-

June 1941. The sun at its solstice in the northern hemisphere looked down on something new and ugly: Jews in the Soviet Union being forced to the edge of a pit and massacred by Nazi *Einsatzgruppen*. By the following spring, upwards of a million Russian Jews would be rotting in piles in mass graves; and death camps in Poland—Chelmno, Belzec, Sobibor, Treblinka—would be starting their dark, efficient work.

-213-

The Grand Mufti had been in exile since the time of the Arab Revolt. He'd found refuge in Iraq from a British arrest warrant. Later, he'd moved on to fascist Italy, all very much under wraps. In August 1941, he surfaced in Berlin, where he busied himself by broadcasting appeals to the Arabs to overthrow the British, by issuing anti-Semitic rants and by sucking up to Hitler.

-214-

Since June of 1940, the war had raged in West Africa, but it had been creeping ever closer to Palestine. With the deployment of Field Marshall Erwin Rommel and his crack Afrika Korps a year later, the fighting moved into the sands of North Africa. The closer the Axis approached, the more Arab violence subsided in Palestine. How curious, Rivka mused, that things were quieting down. You'd think with the Germans closing in on our borders, the Arabs would be pouring on their fire. But no, it appeared the Arabs felt they could safely sit back and count on the Nazi war machine to deliver them from British tyranny.

-215-

As to the Jews, there was no change in tactics for all those who'd all along been practicing havlagah. Nor for the Irgun and the Stern Gang, whose violence against the British didn't abate one bit and wouldn't, they announced, as long as the Jews lacked their proper homeland in Palestine.

-216-

As a volunteer organization, the Haganah had been formed for defense. Now, in cooperation with the British military, an elite strike force was formed of a hundred of the Haganah's best men, Avram among them. Called the Palmach, its primary purpose was to strike at the Germans in the event of their victory over the Allies in North Africa, followed by their occupation of Palestine. Among themselves, the Palmachis had an additional latent purpose: to fight attacking Arabs in the event of a sudden British retreat from Palestine.

-217-

Palmach: short for *Plugot Mahatz*, striking force

-218-

Work with the Jewish volunteers went on all that spring and summer of 1941. British army personnel drilled dozens of raw rookies and initiated them into one or two of the special arts of war: sabotage and explosives, reconnaissance, sniping, communications, machine guns and mortars. Regular Haganah and some Palmachis were given supplementary training. When Avram was called in for specialist training in company command, he ended up staying on as an instructor in basic training. He had a way with the "crows," they said.

~219~

Crow: British military slang for a newbie. Arising out of the first World War, the term derides inexperience. It was reputed to be an acronym for Combat Recruit Of War, though army wags commonly rendered it as Can't Read Or Write.

~220~

It was about this time, autumn of 1941, that Avram came home sporting a handsome black mustache and beard, which he trimmed meticulously every morning. Rivka, watching him, asked, "Are you training young women in the Palmach?"

"Sometimes. Why?"

"They wear short shorts, I hear. Very short shorts."

In the mirror, his eyes met hers. "Is that so? I hadn't noticed."

Better to be led around by a young chippie, Rivka reflected, than be ordered to your death by a British officer. Avram, because he was involved in training, hadn't been called for the first Palmach-British joint operation. Twenty-three high-spirited Jews led by a rock-ribbed British commanding officer set out for Lebanon by sea—and were lost, no one knew how. True, things were said to be going somewhat better now—well, they could hardly go worse. But there was that buddy of Avram's who'd served with him in the night squads. He was sent to the Litani River in a combined Australian-Palmachi detail. As he was reconnoitering the enemy from a rooftop, the glint from his binoculars struck the squint of a Vichy French sniper, and he lost one startled brown eye. Sidelined now, and with what sort of future ahead of him? Only in his mid-twenties, this Moshe Dayan. A pity.

-221-

The United States entered the war after the bombing of Pearl Harbor in December 1941. "I think this is good news," piped Shimshon. "But is it good for the Jews?"

Rivka had to bite the inside of her cheek to hide her amusement.

-222-

Never had the Stern Gang shaken Rivka down for support. Still, it was a relief when, in February 1942, Avraham Stern got rooted out of his hidey-hole in a wardrobe in an apartment in Tel Aviv. It happened that the British police found a damp shaving brush there, which gave away his presence. He lunged for escape through a window, and a quick-handed constable shot him dead. Soon, other members of the Stern Gang were being arrested and imprisoned. Rivka lifted a private toast to their disappearance.

-223-

Ever since Nazi forces had occupied Paris in June of 1940, life in the city had grown increasingly dreary and comfortless. When an order went out requiring all Jews to wear the yellow star, Faye balked. She was Jewish—Jorg, Christian—neither one of them observant. She had a Canadian passport, and none of her papers listed her religion. She resolved not to don that Nazi badge of shame.

Their life was quiet, she wrote Elli in May 1942. "You'd hardly recognize us, my dear niece. Marie and Cook have both gone away into the countryside. We rattle around these vast rooms all on our lonesome. No more of my salons jam-full of writers and artists rubbing their shabby shoulders with Jorg's wealthy patrons and their flighty socialites. Of course, Jorg continues to deal in art. A number of military gentlemen have become steady customers. Oh, and sometimes we use your old bedroom suite for visiting artists."

Was that last line code, Elli wondered, for hiding Jews? Hard to know. Faye's letters got through infrequently, after being smuggled from Paris to Vichy. First, the Vichy censors had to pass them, and then in Palestine again they came under the eyes of censors, British this time. "We live a quiet life" Elli took to mean "it's grim here." Jorg's "military gentlemen" she understood to mean German officers, and she had no doubt that Jorg was doing all he could to mislead them in their connoisseurship.

That there was no word about Gena chilled her. Jorg had taken the young artist under his wing and promoted his career as a painter. Surely they were in touch regularly. For some reason, Aunt held back from mentioning Gena. He and his wife, a ballerina, were both Russian emigrés, both anti-Soviet. His wife, Elli surmised, reading between the nonexistent lines —his wife, Sofia, must be Jewish.

-224-

There had long been rumors, of course, and they'd been countered by the usual denials. In wartime, false accusations of enemy atrocities are always rife. Now, though, intercepts of German communications coming out of the Soviet Union confirmed eyewitness accounts and made it conclusive: Jews in the Ukraine and Byelorussia were being slaughtered by the Nazis on a grand, a staggering scale. Word raced through Palestine about a Nazi drive to exterminate all the Jews under their control. "Does there exist sanity anywhere on this earth?"

raged Moshe, pacing the floor. Elli, frozen to her chair, shook her head in despair. Once she'd believed the Great War was the worst catastrophe she'd ever in her life have to witness. How young she'd been then!

-225-

From New York in May of 1942 came the call for a Jewish commonwealth in Palestine. Zionists at a conference in the Biltmore Hotel announced their determination: no longer would they accept the hazy concept of a "Jewish homeland;" their goal was nothing less than a Jewish state that, following the war, would be "integrated into the structure of a new democratic world."

-226-

In June 1942, Rommel's tanks rolled over the British at Tobruk. Pillars of dark smoke billowed from the port as the Germans mopped up thirty-three thousand British prisoners. What was left of Britain's forces retreated behind their defenses at El Alamein, a railway stop on Egypt's coast, and Britain's last defensive position in North Africa. The Afrika Korps was now only sixty miles from Alexandria, crouching to spring. No one predicted a British victory. In Cairo, King George's civil servants were burning their papers. Along the Nile delta, military engineers were flooding key positions to fend off a Nazi takeover of the Suez Canal. In Palestine, anyone British or Jewish trod on tiptoe, the hairs raised along their necks. Moshe got a phone call from Freddie Williamson. "I've got a bag packed and ready," he said. "I'd advise you do the same. I feel responsible, you know, for bringing you out here."

-227-

There was every reason to anticipate defeat. Where had the Axis powers not been victorious? Throughout Europe, they'd triumphed. True, they hadn't conquered England, but the London blitz—near-nightly bombings between September 1940 and May 1941—had killed tens of thousands of civilians and destroyed millions of homes. The blitz stopped only when Hitler called it off, distracted by the Soviet Union, where his troops penetrated deep and enveloped several armies. Sevastopol had been taken, and his troops were advancing on Stalingrad. Leningrad was under siege, and the Mediterranean island of Malta. German U-boats prowled the waters and coastlines of the North Sea and the Atlantic. Nor were things going any better in the islands of the Pacific, where Japan held the Asian rim securely under its thumb. Much of Burma had been taken. Calcutta, Ceylon, even Alaska and Vancouver were vulnerable. Already Vancouver had been shelled.

-228-

The battles for the last positions before Alexandria are hard.
   —Field Marshall Erwin Rommel, July 3, 1942
   letter to his wife

-229-

The first of two battles fought at El Alamein began early the morning of July 1, 1942, with an advance of Axis troops over the flat, scrubby terrain. To their north was the sea, to the south the Qattara Depression, an area the size of Lebanon lying below sea level. 'Outflanking' was Rommel's go-to maneuver. Qattara, full of sand dunes and salt marshes and bounded on its north by steep escarpments, ruled out that favorite Rommel ploy. At best, the line of battle could be forty

miles wide. The advance that day took longer than he expected, the troops not reaching their positions until fairly late
in the afternoon. Nor did things improve for the German and
Italian forces in subsequent days. Nearly the entire month
wore itself out in repeated attacks and Allied counterattacks, a
battle reminiscent of the stalemate of the Great War, rather
than the mobility of this one. The Axis brought off no break-
through, the Allies no rout, and the first battle of El Alamein
fizzled to a standstill.

On October 23, the second battle of El Alamein was
launched. Along overextended, insecure supply lines, the Axis
had done all they could to reinforce their troops and matériel.
The British were fighting under new leadership. Lieutenant-
General Bernard Montgomery had command of roughly
200,000 troops from the British Empire, Greece, Poland and
France, as against some 115,000 German and Italian troops.
Montgomery had a thousand tanks at his disposal, the
Germans five hundred fifty—though half of those were worth
double, being panzers of the Afrika Korps. Most important,
Montgomery had the support of the Royal Air Force. Quick
superiority in the air was key in this battle, as in this war. Its
role was conclusive in destroying Rommel's fast-moving, lethal
tanks.

The German troops had used the three months since the
last battle to place half a million land mines in a maze
overlaid with barbed wire. This they dubbed "the devil's
garden." Rommel had taken ill and was still recuperating in a
German sanitarium on the moon-washed night Montgomery
kicked off his offensive with a thousand-gun bombardment.
Demonic heat, light and destruction blasted the enemy for
five-and-a-half hours, the objective to clear two paths through

the minefield garden for his infantry. Within two days, Rommel was back with his troops, but by then Montgomery's bombardment had done its work. The battle had become an ear-splitting, nerve-rending, sweltering furnace of dense and lethal brawling. On November 2, Rommel begged permission from Hitler to withdraw. The Führer replied, "It would not be the first time in history that a strong will has triumphed over the bigger battalions. As to your troops, you can show them no other road than that to victory or death." For many it was death—or imprisonment. Montgomery's forces broke through the Italian lines on November 4, and Rommel's surviving troops started their sour trek back into Libya.

Church bells throughout the British Empire—silent since 1940—rang out their jubilation. At long last, it was possible to believe that Hitler was not invincible!

-230-

Before Alamein, we never had a victory. After Alamein, we never had a defeat.   —Winston Churchill

-231-

With the threat to Palestine removed, the British ordered the Palmach disbanded. Fat chance of that! While serving under the command of the British, Palmachis had been marshaling their own secret plans, which they now activated. Palmach platoons were redeployed to the kibbutzim to live as the residents did, receiving food and shelter in exchange for their agricultural work and enhanced protection of the settlement. They got seven days off each month. The rest of their time was taken up with work and training.

-232-

The immediate threat from the Nazis to the Jews of Palestine may have evaporated, but not the ongoing threat from the British, who now asserted Palestine's utter incapacity to absorb even one more Jewish refugee, stateless and homeless though he or she might be. The Irgun, infuriated, called for the Yishuv to arise and demand a government of their own. Okay sure, but let's beat the Nazis first, was the Yishuv's tepid response.

One way and another, though, Jewish people kept on settling the Land—on the edge of the Judean and Samarian hills, in the Huleh valley, around Hebron, near Gaza and south of Be'ersheva—moving into the Negev, proving it possible to farm there, to prosper in date palms, pomegranates and olives. No matter what the law said, there was always an Arab willing to sell land to a Jew—or in such financial straits as to make it impossible for him not to.

-233-

For two nights in March 1943, *We Will Never Die* was presented in New York City at Madison Square Garden. Financed through Peter Bergson, the pageant was produced by Billy Rose, directed by Moss Hart and scored by Kurt Weill. It starred Edward G. Robinson and Paul Muni. No wonder it attracted an audience of forty thousand!

The show traced Jewish history from Abraham onward, with a moving climax that trumpeted the continuity, the indestructibility, of the Jewish people. From New York, *We Will Never Die* traveled to Boston, Philadelphia, Chicago and Washington DC, where Eleanor Roosevelt saw it at Constitution Hall. Her next "My Day" column, syndicated in

newspapers nationwide, recounted the plight of Europe's Jews
—the first report many Americans had of it.

-234-

The modern Parisian suburb of Drancy had been
conceived, designed and partially built in the 1930s to
demonstrate the feasibility of safe, affordable urban housing.
It was nicknamed *La Cité de la Muette*—the Silent City—
because of the promise its architects held out of a tranquil and
contented way of life for its residents. The first pale-yellow
brick apartment block was completed before the war, a four-
story, U-shaped structure with a deep center courtyard.
Construction had only just begun on five adjacent residential
towers when the war started, and the near-empty facility
northwest of the city was turned into police barracks. When
the Nazis took Paris, with arrests mounting in and around the
city, they converted Drancy to a transit camp for temporary
internment of those who'd been rounded up. Sooner or later,
most of the prisoners would be transported to concentration
camps in the east. Drancy would serve also as a camp of
ongoing detention for foreign Jews.

Initially, French police did the round-ups and guarded the
inmates. These gendarmes could be bribed. Then, in July
1943, Drancy was given over to the governance of one Alois
Brunner, German officer in the SS.

-235-

Later that summer of 1943, Winston Churchill persuaded
the Mandate government to allow into Palestine any Jewish
refugees who could find their own way to Turkey. Boatloads
wallowed into Haifa carrying exhausted survivors from
Romania and Transvitria. Elli waited around on the docks to

meet them. She examined their anguished eyes, which burned with terror.

-236-

Howling and disaster, Father, go endless on and on.
—Nathan Alterman

-237-

October 1943

My darling Nellie,

I have bad news, and no way to temper it. Your Aunt Faye has been arrested, whether for her religion or her nationality I cannot say. I don't know how the SS could have identified her as a Jew. I can no longer look at my neighbors or speak to them. I suspect everyone of informing against us.

She was taken two weeks ago, and I've been on a campaign since then to try and free her. The best I can tell you is that she is being interned at Drancy, just outside of Paris. I have good reason to hope that she'll be held there indefinitely.

I am trying—though without the least success—to visit her. I've been able to lay my hands on a recent photograph of the facility. I knew it from before the war as an architectural gem, a sanctuary for city workers. It is no longer that. The center courtyard has been enclosed with barbed wire, and it teems with people. I'm told that your aunt is likely to have been placed inside the old police barracks. That's still behind the barbed wire, but at least she'd be protected from the weather.

We can only hope for the best. Faye is a strong-minded woman, and if in nothing else, I have infinite faith in her.

My love to you, Morris and Marian,

Jorgen

-238-

Three walls were bare concrete, the fourth all window. About fifty women were assigned to this one small room. Every ten of them shared a single bar of soap. Water trickled out of a faucet into a wooden trough. Laundry was strung on lines criss-crossing the space overhead. A dozen straw-filled mattresses took up much of the floor, along with a few stools and a single chair with a broken rung. The air was stuffy and humid indoors, dry and cold outdoors, where they were made to stand for roll call sometimes once, sometimes twice a day. Day and night loudspeakers accosted Faye's ears. The latrines were unspeakable.

-239-

In November 1943, fifteen miles west of Jerusalem, twenty Stern Gang members tunneled their way out of the prison in Latrun. Lehi was back in business.

-240-

What a trick God had played on her when he made Rivka a mother! He'd given her these helpless infants, these tiny beings into whom she'd thrown the whole of her soul: adoring, instructing, protecting; keeping in sight, keeping in mind, keeping in heart, keeping under her roof, her blankets, her care. Feeding and nurturing and scolding and checking up on and sometimes being so furious at because in some way they'd disappointed her. At first all they were, and entirely, was potential; they could become anything. Then they showed her, slowly, inexorably, who they were and would be. And she'd adjusted to them and tried to help them become fully whoever they would be. She thought she knew, she hoped she knew. She was raising each of them to be independent and to leave her.

Now it was Ahuva who announced her departure, leaving her mother bereft. It turned out Rivka had never grasped that a child of hers would actually go. She'd never dreamt what the going would require of her. She'd been too busy, it seemed. She should be happy for Ahuva, but was too scared to be. She was scared for them all, because sooner or later they would all leave—exit—walk out the door into a world where she couldn't follow, full of trouble and pain and sorrow—where she'd be needed to protect and guide them. She wasn't ready for their absence, but neither were they ready for hers, really not. In the years since they were born, look how much Rivka herself had learned. And look how very nice to spend time with her firstborn had become.

-241-

Leila's children, too, had been disappearing from her side. Not the boys. The boys, in the main, brought home wives and settled down to make children of their own. Leila was rich in sons, and soon in grandsons. Zeinab, her daughter, her darling, her eldest, had been the first to leave. Married at fifteen, Zeinab had gone to live with her father-in-law's family in the village of Deir Yassin. Rivka, too, missed Zeinab, a sedate child with three fine beauty marks that seemed to dance in a line from her forehead to the tip of her nose to the middle of her chin.

-242-

Deir Yassin: a village perched on a high, stony ridge close to Jerusalem. An ordinary Arab village ringed by trees of olive and pine, where families had lived for some seven hundred years. Traditionally home to stone cutters, its narrow streets were lined with limestone houses of one or two stories, prosperous homes sporting arches and sturdy iron gateways. A mosque bounded the village at one end, the remains of a monastery at the other. Horses, camels, mules and shank's mare were the means of transportation in and out. Nearby stood a Jewish village, Givat Shaul. The women from Deir Yassin—Zeinab included—went there almost every day laden with olives and fruit to sell. They came back with the chicken and meat they'd purchased or traded for.

-243-

Moshe and Elli offered to put her up, but Ahuva had no interest in studying at the Hebrew University in Jerusalem. Instead, she found a job typing at a Tel Aviv architectural firm. The construction business was so hectic that even Ahuva's shaky office skills were in demand. Tel Aviv lured modernist architects who'd fled Germany, bringing with them their Bauhaus aesthetic and International Style. Since 1933, thousands of scrumptious buildings had gone up in a dazzling rush of creativity. In her off hours, Ahuva started seeing a young man whose mop of curly ginger hair had drawn her in. Soon her narrow rented room barely saw her.

It's not what you're thinking.

At night, secretly, he was training her in the fundamentals of robbing banks.

1944

-244-

A calamity was devouring European Jewry.

To Menachem Begin, leader of the Irgun, it was glaringly plain and certain that the British would never allow the Jews to immigrate freely. If he wanted to save whoever still survived, Begin concluded he'd have to find a way to get the British to abandon Palestine. On February 1, 1944, the Irgun announced "There is no longer an armistice… in Eretz Israel." From then on, the group made open revolt against the Mandate—but a revolt cognizant of wartime all the same. Irgun's stratagem had nothing to do with threats or assaults on the military. Rather, it aimed at humiliating the Mandate administration. It would turn Palestine into a "glass house" before the nations of the world. It would entangle the British in the world's attention and force them to suffer the world's contempt.

With the Stern Gang pledging its cooperation, the Irgun set to work. On February 12, the immigration offices in Jerusalem, Tel Aviv and Haifa were bombed. February 27, the income tax offices in Jerusalem, Tel Aviv and Haifa were bombed. Lehi members were putting up posters on February 14, when by happenstance they were approached by two British policemen, whom they shot dead. Again Lehi on March 13 killed a police officer, who was a Jew. March 23, two more British policemen were killed and a third wounded; and the criminal investigation department of the police had its offices attacked in Jerusalem, Jaffa and Haifa and also bombed in Jaffa and Haifa.

-245-

Menachem Begin: born Mieczysław Biegun in Poland, 1913, was a "notorious terrorist" in those years. His tactics were deplored not only by the British, but also by the Jewish Agency. A lifelong political, economic and military conservative, he would nevertheless become the State of Israel's lauded peacemaker when, in 1978, he would take part in the Camp David Accords, leading to a peace treaty with Egypt and a Nobel Peace Prize for him and Anwar Sadat.

-246-

The five-year plan of the White Paper lapsed in April 1944. "Not that it makes a particle of difference," muttered Shimshon.

Rivka spied a developing shadow along his upper lip. She smiled.

"What?" he challenged, his voice cracking, but her smile only broadened.

-247-

Despite the Irgun's insurgency, Britain at long last commenced training and arming a fully-Jewish brigade to serve at the front. Not to be outdone, the Grand Mufti in Berlin clamored for an Arab Islamic force to be trained and armed by Germany.

"Please God, nothing comes of it," murmured Rivka. "Say what you will, those damn Germans are crack soldiers. They'd whip the Arabs into shape."

-248-

Nothing did come of it.

-249-

On Monday, June 6, on the beaches of Normandy, under heavy fire and facing fierce opposition, the Allied armies gained a toehold in France.

-250-

Tali left on a scouting trip, his rucksack bobbing jauntily against his shoulders. When he didn't return after a week, Rivka made inquiry of Yudi, to no avail. Yudi said not to worry, Tali would be back soon. Ditto the second week. She couldn't worm another word out of Yudi, so she called the scouts, who claimed no knowledge of the trip. How could this be?

A third nervous week crawled by before she got terrible word: Tali was in jail, a boy only sixteen years of age! It turned out he'd been training with a Palmachi scout by the name of Shimon Peres on an expedition through the Negev. A clutch of boys. A dozen camels. Revolvers, grenades.

"Tell me please, son of mine, what did you think you were you doing in that trackless wilderness?"

"Drawing maps, making friends with the Bedouin—"

"With a grenade in your pocket you made friends?"

"Ima, those were just in case."

"In case what?"

"In case we needed them."

They'd hiked all the way to the Turkish border point at Um Rashrah, where they were all arrested, transported back through the desert and thrown behind bars in Be'ersheva. Avram had had to go down there and get Tali out.

-251-

Um Rashrah: modern day Eilat

Shimon Peres, born Szymon Perski, was twenty years old at the time of his escapade in the Negev, a closed military zone. In later years, he was to become a member of twelve cabinets in Israel, a prime minister of Israel and a president of Israel. A man of peace, he would engineer the Israel-Jordan peace treaty and win the Nobel Peace Prize, along with

Yitzhak Rabin and Yassir Arafat, for the Oslo Accords. He was a lover of literature and would write poetry during long and weary cabinet meetings.

-252-

The two women understood something good was happening off westward. When the wind was right, they caught the prolonged thunder of fierce barrages. Their German guards wore unsettled looks, and their roll calls in the trash-clogged courtyard of Drancy grew cursory and haphazard. Sofia chafed Faye's chilly hand between her own. "Hold on," she urged in her Russian-accented French. "Faye, please hold on." Faye was doing her best, but she'd held out so long already and was so very tired.

-253-

When the moment came, and Ahuva stood fixed in place in the bank, her trembling arms refused to point her firearm into some poor teller's wan face. Ahuva's cohorts—no thanks to her—narrowly contrived to make off with a nice haul of cash stuffed into a battered gunny sack, plus Ahuva's sorry self in tow. Thick in disgrace with the whole Stern Gang, she slunk off to Haifa to re-start her adult life, this time as an aid in a Jewish nursery school.

-254-

He had a telegram from Jorg and sped directly to the clinic in East Jerusalem. He found Elli examining the inflamed eye of a spindly ten-year-old boy. Something made her glance up. Moshe's dear face, so lacking in guile, told her enough. "Who?" she yelped. Not Marian. Oh, don't let it be Marian.

"Faye. Of dysentery."

If he said more, she didn't take it in. Her knees gave way, and she slumped into his arms.

-255-

The Allied advance engulfed Drancy, and on the seventeenth of August, neutral Swedish representatives assumed control of the camp. They, in turn, put its daily welfare into the hands of the Red Cross. Speedily, the foul condition of the place abated. Alas for the foul condition of the inmates, many of whom were beyond remedy or respite. Sofia, Gena's wife, was among those too sick to be saved.

-256-

Paris was liberated from the Nazis on August 25. As soon as her first small crop was harvested, Rivka shipped oranges to Gena and to Jorg, but the hope-laden crates returned back to her, the sweet fruit rotting.

-257-

The Irgun-Lehi insurgency continued through Palestine's spring and summer, even as the British clamped down on the country with searches, roadblocks, cordons, arrests and fines.

-258-

Lord Moyne was an easy mark in his customary bow tie and aertex cotton suit. He sat forward from the backseat of the car slowing to a stop in front of his official residence in Cairo. An idle postprandial silence held the Egyptian air suspended, so too the street, so too the neighborhood. His driver, Lance Corporal Arthur Fuller, got out and reached for Lord Moyne's door. From nowhere, it seemed, or from the inexhaustible shrubbery—came a man running—came a gunshot—Fuller on his back on the ground in a gathering puddle of blood—while looming up a second man at the car door—three bangs like drumfire, Lord Moyne's hand raised to ward off the next whomp, fingers smeared crimson.

-259-

From *The Jerusalem Post*, November 7, 1944:

Murder of Lord Moyne
Minister Resident Shot in Cairo

CAIRO, Monday....

The assailants, who were arrested, are not Egyptians, it is officially stated. The Egyptian Government has issued a statement declaring that it is "shocked by the outrage." An earlier police announcement said that the men wore European dress. In addition to inflicting fatal injuries upon Lord Moyne they also killed his military driver who tried to stop them.

-260-

The assassins' names were Eliahu Bet-Tsouri and Eliahu Hakim. They were arrested on their rented bicycles just streets —and minutes—away from the crime. They went after Lord Moyne because he was the highest British official within the Stern Gang's reach—a reach, be it noted, that could stretch beyond the borders of Palestine; and also because they thought him the chief architect of Britain's policy against Jewish immigration; because he was to them the mirror of Arabist, anti-Semitic and anti-Zionist conviction; because he advocated for a "Greater Syria"—a federation proposed to secure British interests in the region, overspreading Syria, Transjordan and portions of Palestine and Lebanon; because they aimed to dramatize before world opinion the impact of Britain's imperialist policies. For all these reasons, they murdered him—or perhaps for none of them. True, Lord Moyne had made anti-Semitic remarks in public, but he also had promoted the partition of Palestine. So maybe it was the office, British minister of state in the Middle East, rather than the man himself, that the assassins attacked.

-261-

The Saison: hunting season

-262-

Now it was open season on Jewish terrorists, even among Palestine's Jews themselves. Zionist socialists and all they stood for pitted themselves against Jewish militarists and all they stood for. Jews savaged one another in word and print. The newspaper *Ha'aretz* accused the assassins of having "done more by this single reprehensible crime to demolish the edifice erected by three generations of Jewish pioneers than is imaginable." From the outraged Jewish Agency came an incitement of the Yishuv to "cast out" the Stern Gang, to "deprive them of all refuge and shelter, to resist their threats, and to render all necessary assistance to the authorities in the prevention of terrorist acts."

It went beyond bitter words. Stunningly, the Jewish Agency gave lists to the British authority, lists of the names of hundreds of members of the Stern Gang and the Irgun. Rivka would have rejoiced, had she been confident that no one in her own household could possibly be among those names.

British prisons filled. So did secret Haganah lockups where

captured Irgun members were interrogated none too lovingly by their Jewish brothers. "Can you imagine," Avram told Rivka, "who remains free among the Stern Gang have had to make an oath to Haganah's underground. An oath that they won't assassinate Churchill."

"Churchill? *Churchill?*"

"I shouldn't have told you." If he hadn't told her, she wouldn't be wigwagging her arms about like—

"A staunch friend to the Jews, and they'd think of assassinating him?"

"I shouldn't have mentioned it."

He didn't know how to talk to her anymore. Mostly, they nattered past each other. Mostly she spoke of budwood, of black rot, of growth stages, of yield; he of deployments, of volunteers, of mines and mortars.

-263-

Eliahu Bet-Tsouri and Eliahu Hakim were sentenced to death a little over two months after the murder of Lord Moyne, and they were hanged—singing "Hatikvah"—two months after that. On the very day of their execution in late March of 1945, and also in Cairo, the Arab League was formed. Its stated purpose was to unite Islam throughout the Arab lands of North Africa and the Near East. Palestine, it declared, "constitutes an important part of the Arab world and the rights of Arabs cannot be touched upon without prejudice to peace and stability in the Arab world." Not an Islamic army yet, but formidable enough.

-264-

Thirty years later, in 1975, Egypt would exchange the remains of the two assassins for twenty prisoners held by the

Israelis. After lying in state in Jerusalem, Eliahu Bet-Tsouri and Eliahu Hakim would be buried in the military section of Mount Herzl—that place of ultimate homage—in a state funeral with full honors. Times—politics—would have shifted by then, and the State of Israel would rank the two young men as "heroic freedom fighters."

1945

-265-

Berlin fell to Soviet forces on May 2, 1945.
Haj Amin al-Husseini decamped into France, where he was spotted as a Nazi collaborator and held under house arrest in Paris.

-266-

From *The Palestine Post*, May 7, 1945:

WORLD AWAITS CEASE FIRE

-267-

From *The New York Times* May 8, 1945:

THE WAR IN EUROPE IS ENDED! SURRENDER IS UNCONDITIONAL V-E WILL BE PROCLAIMED TODAY

-268-

More than thirty thousand Jews from Palestine and about six thousand Arabs had been serving with the British army in Greece, Crete, North Africa, Italy and Northern Europe. Soon to be demobilized, they would carry their fighting skills home with them.

-269-

So the war was over, and what was the world going to do with all those leftover Jews? Hitler hadn't quite finished the job, and the Jewish remnant didn't look kindly on going back to the places in Germany, Poland, Czechoslovakia, Hungary and wherever else, where they hadn't been wanted in the first place, and where they no longer had any community. Some of them who tried to resettle were murdered. In Poland alone, hundreds—perhaps thousands—lost their lives in pogroms. At best, they got home and found their houses inhabited by strangers. It was explained to them that nobody thought they'd be back. They were looked at like ghosts. They looked like ghosts.

They trudged, they slogged, they straggled their way into the DP camps, where they could be fed and clothed and sheltered, though admittedly in repurposed concentration camps or prisoner-of-war facilities. Some of them hoped to settle in America, but that prospect was improbable unless they had a relative already living there. Most of them longed to go to Palestine. They knew little about the place and even less about Jewish problems there, but they felt it as a future worth fighting for.

In the DP camps, they crowded into Hebrew classes set up by the Joint.

-270-

DP: Displaced Person. At war's end, about a million displaced persons passed through camps in Germany and Austria. Among them were between 200,000 and 250,000 Jews. The others had homes they could return to, or if not, job offers in faraway lands needing able-bodied workers. Thin and frail and haunted, the Jews who stayed, languished.

The Joint: The American Jewish Joint Distribution Committee, a philanthropic organization. It was started during World War I, when Henry Morgenthau, Sr., America's ambassador to Turkey, wired Jacob Schiff in New York to raise funds to reduce the wretched condition of Jews in Ottoman Palestine. Relief efforts continued beyond the war both in Palestine and in Europe. Upon the rise of Nazi Germany, the organization revised its mission to focus on those refugees. Their rescue continued throughout the war and in its dismal aftermath.

-271-

The operation to bring Jews to Palestine was called *Aliyah Bet*. After the war, the boats of Aliyah Bet were organized by an arm of the Haganah. Those that left soonest after V-E day did get through. From ports in Italy and Greece, they crossed the Mediterranean carrying survivors of the death camps. But first, to get to the boats, if you were coming south through Italy as most did, you'd have to get by the Tommies at the northern border of Italy. You'd be in danger there of arrest and imprisonment. The British continued to assert that Palestine simply could not admit most Jewish refugees. This was based on the immigration restrictions of 1939—despite the relevant White Paper having sunsetted in April of 1944.

-272-

The death of President Franklin D. Roosevelt in April 1945 had elevated his unprepared vice-president, Harry S. Truman. Regarding Palestine and the DPs, the new president had been rightly christened—he was harried beyond endurance on all sides: by Zionists, by congressmen and senators of all slants, and by his own state department, which had its eye on Middle Eastern oil. He dispatched Earl G. Harrison to Europe on a fact-finding mission to inspect the DP camps and inquire into the conditions and needs of the DPs. Harrison was well suited to the job, having been Roosevelt's Commissioner of Immigration and Naturalization as well as the United States representative on the Intergovernmental Commission on Refugees. An attorney, he was also dean of the law school at the University of Pennsylvania. Harrison drew together a handful of trusted advisers in a delegation that set out early in July. At the time, there were an estimated 250,000 DPs in the camps, 138,000 of them Jewish. Without delay, members of the delegation toured two dozen or more camps, interviewing DPs and officials alike. On August 24, Harrison delivered the written report of his findings. Its conclusion, in brief:

> The only real solution of the problem lies in the quick evacuation of all non-repatriable Jews in Germany and Austria, who wish it, to Palestine. In order to be effective, this plan must not be long delayed. The urgency of the situation should be recognized. It is inhuman to ask people to continue to live for any length of time under their present conditions.... The civilized world owes it to this handful of survivors to provide them with a home where they can again settle down and begin to live as human beings.

The Jewish Agency had already demanded of the British one hundred thousand new immigration certificates for immediate use. The British had refused. In mid-August, having received Harrison's preliminary report, Truman said in a press conference that his policy was to "let as many Jews in Palestine as possible and still maintain civil peace." Once he had the final report in hand, Truman sent a note to British Prime Minister Clement Atlee urging a hundred thousand visas be released.

-273-

The more boats that made for Palestine's shores, the better the British became at intercepting them. By fall of 1945, very few were getting through. They'd be caught and towed into Haifa, where the crushed refugees would be ordered ashore and taken to the camp at Athlit twelve miles away. There, men were separated from women, and all were concentrated behind walls and barbed wire, overseen from watchtowers. Huddled there, still they nursed dreams of one day being free in this Land where all their hopes converged.

-274-

At the beginning of October, six Palmachis infiltrated the camp at Athlit in the guise of teachers of Hebrew and physical education. Their mission was to ready the inmates and the site itself for an operation that would be carried out on the night of October 9-10. This they did, all according to a plan devised by a serious-minded young redhead by the name of Yitzhak Rabin. It was the first anti-British action to be undertaken by Palmach.

On the selected night, Arab auxiliaries guarding Athlit's perimeter discovered at the point when they needed them that not a single one of their rifles would shoot. Rifles with broken firing pins never do. Efficiently, the guards were overpowered and silenced in the darkness. Nearby, British soldiers slumbering in their billets went undisturbed and unaware that an evacuation of the inmates was getting underway. All was remarkably noiseless. Survivors of the concentration camps—even small children—knew how to keep their mouths shut. At a spot not far away, a string of trucks waited to take them to safety on Mount Carmel's northeastern slope. Some had already loaded up and were gone, when a British lorry happening by decided to stop and investigate.

Man plans, God laughs: happenstance is the one thing a

good plan can't control. The British opened fire—and were silenced. Meantime, the remaining Jewish trucks took off with those who'd already boarded. But half of the evacuees hadn't yet reached the meeting place. Now they were left to scale Mount Carmel on foot, many with children on their backs. A harrowing night for them and the Palmachis trekking along with them, making their slow way toward safety at Kibbutz Yagur.

-275-

Yitzhak Rabin was born in Jerusalem in 1922. He joined the Haganah at the age of fourteen, the start of a 27-year career as a soldier, officer and chief of staff of the army. He would become Israel's ambassador to the United States (1968-73) and serve as Israel's prime minister—the first sabra to hold that office—then minister of defense, then prime minister again. Having signed the Oslo Accords to foster peace with the Palestinians—and a peace treaty with Jordan—he was assassinated in 1995 by one of his disgruntled countrymen.

-276-

A knock at her door in the predawn woke Ahuva. The call for action was spreading like a sear of flame through Jewish Haifa. It brought news that the British were getting ready to force Kibbutz Yagur's gates in order to re-arrest internees who'd escaped from Athlit. The British did try to do just that, but by noon on October 10, the place had filled with a mass of volunteers, Ahuva among the hundreds of others. Like the Children of Israel on the safe side of the Red Sea, they milled about, singing, dancing, having a holiday. In that crowd,

208 refugees became like so many women of valor: who could find them?

-277-

The Mandate had a long habit of deporting Jewish prisoners. Somewhere deep in Kenya, a camp was reserved specifically for Lehi and the Irgun. Godforsaken holes were operated, too, in Eritrea, Sudan and other African whereabouts no one had ever heard of. Now a sprawling camp was set up on the Mediterranean island of Cyprus to keep the flood of would-be immigrants beyond reach of Palestine. Aluminum quonset huts and tents enclosed behind barbed wire sufficed. Escape from the island was pretty much out of the question. Yet even there, in the wasting heat and squalor, the refugees held out hope.

-278-

You had to smell Cyprus to believe it.
                              —Journalist Ruth Gruber

-279-

October 20, 1945

Ma chére amie, dearest Rivka,

Your beautiful oranges have journeyed all the way from the Holy Land. They bring me sugarsweet memories of you. With your permission I will share this fullness with a painter who lives nearby. He is good artist but not popular like me. He has been a good help since I lost my *lyubimaya moya* Sofia.

I am well. I have thought of leaving Paris, but to live where? Poland, maybe? Here, I am nearest Sofia's spirit, so I stay.

Can you send photo of your children?
Gena

-280-

October 22, 1945

Dear Rivka,

The crate of fruit has, indeed, reached me this time. I would have telegraphed at once to let you know it, had I not worried that the very sight of a telegram from Paris would cause you anxiety.

Life has been hard here since the liberation. Parisian citizens have been cruel to anyone who collaborated with the Nazis, and they're anything but careful in determining who has been a collaborator. I think they need scapegoats to account for their years-long subjugation. I am one whose loyalties are suspected. Primarily, I suppose, my very public dealings with German officers were the reason, though it can't have helped that I'm a foreigner in their eyes. The impatient French have been too ready to take things as they appear and to brush off any closer examination. All of which is to explain to you that the oranges have brought me great delight and more. They have in addition brought me a measure of peace, as I've provided my too-nosy neighbors with enough sustenance to quiet their suspicions. Many thanks. Your generosity touches me deeply.

Thank you, too, for your tender and funny reminiscence about Faye. This year, the roses she planted in our garden bloomed like never before, *Soleil D'Or* and *Bouquet D'Or*, peach and vanilla. She wasn't here to paint them, but their lingering fragrance wafts her through my heart. I miss her every moment.

My best to Avram. I wish you health and joy, and success in besting the British in your quest for a commonwealth of your own.

Jorgen

-281-

The Saison had been called off prior to the war's end, once Germany's defeat was in the bag. That fall, Ben-Gurion, as head of the Jewish Agency, banged together the heads of the Irgun and the Stern Gang and the Haganah, insisting they all work together, coordinating their strategies. Over the next eight months—before the deal fell apart—the resistance movement's explosives would bring havoc to British coast guard and police stations, trains and electric substations and military depots. Together, the resistance would loot British payrolls and plunder British arms caches. Between Jewish destruction and Jewish theft, Britain would be out millions of the pounds they'd invested in Palestine.

-282-

The groups were like brothers who couldn't get along. They sneered at each others' methods and squabbled incessantly over aims. But like brothers, they couldn't get along without each other, either.

"Each of us serves a part, I suppose," remarked Avram with a shrug.

Rivka grunted. She'd seen it all before: a country tearing itself apart; a ruling class that understood nothing; a population divided and scrapping; a volatile, violent minority taking the lead. She'd witnessed all this in Russia in 1917 and knew how suddenly things could go bad. It was incomprehensible that she should live to see her own people waging an all-out war, an undeclared war—against the British, no less —over the issue of immigration. Incomprehensible that so few of her people still believed in a country to be shared in a spirit of equality with their Arab neighbors. Incomprehensible that the Jews could place their hope in the actions of Etzel, Lehi, the Stern Gang—different names, but always the same criminals and terrorists who would stop at nothing. They thought they could blast open the doors to Europe's Jewish remnant, that they could build, like an overnight settlement, a Jewish majority in Palestine. No good could come of an evil beginning. No structure stands long on sand. "We weep, and the Arabs laugh," she told Avram. But here's what she really meant: I fear for what we are becoming.

-283-

For the most part, Palestine's Arabs sat back and watched. And worried.

-284-

Why was Avram suddenly home so much? Almost three full weeks now, and not a single night away. He claimed he was training the new kibbutzniks who'd decided to settle atop the hill south of Ness Ziona. This corner of Rehovot seemed an odd location for pioneers, but many of them were said to be bakers, so maybe not so odd a place after all. If Avram weren't so close-mouthed about it, she'd have thought nothing of it.

-285-

On October 31, the temporarily united Jewish Resistance Movement sabotaged the Palestinian Railway, not at a single spot, but at a hundred fifty-three separate ones. Ahuva rolled over in her sleep, disturbed by the rumbling in Haifa.

-286-

At a press conference in November 1945, British Foreign Secretary Ernest Bevin cautioned Jewish refugees not to "get too much at the head of the queue."

-287-

The British tended to push harder the harder they were pushed. They'd come out to Palestine expecting to patch things up between the two adversaries, Arabs and Jews—but now in the aftermath of the war, they found themselves the adversary of both, hated by both, and now plagued and harassed by a Jewish insurgency. In the post-war demobilization, the first soldiers into the country became the first to leave it, with a resulting loss of discipline. The British officers who remained in Palestine were, as a rule, less experienced and knowledgeable, and their troops likewise less sound.

-288-

There was this high school kid, Ahuva knew him vaguely. In Haifa, it was rare for a Jew not to have some sort of connection with every other Jew. This Asher, he was a sweetie. He'd carried her groceries uphill for her a time or two. One day, they shot him. All he was doing was tacking up some anti-British posters on a wall near his school. For this, they put a British bullet in his hip, then put him straight into jail in Acre. No doctor, no care at all for the wound. He was cooped up and tied to his bed, a maimed schoolboy! For a poster! It could just as well have been one of her brothers.

-289-

It could have been his own daughter, Marian, tied to that bed, hip festering, wound oozing blood and pus onto the mattress, spilling to the ground. Moshe paced the floor of his office, imagining the boy, letting his long-festering anger spill over like pus. For all his former countrymen's outrages committed in the name of keeping order—outrages Moshe himself had been disposed to forgive or ignore or even see reason for (we're no angels ourselves, we Jews)—this attack upon an innocent schoolboy lodging a rightful protest was the thing that galvanized him. It gave him to know that he was fully Jewish Moshe now, and not the least bit British Morris any longer.

-290-

In February 1946, the Jewish resistance movement picked up some munitions in a raid on a military depot. They went on to strike at police barracks and military encampments. In an attack on an airstrip, they wrecked a dozen or so British planes. When two of their own men were killed in a crossfire with the police, fifty thousand mourners turned out for the funeral.

-291-

Time after time, Truman pressed Britain to admit a hundred thousand survivors into Palestine. By June 1946, Ernest Bevin had had enough. He countered, "I hope I will not be misunderstood in America if I say that this was proposed by the purest of motives. They did not want too many Jews in New York."

-292-

Chaim Weizmann, who'd played a key role in negotiating the Balfour Declaration, had a home in Rehovot not far from Rivka's place, and they'd cross paths from time to time when she went about her errands. One day she chanced to hear him remarking that the advent of Jewish terrorism was deplorable.

Of course it is, she thought.

But also tragic—he went on to say—since it arose from despair of ever securing justice for the Jewish people through peaceful means.

If it was tragic, did that make any difference? Did that make Jewish terrorism less deplorable, or more acceptable? She'd have to think about this word *tragic*.

-293-

Weizmann would go on to become the first president of the State of Israel.

-294-

A year under house arrest had passed pleasantly enough—and without incident—when one more time, Haj Amin al-Husseini proved his flair for slipping away undetected. His baffled captors in Paris found themselves unexpectedly without their quarry. He, meanwhile, delivered himself to Cairo, and took up where he'd left off as mufti in exile. News of his escape flew through Palestine, and celebratory bonfires blazed up in village after village. In Zarnuqua, Leila's husband and sons went the rounds exchanging handshakes with other Muslims, tears of joy starting in their eyes. The lifting hearts of the women sent warbling ululations sailing into the air.

-295-

Why should you Jews come here?—asks the Arab.

Answers the Jew—Because this Land was our home for over 1,600 years. It was we who abided here, despite the conquering Assyrians, Babylonians, Persians, Greeks and Egyptians. Then the Roman invaders threw us out—toppled Jerusalem—and sowed the Land with salt. But even so, some Jews stayed on in the holy cities. Always in Safed, in Tiberias, in Hebron and yes, in Jerusalem, too. Not to mention that the Land has remained in the hearts of Jews ever since.

A—This was long ago. Why didn't you settle yourselves elsewhere?

J—We did, and prospered, until we were expelled. Let's not review all of history. Let's just take, say, five hundred years in Europe alone. Between the year 1000 and the year 1500, we Jews suffered expulsion from the Crimea in the year 1016; from Germany in 1012, and again in 1096 and again in 1192; from Silesia, 1159; from England and Wales, 1290; from France, 1182 and again 1306 and again 1420; Provence, 1394 and again 1490; Austria, 1421; Spain and Sicily, 1492; from Cracow, 1494; from Lithuania, 1445 and again 1495, and from Portugal, 1497. Wherever we go, we're guests, wanderers living at sufferance of other people. If what we've endured under the Nazis doesn't convince you, I don't know what will. We must have our own homeland.

A—Fine. Good. Have your own homeland. But not here in my house. Go find yourself an empty house.

J—But this was my house once, and I did not leave it voluntarily.

A—A thousand years ago?

J—You have all the rest of the vast Arab world. Why insist upon this small patch, where you've never prospered?

A—Because it is my home. Not yours.

J—Well, we'll see about that.

A—Inshallah.

J—Inshallah.

-296-

Freddie Williamson phoned him—Freddie, whom he barely saw these days, except at official receptions. Freddie said he felt himself responsible for their being in Palestine. Actually, what he said was, "The fact that we Britons saved your Jewish skins at Alamein doesn't alter the fact that I got you out here in the first place"—but Moshe chose to notice only the latter half of Freddie's sentiments. And now the brisk voice on the phone confided that a remarkable advice had come down from above. He read it to Moshe in full. It was addressed to British officers and administrators, calling for their families to evacuate Palestine, inasmuch as the Mandate could no longer assure the safety of women and children. Moshe brooded over it for the rest of the day.

That night, after an unusually silent dinner, he cleared his throat and urged Elli in strongest terms to take Marian and go.

Elli stirred a spoonful of sugar into her tea, unmindful that she'd already done so. For the first time ever, she found herself disappointed in her husband. How could he suggest she decamp at just this time? "I cannot, will not, leave. Not now. Anyway, we've both lived through far worse, haven't we."

"Won't you consider it, for Marian's sake?" he implored.

"Don't you know me at all?"

She let him discuss with her whether there was anyplace out of danger, anyone they trusted, to whom they might send their daughter. He discussed it with her, but no. There were only Jorg and Gena, two broken widowers back in Paris, neither of them equipped to deal with an adolescent girl.

-297-

An Anglo-American Committee of Enquiry was formed at the beginning of 1946. It aimed to assess current conditions in the Mandate and Europe, identifying problems and recommending solutions to them. A dozen members, half of them British, half American—diplomats, scholars and politicians— met in Washington DC and London, in the DP camps and Palestine, holding hearings and meetings everywhere, wanting not to overlook the representatives of any party.

The Jews had a great spokeswoman and fundraiser in Golda Meyerson (later Meir). In March 1946, she challenged the committee, "How can you know what it's like to be a member of the people whose every right to exist is constantly being questioned?" Maybe not an exact quote, but close enough. "We want to be masters of our own fate," she went on. "Just our own fate and no one else's." It was good stuff, but it made no ultimate difference to the decision makers in Britain's government. She might just as well have been spluttering. And she wasn't alone. The Anglo-American Committee report that came out late in April recommended by unanimous vote of its members that a hundred thousand Jewish survivors be admitted immediately into Palestine. Where Britain was concerned, they, too, might just as well have been spluttering.

-298-

It was in April, too, that the British caught wind of two Palestine-bound ships making ready to put off from the Italian port of La Spezia. His Majesty's government had a little talk with the Italians. Aboard the ships, the refugees were awaiting departure when an order came for them to disembark. They refused; they declared a hunger strike; they warned that they were prepared to die, and an attempt to remove them by force would prompt their mass suicide. The Italians paled as they envisaged a thousand survivors subsiding into corpses right there on the fabled shores of the Riviera. The optics of it came home to the British as the affair began to draw international scrutiny. Not long after, the two ships, the *Dov Hoz* and the *Eliahu Golomb*, were given the go-ahead to sail unimpeded. On May 13, they made port in Haifa, and every single one of those refugees was handed an immigration certificate.

-299-

Dov Hos and Eliahu Golomb, the men for whom the ships were named, were born in Byelorussia within a year of one another. Both made aliyah to Palestine with their families, both were among the first graduates of Herzliya High School in Tel Aviv, both were founding organizers of the Haganah and both served as members of its command. Both married sisters of Moshe Shertok (later Sharett).

Dov Hos (1894-1940) became a pioneer in Israeli aviation.

Eliahu Golomb (1893-1945) spent time abroad in the 1920s organizing pioneer youth groups and purchasing arms for the Haganah. In the 1930s, illegal immigration was organized and financed largely at his direction. A founder of the Palmach, in the 1940s he trained many of its fighters. Personally, Avram found him overbearing, but when he died of heart failure on a hot June day in Tel Aviv, Avram wept.

-300-

A full moon poured its light over Palestine the night of June 16, but most on-duty British police and military stood watch as if in a fog, their attentions distracted by Palmachi flimflam. Operation *Markolet*, the Night of the Bridges, targeted ten bridges that linked Palestine to Lebanon, Syria, Transjordan and Egypt. Their fall would cut Palestine off from its neighbors. Concurrently, some fifty dizzying actions and ambushes were put in play over a wide area, making the true mission hard to suss out. Most guards remained unsuspecting at their bridgeheads while boluses of TNT were gently set in place along the supports below their feet. Unsuspecting, that is, until the Palmachis called out a warning to them that the span would blow in a minute or two. Nine road and railway bridges collapsed into rubble that night. Only at Nahal Kziv were the charge setters spotted in time. Fourteen Palmachis were killed in the firefight that followed.

The next night, Lehi attacked and damaged two railway workshops in Haifa, with eleven killed.

Soon after, in Tel Aviv, the Irgun seized five British officers who were peaceably lunching at their club. Two of the officers were let go to deliver a ransom note. It said the lives of the other three rested on what would happen to two Irgun members being held by the British and lately sentenced to death.

-301-

All this damage to Palestine's infrastructure, all this danger to British lives was grievous enough. But all of that together was less confounding for the British than the galling damage done to their country's prestige in the world. And to think it came at the hands of the Jews!

-302-

The massy stone headquarters of the Jewish Agency bristled in west Jerusalem like a fortress, stout, determined and stiff necked. The agency's executive council resided there along with an elected legislature and administrative offices, and the Haganah central command, as well. A half-mile away in proud resplendence stood the King David Hotel, where the British had taken over the south wing for their administration. Along with the British, Arabs and Jews staffed the offices, all working amicably side by side.

Just across the road from the King David beckoned the Y, a landmark of the new Jewish culture. It housed not only a swimming pool, but also a gym with a wooden floor—both features rare enough then to be glamorous. From the Y's auditorium, Voice of Israel, the Jewish radio station, broadcast live concerts. The football club Beitar Jerusalem ran scrimmages in its field out back. British soldiers and policemen frequented these practice sessions to scope out the players, since—as everyone knew—the Beitar clubs went hand-in-glove with the Irgun.

-303-

Marian had a boyfriend who played with Beitar Jerusalem.

Moshe and Elli were stewing over this calamity the day Rivka—whose business had brought her to Jerusalem—stopped in for a visit, bringing a bakery-bought cake. She'd never seen Moshe in such ill humor.

"She's only seventeen," he fretted, not for the first time. "Still but a schoolgirl, and the boyfriend twenty-one."

Elli concurred. "A girl stepping out with a full-grown man? In a few years, the difference in their ages might not matter, but for now—"

Rivka pointed out that Elli had been only sixteen when she became a nurse in the Great War, and Rivka herself only Marian's age when she'd become a foot soldier in the Tsar's army. For that matter, how much older a man was Avram than Rivka—or Moshe than Elli? More than a mere four years.

"This is different," protested Elli.

"How so?"

"He plays football for a living!"

Rivka doubted he got paid anything for playing, but all she said was, "Maybe it's not all he does." She meant the Irgun, of course, in case Elli wanted an opening for acknowledging the unsaid.

Elli winced. "If that's true, I don't want to know."

"Fair enough."

"He'll probably end up in internment in Africa." Several of his teammates already had been shipped off.

"That's one way to get him away from her," Moshe mused.

"Grand, let them make a martyr of him. We'd have her mooning around, unwilling to look at another boy."

-304-

It was about this time that Jews started making, rather than importing, their weapons—their Sten submachine guns, their grenades and mortars—in underground factories. Literally, they worked under the ground. Nine millimeter cartridges for the guns were manufactured inside Rehovot's Kibbutz Hill, twenty-five feet below the laundry and the bakery. Avram had seen to the top secret set-up there. Weeks spent at home, he aching to involve Rivka, to involve the boys; but no one was to know except those who absolutely had to know. Other than the forty-five young people involved in the manufacture, and some of the bakers and launderers, even other members of the kibbutz hadn't the least idea of what was going on. British soldiers got their shirts done at the excellent laundry. On occasion Rivka bought cakes at the sweet-smelling bakery. So far the secret was safe, and the Haganah intended to keep it that way. The cartridges they needed would have been hard to duplicate anywhere else.

-305-

Why was Rivka barreling toward him down the orchard lane, bounding over ruts and furrows, her cheeks aflame, her unclosed mouth singing out, "I can't believe it?" In confusion, Avram caught her in his clueless arms. She shrieked, "They're making flame throwers!"

"What?"

"Right here, underground!"

He shushed her, eyes darting to assure himself no one was near enough to overhear. "Come with me," he grunted. He double-timed to his tool shed, she following after. When both were shut inside the semi-dark, he growled, "Now what's this all about?"

"I heard there's a factory somewhere in Rehovot, under the ground."

"Shhh. You heard this from a reliable source?"

"You think I'd pay attention to rumors?"

"Who told you this?"

"Avram, what does it matter? They're making flame throwers!" Her voice rising, resonating in the small space.

"Calm down," he said, the very last thing any man should tell a distressed woman.

"Calm down?" screeched Rivka. "You call this a Jewish occupation, making flame throwers?"

It had been the right thing not to breathe a word to her about the bullet manufactory—that was obvious now. He had no knowledge of flame throwers being made anywhere in this vicinity, but he'd warn the Haganah just in case. He convinced her it was her duty not to let slip even a hint of this to anyone else, and to warn her source, too, to keep mum. True or false, Jewish lives might depend on their silence. The police relished every chance to make examples of those they caught thumbing their noses at British authority.

-306-

Betrayal: the sentiment common to every side in Palestine. A brooding sense of being done wrong was the one thing they all shared.

-307-

The code name was Agatha. The mission was to stifle the Jewish insurrection. The method was to nab its leadership. The means was a kingsize muster of thousands of British police and military. H-hour was before dawn on June 29, a Shabbat. All across Jewish Palestine, squads pounced: on Jewish Agency offices; on the homes of its executive council and of the heads of the Palmach and of other underground partisans. They weren't done until they'd nosed into the nooks and crannies and hidey-holes of myriads of settlements. For two weeks the Land was poked and prodded and raked clean, and when the dust settled, 2,718 people had been taken into custody. Officials of the top Jewish organizations found themselves behind bars. Among them was Yitzhak Rabin. For his arrest no less than four platoons of paratroopers had been sent out—three to storm his apartment, one to girdle the outside of the house.

Three truckloads of documents and fifteen caches of arms were taken in Agatha's raids, as well. Kibbutz Yagur alone yielded up a gargantuan stockpile of rifles, mortars, revolvers and grenades, plus hundreds of thousands of bullets. Not a single one of its men escaped imprisonment.

Who would question Agatha's spectacular accomplishments? And yet: its mission went unfulfilled. For one thing, the Yishuv's dominant leaders, David Ben-Gurion and Moshe Sneh, were out of the country and thus evaded arrest. For another, those three truckloads of confiscated documents might reveal new intelligence, but nothing that would truly damn the organizations or their leaders. Any ticklish information had been weeded out weeks before the raids. The Jewish Agency had been tipped off to Agatha well in advance.

-308-

David Ben-Gurion (1886-1973) arrived in Palestine from Poland in 1906, already a committed Zionist. Initially a farm worker, he soon volunteered to guard Jewish settlements for Hashomer. By 1912, he was studying law in Istanbul. It was then that he Hebraized his name. A central force in Labor Zionism, he was a founder of the Histadrut labor union. By 1935, he was serving as chairman of the Zionist Executive and head of the Jewish Agency.

Moshe Sneh (formerly Klaynboym) attended school and college in Poland, where he earned an MD in 1935. The same year, he became a member of the Zionist Executive Committee. He entered Palestine five years later, having escaped Warsaw, then Vilna, at the start of World War II. Immediately, he joined the Haganah. By 1945, he was a member of the Jewish Agency's executive board, heading its immigration department and later its political department for Europe. On "Black Sabbath"—the Jewish term for Operation Agatha—he was chief of the Haganah command.

-309-

A reprisal for Black Sabbath was to be expected.

-310-

The death sentences hanging over the two Irgun members were commuted to life imprisonment. With that ransom paid, the British officers who'd been kidnapped were set free, though brashly and humiliatingly so. The three of them got crated up together and the box dumped at the handsome front door of the club where they'd been stolen from their lunch.

-311-

At the height of the sun in the heat of a Jerusalem July day, seven Arab milkmen wheeled their milk churns past the security guards, rolling right on through the kitchens and beyond into the nightclub at the south end of the King David Hotel.

Except they weren't Arabs. And they weren't milkmen.

They were Irgun out to avenge the thousand injuries of Operation Agatha and—while they were at it—raise the stakes for the British. They set the charged milk cans down beside each of six supporting columns and left the hotel, touching off a small explosive device outside as a diversion for their getaway. They had a car waiting just around the corner near the French consulate. A warning phone call to the hotel switchboard allowed some fifteen or twenty minutes for clearing the place out, but the looming peril was either ignored or overlooked, or else the call was misdirected. Or perhaps it happened, as recorded in the Irgun's archives, that a certain high-placed British official did get the alert in time to evacuate the building—but instead he bellowed, "I am here to give orders to the Jews, not to take orders from them!"

Three hundred fifty kilograms of explosives blew up, bringing down the administrative offices of the British Secretariat, where the trove of documents taken in the Black Sabbath raids was believed to be stored. File clerks, typists and sundry other office workers were killed in the blast—Britons, Arabs, Jews, Armenians. They were a jumble of ages and backgrounds, Christian and Catholic and Muslim and Hebrew, veterans of the Great War, of the Jewish battalions, volunteers to community organizations, refugees from Germany. Ninety-one people in all perished, among them a telephone operator nineteen years old, a newly-hired young woman just days at her job.

-312-

Moshe was kept at work coping with grisly wounds and burns and mutilations from the King David bombing. Marian was expected home at five o'clock. She didn't come home, and she didn't call. Alerted by Elli, who'd already checked with the city's hospitals, Moshe got away as soon as he could and went the rounds of the morgues, pleading and bargaining with God not to let him find his daughter at any of them. Rivka ran her truck up to Jerusalem and sat with Elli, waiting. Elli's lowered eyes stayed fixed on her fingers wringing themselves. She willed her mind to be blank, but who in such circumstances could keep from picturing the worst? Certainly neither of these two women, whose unspoken dreads produced monstrous processions in their minds of the ways in which a girl could die or be maimed for life.

-313-

You have made my days a mere handbreadth.

—Psalm 39

-314-

Marian's boyfriend never belonged to the Irgun, nor was he in on the bombing of the King David Hotel. His football team had made it to the second round in the Maccabi games, and though they'd lost to Tel Aviv a couple of months earlier, still they went on practicing. He had a scrimmage at the Y that ran most of the morning, and Marian had come to see him play. At half past noon, they left the field and went inside the Y for a gulp of water. He wanted to freshen up in the restroom. Marian waited just inside the Y's wide glass front door, idly peering through one of its small panes. Across the road, the hotel was a handsome sight, its pink limestone facade dotted with balconies.

Jerusalem's first modern luxury hotel, the King David had been open for business since 1931. Among its guests and residents had been King Alfonso VIII of Spain, Abdullah of Transjordan, Haile Selassie of Ethiopia, and George II of Greece. It was constructed in the shape of the letter I with its wings on the north and south. By 1946, all six stories of the south wing and three floors of the connecting corridor were utilized as central offices for the Mandate government, military and police. The lounge off the marble-floored lobby was a chic watering spot for the well heeled and the well connected. At that hour it was serving pre-lunch aperitifs.

At 12:37, just as a bus belched by, there came a rumbling, throbbing, shuddering roar that Marian felt beneath her feet. Across the way, the walls at the southwest corner of the hotel seemed to belly out, then to waver, then to be eclipsed in a cloud of heavy brownish-gray smoke. A hand's grasp at her waist, and then her boyfriend's nasal voice saying her name in her ear as he pulled her back from the glass. She had only the moment to notice his soapy underarms, his damp shirt shoveled into his waistband, before the lobby exploded in screams and shouts and people running, jostling, colliding, some trying to push their way in through the door and others trying to push their way out. No sooner did the dense column of smoke billow away into the empty sky than they joined the ones pushing out.

The acrid air was filled with dust and coughing. Debris pattered down on them. It clicketed onto the pavement and rained onto the heads of dazed and staggering cheaters of death. The blast had ripped upward through the south wing, tearing out its westernmost half. To Marian's disoriented senses someone appeared to have strung lines of tattered laundry across a gaping space, above a hill of smoldering stone. Muffled cries came out of the hill. Crumpled iron stuck out, and jagged wood. A man hailed someone from an open platform high up the ruined building. His dusty clothes were blood-splattered, his face twisted, yelling out that he was alone up there and stranded. Anti-terrorist sirens drowned him out with their sudden wailing.

Others on the street fled from this vast incoherence— sensibly, since who knew if there might be another blast coming? But those two, being naive and invincible and impulsive, jogged toward it. Shards of glass and tile crunched under their shoes. Police cars, armored cars and army jeeps were rushing to the scene; being young and fleet, those two already were there, trying with bare hands to excavate people out of the hill of wreckage.

It was bad. Wounded, moaning victims were buried so deep, and body parts emerged wherever they dug. Then the police announced a curfew and forced them away. They went back into the Y, which was turning itself into an emergency aid station, where they did what they could for people lacerated by flying needles of glass.

-315-

When Marian finally got home, stained in the blood of the survivors, she sank down exhausted, reluctant tears trickling through the dust caked on her chalky face. She apologized: she'd tried to call home, but the telephone booth.... A gesture of impatience, of helplessness. More than food, more than anything, she craved a shower. Since there was no letting go of her, Elli loitered outside the bathroom door. Not meaning to listen, she took in the deep sobs wrenching out of her daughter's inmost hollows. With a heavy heart she waited for these fierce spasms to subside. At last the shower handles squealed shut, and Elli tiptoed away. By the time Marian came out freshly dressed and clear of face, she was her composed self again. Marian was that way. She didn't like to show any weakness.

-316-

The following afternoon, July 23, at three o'clock, traffic stopped in Jewish Jerusalem and all work halted for a minute of silence.

The names of the dead were printed in the newspapers.

In a statement in *The Palestine Post*, the executives of the Jewish Agency and the Vaad Leumi expressed their horror "at the dastardly crime perpetrated by the gang of desperadoes who today attacked the Government officers and other citizens, British, Jewish and Arabs." They expressed their deepest sympathy to the relatives of those murdered or injured. And they called upon the Yishuv in Palestine "to rise up against these abominable outrages."

-317-

From all the established Jewish organizations came similar statements of condemnation. Rivka read them, believed them, was sure that none of the Jewish leadership had known of this misbegotten plan, was sure it had been solely the covert work of extremists. It was an act of terrorism to shock the world. What tormented her as she drove from Jerusalem back home to Rehovot, was who in her own family might have known about it, and who might, God forbid, even have had a guilty hand in it?

-318-

He found her in the kitchen frying up schnitzel. She said, "I don't know you anymore."

Avram grinned. "No? So how is it you talk to a stranger?"

"Someone told me you're involved in the hotel bombing."

He took a chair. "Who said this?"

"Just someone. A woman."

"I can't converse with the back of your head. Come sit."

"I'm cooking," said Rivka.

"What woman?"

"What does it matter?"

"It matters because you believed her."

She flipped the slices over, then turned to him. "As a matter of fact, I didn't believe her. You're Palmach, not Irgun. By all reason, if you'd gotten so much as a hint of this terrible deed, you'd have reported it to Ben-Gurion."

His lips pursed. He said nothing.

"But you didn't report it."

"Rivka? Rivkele, what nonsense is this?"

"I want to know what your involvement was, and why." She checked the pan, lowered the flame. He got up and gently took the spatula out of her hand. Her nostrils flared.

"You have no cause to suspect me," he said.

"There's blood on your hands. I can smell it."

"Oh yes, this from the girl warrior—the Russian bearess— the spy who killed—how many? Did you even keep count back then?"

"That was in war, in self-defense. This at the King David? Is the murder of innocents! I've never spilled innocent blood. Never."

"I see." He turned off the flame and transferred the food to the rack she'd prepared. "So tell me, Rivka, in this country where can you find innocent blood? A child maybe?"

"Don't make fun of me."

"But only under five years of age, say. One who's never thrown a rock."

-319-

Out in the shed, Avram paced to and fro, taking apart each of the rifles he owned, cleaning, oiling, re-assembling, all the while muttering to himself. "'David Ben-Gurion, David Ben-Gurion.' It's all I hear. 'David Ben-Gurion says this. David Ben-Gurion says that. Shhhhh—on the radio—be quiet, it's David Ben-Gurion talking.'

"So who does she think he is, this David Ben-Gurion? I knew him fresh from the old country, Lithuania or Poland or wherever, when he was a runt, the *pitzkele* David Gruen, who couldn't utter a decent word of Hebrew. And now the world holds its breath when he speaks. It would be nice if Rivka would give me half the ear she gives to the great David Ben-Gurion.

"'We shall fight the war as if there were no White Paper and the White Paper as if there were no war.' Pretty words, but what did they mean? Only that he could sit up there safe in his high office at the Jewish Agency while the rest of us were out fighting the war or fighting the White Paper. Well, I'm still fighting the White Paper, little man. Unless it goes, there's no place for Jews on this earth. Yet restraint he still calls for, this David Ben-Gurion.

"Oh yes, I knew when I met you that you would become a someone. Your eyes told me so, your burning dark eyes. But that you would become David Ben-Gurion? No, never could I imagine this. Never did I think it would be you telling me when to stand up for myself and when to bend over and kiss British arses.

"You know—you must know, I'm sure—the location and content of every cache of arms we've toiled and sweated to hide away, of every hidden factory, every secret plan for bombing railways and police depots, for freeing our compatriots from British jails. How can you not know? In this country, every Jew knows when every other Jew crouches to take a shit. But oh, no, you weren't aware of this plot against the King David Hotel. A heinous crime, now that it's been successful, no? You hypocrite!

"And still my Rivka swears by you. My beautiful Rivka, who once blazed with youth and strength. And such passion—for me, for the Land. Now she says she doesn't recognize me. 'To murder innocent people, Avram?'

"Come on, Rivka. You tell me who, over the age of five, is innocent in this cursed holy land. Arab children of three and four throw rocks at you when you cross the wrong street in Neve Tzedek, isn't it so?

"'Don't make fun of me,' she says. 'Random violence won't bring us the good and righteous society we dream of.'

"Oh, and you think the opera will? Toscanini will? Half-naked ladies dancing barefoot will? That's your way to win the Land?

"'You want a new Jewish home with a new Jewish outlook, then you need a new Jewish culture,' she says. 'Or would you rather we hear Teutonic music by that bigot Wagner and read poetry by some Stalinist anti-Semite?'

"I watch the passion in her stare turn to hatred, then go cold. And she wonders why I stay away. I stay away to fight. To fight for her, for my children. Someday, maybe my name will mean more than Ben-Gurion's. If not to her, then maybe to the Land."

-320-

The Palestine Post of July 24, 1946, reported that Jerusalem's Chancellor Road was crowded for the funeral of four Jews. Many thousands of their countrymen, it said, "moved slowly and silently along the street toward Mount Scopus, with hardly a word breaking the stillness. Their faces were set and expressionless." It was as though, along with the victims, they were burying their own cherished hopes.

-321-

Also smashed beneath the collapsing wing of the King David Hotel was the short-lived Jewish combined resistance movement. Cooperation and support among the Yishuv's underground organizations lay dead in the rubble.

-322-

In a show of strength, the British made another sweep for hidden weapons, a relentless one, a productive one. Down in the basement of Tel Aviv's main synagogue, they uncovered a substantial armory belonging to the Stern Gang. A hunt—with wholesale arrests—for the organization's leaders followed. Yitzhak Yezernitsky (later Shamir) almost made a clean getaway. He disguised himself as a rabbi in black hat and long black coat and bushy dark beard, but his true identity was betrayed by his even bushier dark eyebrows.

In a way, Menachem Begin was luckier. Often, he'd ducked capture in his disguise as 'Rabbi Sassover.' This time, he made for himself a tidy bolt-hole in the rafters of his apartment. He went undetected even when conscientious British soldiers thoroughly ransacked the place. So far, so good. But next they camped out in his garden expecting him either to come out or come home. Four days they stayed. Four days in that cramped margin above the ceiling without food or water, ninety-six interminable hours waiting for them finally to decide that Begin wasn't going to be found there, after all.

-323-

At the Alvin Theatre in New York City, on September 5, a new production premiered, backed by Peter Bergson. The show was called *A Flag is Born*, and it was written by Ben Hecht, scored by Kurt Weill, and directed by Luther Adler. War journalist Quentin Reynolds narrated the play, which portrays the chilling hardships of three concentration camp survivors—played by Paul Muni, Celia Adler and a young Marlon Brando—in their attempt to reach Palestine. At the play's finale, Brando's character steps forward to confront his audience. "Where were you—" he charges—"when the killing was going on? When the six million were burned and buried alive.... Where was your cry of rage that could have filled the world and stopped the fires?...A curse on your silence. And now speak a little. Your hearts squeak—and you have a dollar for the Jews of Europe. Thank you! Thank you." When he'd finished, there came an announcement that all funds raised that evening would go toward ships to carry Jewish refugees to Palestine.

The play would run three months—120 performances—in three successive Broadway theaters, and then move on to five other American cities. At the Maryland Theater in Baltimore, on February 12, for the first time Black playgoers were admitted in unsegregated seating.

The show would raise some $400,000 in ticket sales and nearly twice that much in donations to support Jewish immigration into Palestine.

-324-

That most of the Jewish Agency's executive were either out of the country or in British prisons didn't stop their messages from getting through. They gave out the word for settlement in the Negev, and on Yom Kippur that year, the desert bloomed overnight with eleven kibbutzim.

-325-

It all continued through the last months of 1946—the searches and confiscations and arrests, the interception of ships; the concealment and assimilation of the few refugees who got through, the swift construction of settlements, and most of all, the endless assessments and re-assessments and arguments about what the Jews ought to do or not do, what they ought to accept or reject and how they ought to conduct themselves. It was clear to every Jew that some form of their own sovereignty was needed. It was equally clear that they could tolerate no restriction on bringing in the survivors from Europe. But how and when and what amount of pressure and of what sort ought to be exerted—not only did everyone have a different opinion. In most cases everyone had at least two opinions and was at war within himself.

That December the British upped their game once again, not simply imprisoning Jews found with arms caches—but flogging them, too. In retaliation, the Irgun captured and flogged a British major and three sergeants. Rivka fretted, "If only the British would get out of the way, we could solve our problems with the Arabs ourselves." Yudi convulsed into jeering laughter so giddy, he fell off his chair and spilled hot nana tea all over himself.

-326-

On Cyprus by year's end more than fifty thousand would-be immigrants from thirty-five ships were penned in behind barbed wire, guarded by British troops. To keep some semblance of order, more soldiers kept having to be deployed and more police recruited. One way and another, Palestine was costing the British a small fortune. Back in England, post-war shortages of food and fuel made everyone touchy. India would soon be lost to the Empire. To that humiliation add the whole world's condemnation of the imprisonment of Holocaust survivors.

-327-

Out of the blue, Moshe received another phone call from Freddie Williamson, this time at home.

"I must cut off all further communications with you," he said. "Orders from above."

"All right."

"I'm sorry, but it must be done."

"I understand."

"Best of luck to you, Morris."

"To you, too."

"Goodbye."

Freddie clicked off, leaving Moshe with the phone receiver in hand, a bemused frown on his face. "That was odd," he said.

"What was?" asked Elli.

"I think I've been dear-Johned. But there was no need, you see."

-328-

Americans were polling ever more favorably toward a Jewish state. By year's end, the margin was two to one.

1947-8

-329-

 senseless, squalid war.

—Winston Churchill

-330-

At home in Britain, people had had a bellyful of Palestine. Too much money, too much time and energy and prestige had disappeared into that black ungrateful sinkhole. His Majesty's government in February 1947 declared its intention to hand over the problem to the United Nations. Britain was calling quits to the Mandate.

-331-

A British capitulation was something to crow about—and, as the Irgun saw it, something to prompt further action along the same lines. They blew up the British Officers Club in Jerusalem, they raided police stations throughout the Land, they sabotaged railways, they harassed British troops and kidnapped more officers. Sometimes Rivka wondered: does the Irgun mean to undermine our struggle to make a homeland here? You couldn't help thinking about it. Besides, thinking about it distracted Rivka from worrying over her children. It was normal, she told herself, that she hardly saw them anymore. At their age it was normal to be out and about, visiting friends, attending classes, hanging around the streets, whatever people in their teens and early twenties did. She wouldn't know. At the boys' age she'd been fighting a war. At Ahuva's age she was already married and starting a family, with the urgent hope for a better future for those very children. Shimshon was still around, and it took all her restraint not to smother the boy in unwanted attention. He was so quiet, so solitary and inscrutable, but at least he was there at the table for breakfast, lunch and dinner.

-332-

Having an early faculty meeting, Moshe rushed through breakfast, didn't see Marian (still asleep, or at least lying abed reading—her first class wasn't meeting until the afternoon). He gave the crown of Eleanor's head a peck as she sat reading the newspaper over her coffee, and took the bus up to the university. The bus lurched and lumbered its way through Jerusalem's suburbs, which kept on growing despite violent disturbances and worse retributions. Just yesterday, the British had executed Dov Gruner, captured a full year ago in an attack on the Ramat Gan police station and imprisoned all this time in Acre with a jaw shattered by British gunfire. In 1939, this man Gruner had volunteered for the British army and seen action both in North Africa and across Europe. Perhaps in recognition, the British were said to be negotiating for some kind of deal for him. Yet according to this morning's radio, two hours before yesterday's dawning, while Jews were locked down under curfew, Gruner was hauled out and hanged along with three of his Irgun comrades. Britons, Jews, Arabs— Moshe brooded—we're all in some terrible collective dance of death, our arms entwined, our legs jigging of their own accord, our distended mouths spitting at each other. Thoroughly spent, we can't stop, we just keep on, until someday we'll all drop straight into our graves.

The bus started its dreary climb up the long road to the top of Mount Scopus. Through the window, he saw a gap-toothed succession of run-down garages and fly-by-night businesses, most of them in Arab hands. Someday perhaps they'd be torn down, and who knew what would take their place. A posh shopping street? A park for children? New buildings for the hospital? Thinking like a Jew, this April day of 1947.

In bygone Paris, on a balmy April day like the twin to this one, Eleanor had joined the staff at Val de Grâce Hospital. What year was that? 1917? Yes, April 1917, making it thirty years since he'd fallen for her, for her earnest manner, her solemn eyes, her infrequent enchanting smile, and the way she had of bending toward the patients instead of away from them, as most new hires did. Their twenty-eighth wedding anniversary would be coming in July, a thought that made even those scrubby, barren patches of land out there lovely to him. Somehow, Nellie had stayed with him all this time, raised a daughter with him, and so far as he knew been faithful.

-333-

By 1947, the Royal Navy were outperforming themselves at intercepting refugee ships. Take just the three months March through May:

On March 9, the 597 refugees aboard the *Ben Hecht*—a ship purchased and refurbished with funding from *A Flag is Born*—were interned on Cyprus after their ship was rammed and captured by three destroyers.

On March 29, the 1,588 refugees aboard the *Moledet* were stranded after their ship suffered engine failure about thirty miles off Palestine. They were transferred to British ships and interned on Cyprus.

On April 13, the 2,641 refugees aboard the *Theodor Herzl* —six hundred of them children—resisted when two British ships bore down on them. Three of the refugees were killed; the rest were interned on Cyprus.

On April 23, the 768 "young and organized" refugees

aboard the ship *Shear Yashuv* were interned on Cyprus when their ship was intercepted by HMS *Cheviot*.

On May 17, the 1,414 "emaciated and deadly tired" refugees aboard the ship *Hatikvah*—their ship having been rammed and captured by two destroyers—were interned on Cyprus.

On May 24, the 1,457 "gloomy" refugees aboard the ship *Mordei Hagetaot* were arrested and interned on Cyprus.

On May 31, the 399 refugees from camps in North Africa, aboard the ship *Yehuda Halevi*, were arrested. They were interned on Cyprus the next day under a heavy rainfall and tornado. Two days later, an earthquake shook the island.

There was one semi-exception to this train of arrests: On March 12, amid high seas, the 823 refugees aboard the *Shabtai Luzinski* made it safely, if damply, to shore at Netzanim Beach, north of Ashkelon. There they mixed with local residents who thronged the beach in defiance of a British cordon. The British arrested about a thousand people and trucked them to Haifa. About 240 were immediately identified as locals and set free. Another 700 were sent to Cyprus. Some 325 of those were soon returned to Palestine, and among them were 85 undetected refugees.

-334-

Over a hundred thousand people attempted to enter Mandatory Palestine illegally in 142 voyages. The ships were purchased wherever they could be found, from the US to Scandinavia. They were tired vessels, many decommissioned, most barely seaworthy. Most sailed out of ports in France and Italy, with crews from Spain, Italy, the US, Palestine and elsewhere, overseen by *Palyam*, the maritime branch of the Palmach. Often the refugees were gathered from two collection points in the American sector and taken in secret to the port where a refurbished ship waited. They were crammed in. They lacked everything, except a guttering flicker of hope.

-335-

In English they were called refugees, or survivors, or illegal immigrants, depending on who was doing the talking. In Jewish Palestine they were known universally as *ma'apilim*. The term has no direct English translation. It appears to have come from *vayapilu*, a word in the Torah (Numbers 14:44) referring to the generation of Israelites who were brought out of slavery in Egypt and by God's edict banned from entry into the Promised Land. This ancient word vayapilu itself lacks a clear definition and has been variously translated as sinfulness, hardness, strength and bravery. What seems certain is that ma'apilim focuses not on where the people came from (as does the word 'refugees'), but where they're going. It bears similarity to the word *ha'apala* in modern Hebrew—an alternate term for Aliyah Bet, the movement to bring the Jews into the Land. To make *aliyah* is to ascend, and likewise, ha'apala has been translated as "upward struggle" or "ascension"—going up—which is how Jews are always said to approach the Land of Israel.

-336-

The persistence of hope: In 1947, the Jewish festival of *Lag B'Omer* fell on May 7. Ma'apilim in the Cyprus internment camps that day celebrated sixty-eight weddings—another kind of ascension or upward struggle. Another kind of strength and bravery. A hope for another promised land.

-337-

When she heard that the great Leonard Bernstein would soon be conducting a series of concerts with the Palestine Philharmonic, Rivka could hardly contain herself, cleaving into equal parts excitement and dismay. You'd think for the sake of the maestro all the trouble could come to a stand-down for the space of a measly two weeks. But no, a police station was blown up, a truck demolished; and then some sort of bomb was touched off just outside the concert hall where the musicians were rehearsing. It's a wonder Lenny didn't turn right around and go home to America. Instead, that gracious man crowned himself in graciousness by publicly admiring not only the beauty of the country, but the resolve of his people.

In Jerusalem, he premiered his revised *Jeremiah* Symphony. Rivka was glued to the radio for the broadcast. Tears filled her eyes in the third movement when the mezzo-soprano sang passages from the Book of Lamentations, her liquid voice irresistible and impassioned and glowing like a beacon. "Sublime," Rivka found herself murmuring, a word she'd never before comprehended, much less had use for. Then the long applause surged up, the audience shouting and cheering and stamping their feet. At last, here was something good in the air, something that could unite the country!

-338-

With flushed eagerness Rivka described the concert broadcast for Avram. He only half-listened. His mind was on Palmach business.

"Why do you fight when there's no need?" she sighed.

"How can you say there's no need?"

And in a flash, they were at it again. She begged to remind him that taking the moral high ground was the right thing to do, not to mention the best thing for the eyes of the world. He bowed low to her, taunting her as his homegrown light unto the nations. She accused him of hating the Arabs. He ridiculed her false sentiment in the face of reason. They went around and around, and neither convinced the other of a damn thing.

-339-

How doth the city sit solitary
That was full of people!
How is she become as a widow?
——Lamentations 1.1

-340-

It took a while, because so much was happening. At last, though, Rivka put together the times of Ahuva's absences with the times of Irgun attacks. She'd tried to phone Ahuva on March 1, but the daughter hadn't been home. That was the day the Irgun made an attack on the British Officers' Club in Tel Aviv, their grenades killing twelve outright and injuring thirty. Again, Ahuva had been "out" when Rivka tried calling at the end of March, on the very day the Irgun sabotaged Haifa's oil refinery. Where in Haifa could she have been "out?" Yesterday, the Irgun had brought off a prison break in Acre. Some twenty-eight Jews and two hundred Arabs escaped. Rivka hadn't tried Ahuva yesterday, but when, out of nowhere, Ahuva called this morning "just to chat," Rivka invited her for a special mother-daughter treat: just the two of them at Bernstein's final concert.

She planned just how she'd corral her daughter. If Ahuva was involved in anti-British attacks, Rivka would say she could understand, though not approve. She'd explain how the British were no longer the issue—the United Nations were.

She'd spell out how these lawless activities would only hurt the Jewish position with the United Nations. Over and over in her mind, Rivka kept turning, revising, perfecting the exact words she'd use.

-341-

Bernstein's last appearance in Palestine was an open-air concert on May 10 in the Jezreel Valley. The roads jammed early with people in trucks, in cars, by wagon and on foot. It took hours for Rivka to get to Ein Harod and meet up with Ahuva, as planned. Rivka brought food with her, Ahuva supplied the blankets they'd need. The British curfew ruled out travel on the roads after dark, so everyone would be spending the night.

The ticket holders had seats reserved in an open-air shelter. Some of the others—those who'd arrived early enough —crowded into the aisles. Rivka and Ahuva were among the remaining thousands who settled outside the shelter wherever they could: atop vehicles and boulders or in whatever pinch of space they could find. The two women had just squeezed themselves into a gap between two rocks, their arms about each others' shoulders to buy room for themselves, when abruptly the electric lights went out. A power failure? The crowd buzzed. Someone claiming to be in the know blamed Arab sabotage. No one moved an inch. An announcement was made: an auxiliary generator was being readied. Unfortunately, a bit of time would be needed to boost up sufficient power. The sky grew dark. They munched on the cold chicken and tomatoes and bread that Rivka had packed.

It was 10:30 p.m. when the lights finally came back on. The place went wild as Leonard Bernstein took the stage. How impossibly young he was! And how gorgeous, even only a few inches tall, as he appeared to them: a teeny weeny bar mitzvah boychik. Rivka was reminded with a pang of her dark-mopped brother Mischa at that age.

The pandemonium died the moment the conductor took his place at the piano. Not a wisp of human sound. Then, a romp of music, the opening bars of Ravel's Piano Concerto. Rivka knew the program. It was the same one she'd heard over the radio broadcast from the Edison Cinema in Jerusalem —and just as moving the second time around. The Ravel, Bernstein conducting from his piano bench; Schumann's Symphony No. 2; and then the poignant close, Bernstein's *Jeremiah* Symphony.

-342-

Even with my back to [the audience], I could feel them every second...[going]...up with the *crescendi* and down with the *diminuendi*.   —Leonard Bernstein

-343-

Applause and cries of *bravo* and *brava* and *bravi*, and handkerchiefs waving and rhythmic stomping that gradually waned. Finally a kind of enervation set in, though who could sleep on such a night? They had a few hours of on-and-off dozing, and then Rivka determined it was time. In the pre-dawn murkiness, over a shared thermos of lukewarm coffee, Rivka launched her interrogation. Ahuva's expression turned from concern, to confusion, to abrupt comprehension. Before her mother was quite done, she gave out a rude guffaw. "Me?" she said. "You think I'm a Jewish terrorist? What do you imagine I could do for the Irgun? Sew curtains on the slits in their bunkers?" She railed at Rivka for having not an ounce of sense about children, not understanding her own daughter at all, never paying enough attention to know who she was. "If I were a citrus tree maybe you'd have spared me a thought now and then."

Rivka said, "Tell me what you were doing on those occasions," clumsily keeping her voice steady. Her lips quivered, her eyes brimmed. The Pope's open window in Rome was less transparent. If she'd been home in her kitchen, she wouldn't even have fooled Gena's painted portraits on the wall.

Ahuva said, "I don't have to tell you anything."

Ahuva said, "But I will."

Ahuva said, "I was at the movies. And don't you dare ask me what I saw, because I could just as well make something up. How would you know the difference?" Then she laughed again, braying into her mother's stricken face.

-344-

From a full-page fundraising appeal in the *New York Post*, May 14, 1947:

Letter to the Terrorists of Palestine

In the past fifteen hundred years every nation of Europe has taken a crack at the Jews. This time the British are at bat....

Every time you blow up a British arsenal or wreck a British jail or send a British railroad train sky-high or rob a British bank or let go you [sic] guns and bombs at the British betrayers and invaders of your homeland, the Jews of America make a little holiday in their hearts.

Not all Jews of course.

The only time Jews present a United Front is when they lie piled in the massacre pits.

—Ben Hecht

-345-

And now it became Shimshon, too, who was gone for days on end. Rivka suspected Avram knew where. Predictably, when she demanded to be told, Avram shrugged. Avram's shrugs were a fully developed language in themselves: one-shouldered shrugs, two-shouldered shrugs, with hands engaged, head engaged, or not. Shrugs that said, I know, but I can't reveal it. I know but I won't tell you. I think I know, but I don't want to venture a guess. State secret, army secret, secret of the squad, private secret. Someday you'll know, but not now. So it was natural for Avram to shrug when put on the spot about Shimshon, a long curl of his shoulder, a move new to Rivka even after all these years.

"Are you shrugging in Hebrew or Yiddish?"

"How do you know it's not Arabic?" his eyes toying with hers.

No question, he knew what the boy was up to.

-346-

The story she told herself: in some minor, un-risky way, Shimshon was supporting the struggle against the British. She bore in mind the rumors she'd heard of special kibbutzim where armaments and ammunition were manufactured deep underground. Shimshon was probably running supplies to them. Or possibly helping out down in their workshops all night.

-347-

The United Nations sent out a special committee to investigate and make a report on Palestine. Not 'yet another report,' though. This would be different. This report would go to the nations of the world. And on that committee called UNSCOP there sat not a single Briton.

-348-

UNSCOP: United Nations Special Committee On Palestine.

-349-

Three members of the Irgun had been arrested during the Acre prison break on May 4. They were tried, found guilty and sentenced to be hanged—though generally it was thought that the execution would be put off for the length of UNSCOP's visit. In a fury of reprisal, the Irgun tried a number of times—and failed—to take British hostages. Then, on July 11, they brought it off. Two British sergeants were captured in Netanya, chloroformed and transported to an abandoned diamond-polishing plant, where they were jailed up in a specially built cell in the basement. They were left there with a canvas bucket, a supply of food and water, and cylinders of oxygen to last several days. The cell was sealed with an airtight hatch concealed under layers of sand. The British searched for the two sergeants everywhere—including the old plant—unsuccessfully. The Irgun were threatening to hang the prisoners the moment their own people were executed.

-350-

That same day, July 11, with all eleven UNSCOP members in Palestine, the *Exodus 1947* steamed out of the French port of Sète. This flat-bottomed ship, originally called the *President Warfield*, had been built twenty years earlier to carry upwards of four hundred sightseers on excursions in the sheltered waters of Chesapeake Bay. During the war she'd been given over to the British for transport, but served primarily as a barracks and training facility. After D-Day, she provided military accommodations off Omaha Beach. She was decommissioned stateside by the US Navy in September 1945, and a year later was purchased as scrap for the Haganah. The derelict vessel was refitted with bunks three stories high, with upgraded engines and reinforced fittings and barbed wire defenses. Her crew of thirty-five were mostly young American Jewish volunteers. She was the largest immigrant ship thus far, a floating provocation carrying 4,554 ma'apilim, many of them women and children. She had thirteen bathrooms.

As expected, she soon found herself shadowed by British warships and aircraft.

-351-

Every so often, at varied hours, Shimshon loitered behind the large rock near the road, watching for toads and spiders until the 'taxicab' pulled up. Without a word, he joined the two in the car. Stashed in the trunk were food and water to last three days. Stashed under the seats were their weapons in hidden compartments. Silence all the way to Netanya, not even the radio playing.

Down in the cell, one of the men held a steady gun on the two sergeants. The other, in stillness above, stood guard. Shimshon shuffled back and forth emptying the slops. The prisoners wore ordinary street clothing. If they were sergeants, where were their uniforms? "Are they truly British soldiers?" he whispered.

"Spies," grunted their guard. "Hurry it up."

-352-

On the eighteenth of July the ship stood off Gaza's coast. As the sun rose over Palestine, there came a radio broadcast over the Voice of Israel: "This is the refugee ship *Exodus 1947*. Before dawn today we were attacked by five British destroyers and one cruiser at a distance of seventeen miles from the shores of Palestine, in international waters. The assailants immediately opened fire, threw gas bombs, and rammed our ship from three directions. On our deck there are one dead, five dying, and a hundred-twenty wounded. The resistance continued for more than three hours. Owing to the severe losses and the condition of the ship, which is in danger of sinking, we were compelled to sail in the direction of Haifa, in order to save the forty-five hundred refugees on board from drowning."

When the British sailors boarded—using gas and coshes and ultimately firearms—the ma'apilim defended themselves with steam hoses, cans of kosher beef and piles of potatoes and broken-off pieces of rammed wood from the vessel's skin. A misbegotten skirmish, indeed.

-353-

Tali had an errand to do in Tel Aviv that day. When he got there, he found the city closed down in sympathy with those aboard *Exodus 47*.

-354-

Two of the UNSCOP members were persuaded to make the trip to Haifa's docks to see for themselves what was going on there. Possibly, they had little else to do at the time. The Arab Committee were boycotting them because UNSCOP's purview included a study of the DP immigration issue. Not surprisingly, the Arabs maintained their exclusive right to Palestine: it was their land alone, incontrovertibly, and any inclination to make mockery of such an obvious fact did not deserve the dignity of their attention. Their position was certainly a strong one, but not a flexible one, and in this situation it served them ill.

Tugboats towed the *Exodus 47* to the pier at Haifa. Late that afternoon, the would-be immigrants were instructed to disembark from the crippled ship and to board three sea-worthy vessels waiting to carry them to Cyprus. So they were led to believe. They weren't told of the new British policy taking effect that day with them. Instead of Cyprus, these passengers were to be hauled back to France, back to where they'd sailed from. Cyprus was full, overfull, in fact bursting its seams. The British were relying on this new scheme—in contrast to all the old ones—to scare off 'illegals' who had nowhere else to go.

-355-

Here's what the UNSCOP representatives Emile Sandstrom of Sweden and Vladimir Simic of Yugoslavia, in their starched and spotless linen suits, saw and heard at the tightly guarded docks in Haifa: a pummeled and torn vessel, a jagged hole in its near side through which peered a jumble of wan faces; a gangplank that plunged through another of the holes; a slow spill of women and children stuttering down it, their thousand-year-old eyes darting up with yearning at Mount Carmel; shouts of men holding out against the British soldiers trying to drag them off the *Exodus 47*; bandaged Jews, some staggering or unable to walk after the morning's dogfight and needing to be handed out on stretchers.

-356-

Ever the politician, Ben-Gurion came before UNSCOP with praise for the British. How he managed it without heaving his breakfast is matter for speculation—but he did so, crediting Britain for making the very first effort in modern times to set about restoring Palestine to the Jewish people. He made the further point that Jews living in Britain were treated as equals. Politically, at least, this was true.

Both he and Chaim Weizmann highlighted for UNSCOP how unnatural was the homeless, stateless condition of world Jewry and how unbroken was the ancient attachment to Eretz Israel.

-357-

Most of the time, Avram was off on one mission or another. By rifling through his things, Rivka picked up clues to his orders. He was checking on weapons, he was surveying ammunition dumps, he was drawing up reports of military preparedness. He was—was he?—arming for all-out war?

-358-

UNSCOP was still in Palestine at dawn on July 29, when the three Irgun captives at Acre were executed one by one. On the way to the gallows, each in his turn sang out "Hatikvah." Each must have been heartened when the other Jewish prisoners chimed in from their cells. In their own cell, the three left behind a signed message: "They will not frighten our Hebrew youth in the Homeland with their hangings. Thousands will follow in our footsteps."

-359-

The two captive British sergeants were hanged in retribution that same July day in their underground cell. Their bundled corpses went by 'taxi' to a eucalyptus grove a few miles away, where they were suspended from adjacent trees and booby-trapped to explode. Two hapless British soldiers who found them were blown to pieces in the effort to cut them down.

-360-

Three ships left Haifa loaded up with unwilling Jews from *Exodus 47*. A "floating Auschwitz," thundered one French newspaper upon learning that the decks of the ships were outfitted with high cages. They arrived on August 2 at Port-de-Bouc in a blistering heat wave. Ordered to disembark, the refugees steadfastly refused, and the French refused Britain's demand to remove them by force. The ships languished at anchor in the harbor. The British withheld food to starve the refugees out; the French and the Joint together brought them provisions by launch each day.

-361-

American sailor Eli Kalm, who'd been on the ships, remarked, "Picture yourself on the New York subway. It's August, damned hot in August, and it's rush hour. They've turned off the fans, slammed the doors, and you're left standing up against each other, for…weeks."

-362-

After three scorching weeks, the refugees called a hunger strike of their own. The British, backed into a corner of their own making, on August 23 ordered the ships to sail on to Hamburg, Germany. There, a thousand British troops and fifteen hundred German police forced the homeless wretches off the ships with the ready application of water hoses, truncheons and tear gas. Then came relocation to two former concentration camps, now repurposed for DPs. A military band was playing as they entered the gates.

-363-

As UNSCOP representative Vladimir Simic put it, what

better evidence could you have for allowing Jews into Palestine?

-364-

One rare night, with Avram home at dinner and Moshe and Elli joining them, he divulged, in strictest confidence, that the UNSCOP people had been asking about the Jewish military capability. How would you defend yourselves in the case of war? How many artillery pieces do you have?

"A good sign, these questions," said Moshe.

"So who can guess how many?" Avram asked.

"Ten," said Moshe.

"Six?" ventured Elli.

"One," Rivka said.

"That's one too high," laughed Avram.

"Not funny," said Elli. "What in the world did you tell UNSCOP?"

"We said, 'Oh, sorry, we can't reveal that number—for security reasons, you understand.'"

-365-

UNSCOP issued its report on the first of September, 1947. It was a thorough treatment, covering the history and elements of the conflict, the activities of the committee, religious aspects, the various proposals for a solution to the "Palestine Question," economic considerations, and a host of recommendations for the future. Eclipsing all else, a majority of seven members—from Canada, Czechoslovakia, Guatemala, Netherlands, Sweden, Peru and Uruguay—recommended establishing two separate states, one Arab, one Jewish, with Jerusalem to be set apart under an international trusteeship. The patchy area mapped out for the Jewish state was untenable, but the Jewish Agency took it as a place to start a conversation. They accepted the proposal, subject to discussions on specific boundaries. The Arab Higher Committee rejected the report wholesale.

-366-

To Rivka's amazement, the USSR endorsed the report, proclaiming the unjustness of denying Jews the right to their own state. If only Mischa could have been alive to hear this! Never mind that he'd been murdered by these same Soviets; or that, if not them, he'd have been murdered by the Nazis during the war; or if not them, then in any of a hundred other ways between 1938 and the fall of 1947.

-367-

But how many other countries would support this proposal —and would their number be enough when it came to a vote some three months hence? Zionist lobbyists and their opposites scrambled to work: charming and wangling and jockeying and drawing in and wearing down and prevailing upon and wooing and importuning and inspiring and winning over the delegates of the UN General Assembly, who would decide for or against partition. Up to the last moment all was in doubt—at least to everyone in Palestine crowded around radio receivers, barely capable of breath. Direct from faraway New York, the momentous vote was beaming live world-wide. Time took its own sweet time. The vote snailed along. When at last it was done, thirty-three nations had voted in favor of partition, thirteen against, ten abstaining. Could you believe it? In three months, praise God, Haifa would be open to full immigration. In nine months, the partition would be completed, and the city of Jerusalem would come under the control of the United Nations.

~368~

Thus ends two thousand years of homelessness for the Jewish people.

~369~

In theory.

~370~

The land was not to be handed over without a fight. No one questioned that. The questions were when and how the war would break out. Arab nations in the region were sure to lend their kindred a hand, but exactly which nations? How soon? How much would they involve themselves? Probably they themselves hadn't yet worked this out.

All over Palestine there was dancing in the Jewish streets that night. For the Arabs, there were tears and curses and wringing of hands.

~371~

Blessed are we who have been privileged to witness this day.   —David Ben-Gurion

~372~

They made a bonfire, and neighbors came from nearby farms with their Jewish workers, everyone adding food and drink to a long, laden table. They danced, they embraced, they sang and cried with joy, just as if they had no idea what was ahead.

Yudi drew her aside. "Ima, you know what comes next?"

"All the more important to celebrate tonight!" Rivka threw her arms about him and tried to twirl. It was like dragging a block of wood. "Don't you see, *tateleh*?" she implored.

"But tomorrow?"

"Will be tomorrow," she said, offering a shrug she'd learned from Avram.

-373-

A line of blood and fire.

—Jamal al-Husseini, Arab Higher Committee, regarding the partition borders

-374-

"How can this be the will of Allah?"

Leila sat rigid and stone-faced among her family. They were stunned by the UN vote, not to say incensed. This bitter day, unforeseen and unthinkable, capped a decades-long theft of their country and their destiny.

Could it be that Allah, too, was distraught?

-375-

The UN vote was passed on November 30. That same day, Arab gangs ambushed two Jewish buses, killing a half-dozen travelers and injuring several more.

On December 1, the Arab Executive Committee called a three-day strike, to begin the next day. None of Rivka's Arab workers showed up. Even Leila stayed away, a warning more ominous to Rivka than Yudi's had been.

On December 2, Arabs marauded through Jewish Jerusalem's commercial center, plundering and burning the shops. British police stood aside looking on like sightseers. From Jaffa

Arabs descended en masse on Tel Aviv, only to be thrown back by the Haganah.

No Jew was safe from the hunt going on all over Palestine. Angry bands of armed Arabs were lashing out indiscriminately against men, women, children. They shot up buses and pelted ambulances, they ransacked shops. They cut off Jewish lives and gutted Jewish property wherever they could. Beyond Palestine, in Arab lands throughout the Middle East, zealots duplicated the violence. Synagogues were attacked, Jewish homes and businesses pillaged. Jews faced their untimely deaths in Beirut, in Aleppo, in Aden, in Alexandria, in Cairo....

-376-

The Great Synagogue in Aleppo was burned to the ground, along with homes, shops and a community youth club. Apparently lost in the blaze was the priceless Aleppo Codex, a Hebrew manuscript of the Jewish Bible produced in medieval Tiberias around the year 920. It had been kept in the ancient Syrian synagogue since the fourteenth century, until its disappearance that day in December 1947. Eventually—in 1958—a Syrian Jew showed up in Israel with the smuggled book, or what was left of it. Some forty percent of its leaves—gone missing—have never been recovered.

-377-

For the Jews of Palestine, restraint was no longer the watchword. Retaliation was. On the road from Tel Aviv to Jerusalem, where Arabs from Ramle were assailing Jewish passers-by, the Palestine police moved to bar all traffic. Ben-Gurion, rather than urging compliance, urged Jews to disregard attempts to narrow or circumscribe their activities. In the cities, Lehi and the Irgun were busier than ever, pitching bombs into milling crowds of Arabs, into coffee houses and hotels. You wouldn't want to be an Arab villager, either, for it was open season on them too. Not war yet, not grenades and mortars—but plenty of hectoring and intimidation by Jewish police and troops.

-378-

The British soldiers' red berets had earned them the nickname 'anemone.' They were fast losing all control of the country, and many of them couldn't have cared less. Back home, support for the Mandate was slim. As the year 1947 drew to a close, most of the anemones clung to just one objective—to stay alive until they could get the hell out of Palestine.

-379-

By the second week in December, Rivka had only one Arab employee left. Some—long since thrown off their land—had moved away. Others she'd had to fire: for their hostile asides in the '36 rebellion, or in the war for their hateful sloganeering in sympathy with the Nazis. The rest quit her over the partition vote. All except Leila, who returned after the three days of the strike. Rivka and Shimshon were at the table finishing their morning coffee. Leila came into the kitchen without a word, though with eyes that smoldered. She picked up a dishrag and set to work.

"Good morning," Rivka said.

Leila stood mutely scrubbing. Rivka's big toe poked Shimshon under the table. "Uh, glad to see you," he offered. "I found a new grasshopper yesterday. I think it might be from Africa."

With a muffled hiss, Leila dropped the cloth. "Why?" she

blurted. "Why should we have to suffer from Hitler's crimes? Isn't it bad enough you've had to suffer from them?"

"Living in the same country with Jews? This is suffering?" Rivka shot back. "What have we brought to this country but good? From jobs you've suffered? From good roads you've suffered? From medicine for your children you've suffered?"

"You Zionists want to take over. You want to make us strangers here in our own land."

"I? I want to live side by side with you in peace."

Shimshon got up and left the door hanging open on his way out. Leila shook her head, the ghost of a smile twitching her lips. "But not so your children," she said. "And not so your husband."

"That's nonsense, Leila. To my children you're an auntie, a relative. They're like you—born here, raised here. Your sons, your daughter—are their lifelong friends."

Leila's jaw worked. Rivka had the impression she wanted to say more, but didn't dare. Rivka went on, "I came to this Land from a place of hatred. A place where everyone suspected everyone else and spied on everyone else and sooner or later betrayed their friends." Her fingers curled into a fist. Mischa's soulful face floated before her. "I will not live in such a place again!" she cried, her balled hand slamming onto the tabletop. The cups jumped and clattered in their saucers.

-380-

They had benign code words for everything. Bullets were cherries or plums; rifles were pipes; pistols were sprinklers. Her packing shed and storage buildings became prime real estate. Barrels of cherries and plums, and cartons of sprinklers squatted there amid her oranges and grapefruits. Avram was in and out, checking on his merchandise.

For the umpteenth time, Rivka chided him, "These people you're arming against were your friends."

"What, Rivka? You think they're not doing the same— importing arms, storing them? This is what must be done to bring about the Jewish state."

"Avram, we can live with the Arabs in peace."

He sniggered and snorted.

"What are you hee-hawing about?"

"Rivka, even you and I can't live together in peace. How do you expect to live with people who resent us and want us gone?"

-381-

Moshe and Elli were recruited to ready the Jewish health care system for what was coming. Their part involved developing Magen David Adom, the red shield of David; and then organizing the far-flung clinics, the workers' sick fund and the hospitals into one coordinated entity fully primed for war.

-382-

Jewish military operations were still illegal, and forces were small. Avram, for example, was part of only 2,100 men and women at arms in the Palmach, with a thousand more in reserve. A reorganization of Haganah's forces had been accomplished, and a heightened, covert recruitment effort was in the works. Training got a boost, not just among the troops, but even in the detention camps of Cyprus, where those capable of fighting were drilled in secret, hefting imitation rifles made of wood.

-383-

Over school vacation, Shimshon seemed fidgety. Rivka thought he might be interested in joining the Ganda, a youth battalion that prepared underage children for eventual military service. He gave her his unpopulated stare. "Not necessary," he said.

-384-

On New Year's Eve, Marian threw a small party for her friends from university. It was a quiet affair, with more chatting than dancing and more philosophizing than drinking. Some harmless necking going on under the trees in the garden, but all in all, a far more dignified get-together than anything Elli would have met with at Marian's age. Then again, at Marian's age, all the boys Elli knew had been through the trenches and aide stations of the Western Front. With a shudder of dread she picked out her daughter's luminous face in the lamplight, and went on to scan the other earnest young scholars. According to Marian, most of them had, in the last month, registered for the Haganah.

The old boyfriend was boyfriend no more. He'd disappeared from Marian's side, replaced by this group of students. Her daughter treated all the boys alike with cool friendliness. One of them, Elli was certain, had a crush on Marian, judging by the way he offered to help Elli with the trays of food—and by the way he invented conversation about Magen David Adom, in which he obviously had no interest other than to make a good impression on her.

What would happen to these children in the year 1948? What would their cloudless eyes see? Worse, what deviltry would they themselves be led to do in a firefight, and what would the doing of it do to them? Elli knew full well the passion of war, how it took one's curbs away, how it made animals out of angels.

And what of the outcome? In horror she'd watched ragged processions of refugees with lifeless features traipsing down the sunken roads of Belgium and France. Would it be the Jews this time, or would it be the Arabs? Please not the Jews, not again—too damn often it's been us. But she had no wish to inflict such a fate on her neighbors, either. At least, she liked to think that's what she felt.

-385-

Every day, someone got killed. Every day, someone related to someone you knew. Sometimes just a name you knew, sometimes a face you remembered. Sometimes a friend. For both sides, the same. Often Leila looked sad, often Rivka. Neither spoke of it to the other.

"Get rid of her," Avram said. "She's a danger to us."

She was also the only member of her family who still had a job, still brought in food for her children, Rivka reminded him. The two women were no longer close. No friendship between a Jew and an Arab could bear up any longer. There wasn't sufficient trust.

Well, as to trust, Avram knew the commander of a Palmach platoon who were patrolling a pipeline in the Negev. This commander told his men not to worry about the Arab villagers loitering nearby. The village mukhtar was a longtime friend of his, the villagers harmless. He was as certain of this as of his own name. The unwatchful platoon were attacked, and every last one of those soldiers wiped out.

This was the troubling story Avram told her. Still, how could Rivka fire Leila after all their years like sisters?

-386-

Near the Damascus Gate in Jerusalem, an Arab boy, age fourteen, was waiting for a bus when he was shot down. An Arab family were killed inside their home by Lehi. A Jewish man walking to a funeral was stabbed to death. A mother of six, hanging out her wash, was raked with bullets. Was she Arab? Jewish? Does it matter?

On both sides there were those who claimed that the Zionist plan all along had been to erase the Arabs from the country. Rivka, for one, refused to accept that it was so. As proof, she pointed out how the Jewish Agency had all along condemned violence, right up to this very month of December 1947. Only now was the Haganah announcing its intention to parallel the tactics of the Irgun and Lehi, to keep pace with them in their reprisals. Announcing the intention, mind you— broadcasting it over the radio and papering the country in leaflets. No sneak attack, this, and the only target, as advertised, would be those who savaged Jews. Rivka clung to this in hopes of remaining peaceful with all who shared the peace— even though the way forward would spill the blood of those whose hands were drenched in blood.

-387-

Five January 1948: In the busy time of day, a no-name truck hauling a mountain of oranges clattered over the stony pavement of central Jaffa. It parked just near the clock tower, the driver and his passenger heading into a coffee house close by. Without pausing even to stir sugar into the bitter cups set before them, they took quick, distracted swigs, heedlessly dribbling stains onto their secondhand workers' outfits. Within minutes they left the café and took off on foot for Neve Tzedek. A deafening flash-roar followed not long after. The truck bed, beneath its stacked-up canopy of oranges, had been jam-packed with TNT. The explosion killed at least twenty people—Arabs all—wounded many more, and demolished shops and coffee houses. Where the truck had just been smoked a drift of wreckage. The two men were by then safely under cover in Tel Aviv.

Some of the oranges had been wrapped in thin paper, and some of the papers floated free of the fires the explosion kindled, and one of those singed papers came home to Rivka by Leila's hand. She told Rivka where it had been found, and she told Rivka why. "Stupid, senseless brats!" Rivka stormed. "What did this bogus operation accomplish? What did it prove? Only to crush many a mother's heart alongside my own." Leila half unriddled, half apologized for, the facts she'd known for a long time—but needed the evidence before Rivka would believe it. She was right. Even now, Rivka could scarcely believe it.

Around midnight, Yudi and Tali stumbled into the house, reeking of beer. They blinked when the light came on. They had their arms across each other's shoulders and had been softly laughing over some little joke between the two of them. At once, they registered their mother folded into the easy chair, where she'd been awaiting them in the darkness. It took another moment before they noticed the singed paper dangling from her twitching fingers.

Behold the shit-eating grin on Tali's face, almost instantly mirrored in Yudi's! Their arms shot down to their sides as if ordered to attention. Neither could look at the other. Rivka knew the truth right then, yet she put them through a grilling —arguably for their benefit more than for her own.

"You two recognize this wrapper?"

They nodded, in unison.

"You know where it came from?"

Tali gave a quick wave of his fingers as if it was no matter. As if to say, Ima, you go through thousands and thousands of those papers every year, why ask about just one? She knew she could wait him out.

Yudi ventured, "The packing shed, I suppose."

She shook her head. Sat tight

"It's late, and we're tired."

"I should think so," she said, "after trucking this silent witness into Jaffa." Anyone who didn't know them well would have thought them guiltless as newborns—they had all the earmarks down pat. "Tell me, how did it get singed?" rotating the airy sheet, softly blowing at the burnt matter until some of it separated and floated onto her skirt.

"It won't be traced to you," Tali said. "We can't be the only orchard who uses those."

"Which of you drove the truck?"

Swift sidelong glances. Each of them seemed about to claim the title. At the last moment, each shrugged a shoulder, fallen apples from the Avram tree.

Hazard to her business wasn't what worried Rivka. She didn't fear reprisals, or the police. For lack of better words, it was the vulnerability of her sons' souls that stopped her cold. But she saw she'd get nowhere with these staunch tin soldiers unless she changed her tactics. "Vee haf our methods to make you talk," she Germanized, a guttural caricature of interrogation.

This broke them up. This broke the ice. "I drove," admitted Tali. "Yudi was our lookout."

This asinine, third-rate device. "You're the Stern Gang?" she said.

"Lehi, yes, and proud to be."

"Terrorists."

"No, patriots."

"Patriotic to what, I'd like to know. Certainly not Judaism."

"To a Jewish state," said Yudi.

"Murdering innocent people? Destroying their livelihood? This is what a Jew does?"

"Hunhh, innocent people. Once you live in this country, Ima, already you've given up your innocence. Arab, Jew, we're all implicated," said Tali.

Yudi added, "You're one to talk, you and Abba both. You think we haven't learned from your stories of gunfights and espionage? We've gone the next logical step, that's all."

"Yudi, Yudi *mein yidele*. It's a step in the wrong direction. You're headed backwards, into anarchy."

"Me? I'm headed to bed. So's Tali. We did our job today, and we've earned our rest."

She was left to sit with her recollections. The gone time when they brought her spring wildflowers, lemon-yellow petals already wilting over their pudgy little wrists, their eyes alight with boyish wonder and love and joy in the giving.

-388-

By 1948, Palestine had a population of nearly two million. A little over half of these—1,180,000—were Muslims. A little over a quarter—630,000—were Jews. The rest—143,000—were Christian. Any other religious denomination had negligible populations. Arabs outnumbered Jews two to one.

-389-

The United Nations partition plan jigsawed out parcels for the Jewish state that would incorporate almost as many Arabs as Jews. In the Arab state, Arabs would predominate by a large margin, with Jewish areas like islands in a sea. Conspicuous among these was a cluster of four kibbutzim known as the Etzion bloc. Settled between 1943 and '47, they were located north of Hebron in a position to dominate the road leading to Jerusalem. In January 1948, the 450 Jewish residents of the Etzion bloc were surrounded by an Arab force under the command of Haj Abd al-Qadir al-Husseini, the Mufti's cousin. It's said that Arab women and children came tagging after the men, swinging sacks meant for looting—so sure were they of a walkover. They had reason for confidence. At least a thousand combatants advanced against the settlements.

A hundred-thirty-or-so armed Jewish defenders beat off this onslaught, but they knew it was only the beginning. Head-on attack was never the Arabs' preferred stratagem; starving people out was. Al-Qadir tightened his circle around the settlements.

The British stepped in to arrange an evacuation of the blockaded women and children. The Jewish fighters could have gone, too, but they spurned any offer of rescue. As long as they could hold out, they would be cutting off the Arabs' southern approach to the holy city. The Haganah dispatched reinforcements, thirty-five men making their stealthy way through the hills. The men never reached Etzion, and for the longest time no one knew what had befallen them.

Ambushed: no survivors.

-390-

Days of siege became weeks of siege, and the weeks would turn to months, and the beleaguered defenders were in want of everything—food, arms, ammunition, volunteers.

-391-

The mouths of her young men were full and sculpted like the lips she'd admired once in a photograph of Michelangelo's David. Yudi's especially—not exactly insolent, but so nakedly self-satisfied. Her house had grown more silent than ever. Shimshon stayed in his room when he wasn't at school. Ahuva, at work in Haifa, rarely came home. Yudi and Tali stalked past her with pouted smirks on their faces. They came, they went, and there was nothing anymore to be said.

-392-

Moshe's destination was the old Rothschild-Hadassah hospital on Rehov Harav Kook. He'd been summoned there to consult on a burn patient. Elli had objected to his going. "Must I spell it out for you? The Arab bombing?" On a night not three weeks before, an armored truck with misleading British markings had detonated in front of the *Palestine Post* building. Glass shattered, fire sowed its hot seeds, and shrapnel whipped in whirlwinds. It was something of a wonder that the building survived at all. Editors and press people caught inside weren't so favored. Working late on the next day's paper, they'd been blinded or mutilated or killed. Yet by some uncanny sleight of hand, the paper came out on schedule in the morning. Only two pages of it, but still—. Moshe would never understand how they were able to print it at all. That they did so emboldened him never to hesitate wherever his work might call him. He worried about his family all the time: would Marian be hurt on her way to or from classes; would Elli, traveling from clinic to clinic? Elli worried would he be hurt, and it was as impossible to allay her fears as his own.

-393-

Perhaps for his own protection, Moshe was told that the patient's burns came from an exploded Primus stove. Nonsense: this raw face had been on a raid and through a firefight that went sideways. The patient's name wasn't given, nor did Morris seek it. He wouldn't have gotten the truth anyway. Obviously the man fought with the underground. This hospital had been treating members of Haganah, Irgun and Lehi for so long—must be twenty years—that the British couldn't possibly be ignorant of the fact; and yet healing went on undisrupted. Moshe could only suppose the police were in enough hot water without having to answer for more beastly outrages—such as overrunning the wards, routing injured patients from their beds and hauling them away to dank and septic jail cells.

-394-

To Elli's horror, her forebodings had been off by only a single day. The very next afternoon on Ben Yehudah Street, some Arabs in British military uniforms set off an appalling blast. Or maybe the men driving those three big explosive-crammed army trucks really were British—deserters, perhaps, who took the side of the Arabs. The news reports were unsure and unsettling. Printed photos of the wreckage were indistinct, yet anything but ambiguous. There's nothing unclear about ruined buildings, nothing indefinite about torn limbs, nothing vague about death.

-395-

What Leila asked was, "Why would you put a Jewish king over my people?" What Rivka heard was, "How can a half-Arab country become a Jewish state?" A problem in whatever terms you considered it.

Jerusalem was settling itself out: most of the Arabs living in the Jewish parts of the city were decamping for Arab areas, while most Jews from Arab areas were moving over into the Arab houses left vacant in the Jewish parts. But Jerusalem's swapfest was a special case, because the city was slated to come under UN control. This prospect for tomorrow tended to disentangle its demographics today.

In the Jewish part of Palestine, what could be done with 400,000 Arabs? Would they be willing to move over to the Arab part? If so, would Arabs over there make them welcome? What would happen right here, in Rehovot? Uncertainties gnawed at Rivka. Could Leila's family stay in their village and the village mukhtar agree to live under the governance of a Jewish state? If not, would the villagers go away on their own? Then who would live in their houses? DPs from Europe? Or would the new Jewish state raze the villages? But what if the villagers refused to leave, what then?

Already the things that were going on! Grisly things if you asked her—necessary things if you asked Avram—glorious things if you asked the twins. Just last week, the Haganah had taken over Caesarea. Arabs were living in its thirty-six homes on land leased from the Palestine Jewish Colonization Association. Some of the villagers fled before the Jewish soldiers, but the rest were forced out—"summarily evicted," as Avram put it. Thirty homes were looted and then blown up. The other six were looted, too, and—according to Tali, who told Shimshon—those houses, too, would have been destroyed, except the soldiers ran out of matériel.

Leila had surely heard talk about Caesarea, which meant she knew Rivka had no good answer to the question she posed.

-396-

When Rivka demanded of Avram, "Why Caesarea?" he assured her that Haganah's operations followed from a long-term strategy, nothing haphazard in any combat or destruction. He rustled up a newspaper map of the UN partition plan, and with three blunt fingers picked out the wasp-waisted, virtually discontinuous parcels proposed for the Jews. "First we have to ensure control of these areas, then secure these borders," tracing the lines, tapping at points of weakness. "We'll occupy any Arab village in position to cut off communications between Jewish towns or kibbutzim. Any capable of threatening our existence as a state? Must be evacuated and the whole place razed."

"All others will be let alone?"

"For now."

"Pretty words," Rivka said.

He grinned. "And after that, we'll annex the Jews who are stuck in Arabland, on the far side of the borders."

-397-

The Arabs, too, had a military plan—to cut off Jewish communications and starve the Jews into submission. They took control of the coastal highway south of Jaffa, cutting off the Negev. They took control of Bab-al-Wad and the hills leading to Jerusalem, cutting off the holy city from the coast. Their blockade was on.

-398-

After Lehi killed ten British soldiers (in reprisal for a reprisal for a reprisal), the British agreed they'd keep their troops out of Jewish Jerusalem and allow the Jews there to police themselves—a milestone in their advance toward

Jewish self-government. Already Palestine's Jews were seasoned in managing their affairs through the decades-long leadership of the Jewish Agency, Histadrut and other organizations. When March came, the Jewish Agency and Histadrut pressed further by forming a legislative body, the Provisional Council. By comparison, the experience of Palestine's Arabs in self-government had been slight, random and ephemeral. For centuries their affairs had been largely managed by the Ottomans, followed by the Mandate. The Jews routinely carped and wrangled and fell out among themselves. So did the Arabs, who took to heart their proverb, "I and my brothers against my cousin; I and my cousins against the stranger." But above all else, the Jews felt they couldn't afford to lose this Land, whereas the Arabs felt they couldn't afford to lose face. That the land could be lost was inconceivable to them.

-399-

Now that the British turned all their care to withdrawing from Palestine, the simmering civil war between Arab and Jew boiled over. Alarmed, the United Nations started making noises about stepping in ahead of schedule and taking over all of Palestine, not just Jerusalem. "Too late," countered Ben-Gurion. "We're already on our way to statehood." Marian, who was just then savoring a course in Shakespeare, observed, "He should have quoted Macbeth."

-400-

I am in blood
Stepp'd in so far, that should I wade no more
Returning were as tedious as go o'er.
—*Macbeth* III:4, 1440

-401-

In April, Arab irregulars infiltrated Zarnuqua, Leila's village. They commandeered the houses and bundled off the women, the children and the elderly. Many of these, including Leila, filtered into the nearby village of Yibna (the biblical Yavneh) to await the Arab victory.

-402-

Leila

Who owns the land if not Allah? By the laws of ownership I am told it has never been my land, but by the law of Allah it is my land because my people have always lived here. The law says the land can be inherited; it can be sold. My people are not for sale. Where they go, I and my children go, for my people are their inheritance.

The law says the fate of our land can be the choice of foreigners. Rivka tells me: the Jews will not harm you. Here you will be a citizen. Elsewhere a refugee.

But her people will not survive what is to come, and we will return to live as always. I wish her no ill, yet that is the truth.

-403-

When the Children of Israel stood at the Red Seashore, with Pharaoh's army in pursuit not far behind them, Moses held his staff out over the waters. And what happened? Nothing, according to a story in the Talmud. The waters of the sea were unmoved. The Israelites huddled in terror, some ready to turn back, others weeping and at a loss what to do. At that critical moment, there stepped forward a fellow by the name of Nachshon. He dipped his toe in the water. Nothing happened. He went in ankle deep. Nothing. He moved forward until the water lapped at his knees. Still nothing. His hips, waist, shoulders. At Nachshon's next—and possibly fatal —step forward (and perhaps it's for this that the Talmud instructs fathers to teach their children to swim), the waters parted, and the Children of Israel passed safely through on dry land.

-404-

The lesson of Nachshon is that we cannot rely on God to do everything for us. We must initiate the first step, risk ourselves—and only then can we count on God's help.

Which might come only in the nick of time.

-405-

One warm day she heard him tell Avram he was going "on maneuvers," but Rivka thought nothing of it. He said it so casually, not with bravado, not like any ordinary boy his age. Sometimes it slipped her mind that Shimshon was everything but ordinary.

-406-

In Hebrew, the Tel Aviv-Jerusalem Road.
In Arabic, the Jerusalem-Jaffa Road.
Same road.

-407-

By the beginning of April, Jerusalem's Jews were down to rations that would last only a few days more. The road from Tel Aviv was their lifeline. Along it were trucked all things necessary to the community's sustenance. The tight Arab blockade meant that convoys bringing aid ran a withering gauntlet of bullets and bombs from Arab gunners in the hills commanding the road. Within the city, deadly shellfire rained down from the surrounding hills. Elli scrounged for the family's food and water; the hospitals for medicines; fighting units for ammunition.

Nachshon was the code name for a Haganah operation aimed at opening the way for food, water, medicines and matériel to reach the besieged Jews of Jerusalem. It almost didn't come off, for lack of arms. Fifteen-hundred soldiers were ready, but without guns how could they go forward? Exactly what timely, Nachshonish step someone took to bring on the small miracle is unclear, but it arrived in the shape of a plane carrying Czech armaments. The plane landed on a recently evacuated British airstrip, and was followed not long after by a Yugoslav ship that steamed into Haifa with additional sorely needed weapons. When you name an operation Nachshon, maybe you can expect this sort of last-minute deliverance. Not that the Jewish fighting force waltzed safely through Palestine on dry land. No, there was a gore-soaked battle ahead, and meaner consequences.

-408-

The operation was launched with two attacks, the first—a feint—at the western end of the road near Ramle, where the area commander's two-story headquarters was blown up. Several of the Mufti's senior officers were killed in that attack. The second attack—the focus of the operation—went off almost simultaneously at the eastern end of the road. It targeted the Arab village of al-Qastal, named for a Crusader castle whose ruins overlooked Jerusalem from a high, steep slope.

Leila's son Ibrahim had joined one of the irregular forces operating out of al-Qastal. As a boy, Ibrahim had played with

Rivka's twins; being a few years their senior, he'd been their ringleader. He'd grown to manhood unchallenged in his belief in that superiority. Now his unit came under heavy fire, and the men were forced to retreat. They fled downhill, following the south-westward remains of an old Roman road into the quarry below. Ibrahim crouched with his fellows among the rocks, chucking desultory small stones at a circle they'd formed with larger stones. He wasn't wounded, except in his pride, which smoldered under the insult of the enemy's victory.

Slowly it dawned on him that something was different this time. Always before, when the Jews took a village, they promptly cleared it of people. Sometimes they tore it down, but whether they did so or not, they then withdrew—always. He'd never heard of their operations being otherwise. Now, there were no sounds of Jewish mischief, no signs of tearing down and no signs of withdrawing, either. It looked as if the enemy intended on staying. Well then, Ibraham intended on staying longer. As long as necessary. With an oath, he swore himself to retake al-Qastal.

-409-

This land of the brave is the land of our forefathers.
The Jews have no right to this land.
How can I sleep while the enemy rules it?
Something burns in my heart.

—Haj Abd al-Qadir al Husseini

-410-

Al-Qastal was in Jewish hands, and al-Qastal was crucial to beating the Arab blockade. Ten tense hours passed before the hungry, thirsty, impatient Jews of Jerusalem cheered the first battered convoy rolling in with its load of what could have been manna from heaven. Jewish force had prevailed—for now. The battle for the road was far from over.

-411-

In the night, Ibrahim was among the host of a thousand who reached the outskirts of al-Qastal. Gunshot crackled past his ears, and the ground under his feet shook with the concussion of grenades. The man to his left went down; the one to his right was hit, a spray of blood spitting from his shoulder. And then Ibraham heard the order to retreat. Their assault on the village was a failure.

Worse, they were running out of ammunition. A car prepared to leave for Ramallah. The driver was Ibrahim's brother-in-law, the husband of his sister, Zeinab. The two men embraced before he set out to see if he could find some bullets to buy. Already al-Qastal had been in Jewish hands for a galling four days. Yet Ibrahim felt far from demoralized, and the troops mustering at the bottom of the hill were confident.

They had reason. Haj Abd al-Qadir al-Husseini had arrived, their commander whom they revered, coming directly to them from a meeting in Damascus. It was he who'd led the Arabs in January against Kfar Etzion, he who claimed responsibility for the March bombing on Ben Yehudah Street, and now he who was here among them, ready to lead them in taking back al-Qastal.

In Damascus he'd pressed for weapons to sustain the fight—and had been refused, but his troops knew nothing of that.

-412-

A soupy fog covered al-Qastal at dawn on April 8. Al-Qadir and a couple of his aides grabbed the opportunity to size up the enemy's deployment. They moved silently up the back slope and with deliberate stealth approached the outskirts of the village. But then some wayward clink or glint or shadowed gesture must have alerted a Jewish sentry to their presence. He opened fire, a shot that flung al-Qadir spread-eagled on the ground. The commander's pop-eyed aides scrambled away, plunging headlong and heedless down the track they'd so deftly crept up.

The sentry knelt to empty the fallen man's pockets. Through his teeth there issued a low whistle with each prize he laid out on the ground. In addition to a well-thumbed, pint-size Qu'ran, he found two gold pens, an ivory-handled pistol, and some papers covered in Arabic writing. Here was a man of importance, for sure. On the Arab's hairy wrist, a gold watch. The Jew unbuckled it and slid it up onto his own forearm. It looked very fine there, indeed. With small wigwags he made it gleam as the sun rose and the fog thinned.

Down below, al-Qadir's unnerved aides were reporting that their leader had been taken. This news of his capture flew from ear to horrified ear through the camp, rousing the men and galvanizing their fury. In no time, Ibrahim found himself running at a gallop amid an aggrieved, white-hot and reinless horde. They hurtled up the western slope and burst in on al-Qastal, driving out its Jewish defenders, who retreated northward and eastward down the slope. Ibrahim stopped with his comrades to scour the village for their lost commander. The rest flew on after the enemy. Any Jew they nabbed was interrogated on the spot: a chorus shrieking questions and demands as to al-Qadir's whereabouts and condition. No Jewish answer was as good as any Jewish answer. The captive got a swift knife in the gut and was left to die while his captors renewed their wild pursuit.

According to Ibrahim, the redoubtable al-Qadir still lived when he and his fellows, lustily chanting *Allahu akbar,* broke in upon the village. Inside one of the boxy stone houses, they came upon the cherished leader, who was braced against a wall, cradling his weapon, his fingers lightly on the trigger. Only half alive though feisty as ever, he asked in fading voice, "You've taken back the village?" They nodded. He'd lost a lot of blood, and Ibrahim noted it still leaking in a slow trickle from his wounds. With his last breath, al-Qadir mouthed, "Thanks be to God we've purged the shame."

Jews contradicted this account. Al-Qadir, they claimed, was killed instantly by the troop's crack marksman—or by his lucky shot, which is how Avram heard it from a Palmachi friend who'd been posted in the village that morning. He claimed that when the Arab hotheads broke in, all they could possibly have discovered was their commander's cooling corpse.

Alive-and-dead for the space of a contentious hour, al-Qadir, for a certainty, was carried post mortem to Jerusalem, his body attended by those who'd taken al-Qastal. A gathering multitude joined the funeral procession winding toward the mosque at the Dome of the Rock. It was April 9, a Friday, the Muslim holy day. Shops closed, and every street filled up with Arab mourners. Ibrahim was a tiny dot among ten thousand. Yesterday he'd felt invincible under his commander, a true patriot. Today, he and his comrades shot their rifles skyward in a passion of heartache and bitterness. Who would lead them now, who could fill al-Qadir's shoes? *"Abu Musa,"* they cried out, meaning that their commander—a true Muslim who believed with all his soul in the words of the prophet Muhammad—had come together with the prophet in death.

From Cairo, the mufti Haj Amin al-Husseini sent a eulogy.
"One thing shall not die: Palestine."

But al-Qastal was dying at the same moment that Amin's
message was read out. Deserted, undefended, the village was
seized once again by the Jews. This time they destroyed it.

-413-

Not long past the funeral, a squabbling arose and then a
clear falling out among the officers who'd served under al-
Qadir. One by one, they flounced off, each with his own men
to their home villages. Sick at heart, Ibrahim headed to
Zarnuqua to till his fields. On the way he spotted spires of
gray smoke tapering into a bright and cloudless western sky,
and briefly wondered the reason why.

His wife, his mother, his cousins streamed out to greet him
as a hero, the women ululating, the men cheek-kissing with
him endlessly. He met them in confusion. It struck him that
the selfsame things that made his people strong and himself
worthy—his family, his clan, his village, and his honor—
seemed to make their campaign against the Jews weak and
unavailing.

-414-

Southwest of Jerusalem, even closer to the holy city than
al-Qastal, but without al-Qastal's strategic position, was the
Arab village of Deir Yassin, where Ishmael's sister, Zeinab,
lived.

-415-

That same Friday of al-Qadir's funeral, on the dot of 3 a.m.,
Shimshon set to walking from a dozen paces behind the slow-
moving truck. In the darkness, the sudden blare of its

loudspeaker jarred him as it instructed all Deir Yassin to exit the village from its western end. In reply came a chatter of gunfire—must be from the village guards. Bullets kicked up little jets of sand around the truck and tat-tatted against its sides. The truck swerved. Shimshon halted and watched it wallow into the roadside ditch. It stalled there cockeyed and mute. He wondered, has even a single villager caught its message?

From the street now, and from inside the houses, come shouts and bellows. He's moving forward again. Bullets thrumming past his ears, ricocheting at him off walls. He's bent nearly double. Wooden door: force it open, pull the pin, throw, throw now. Down, get down. *Kaboom!* Arrowing wood, arrowing stone. Now go. Dust choking, eyes stinging. Dusky silhouettes creeping along the floor. Voices screeching Arab names. Unmoving awkward hulk—dead. Solitary limb in a dark puddle on the tiles. Woman dodging him, picking up weapons. Run her down. Beneath her skirt—surprise!

Searching house to house. Rounding them up. Forming a line, men and able boys.

A father's hand on a boy's head. Spindly brat snuggling a chicken. A wisp of memory nudges Shimshon. When he gropes for it, it dissolves.

His mind's gone deaf.

-416-

Leila couldn't come to work anymore, she said. The family were leaving.

"What, not all of you?"

"All of us."

"Where will you go?"

"Lebanon, Transjordan, Gaza...." A small, stiff shrug, or

was it a tremor, smothered? "The men will decide."

"Until they do, you can work here. You'll have use for the money."

Leila looked so dreadfully uncomfortable. Was it the straight talk about money?

"I can no longer work for you." Uncomfortable was the wrong word: eyes that darted, chin that quivered.

"Why, Leila? What have I ever shown you except kindness?"

"It is true."

"And the same has come from you to me."

Her eyes squeezed shut, and she shook her head. "It is decided. Because of Deir Yassin." The horror there had flashed like lightning across Arab Palestine, arriving before the newspapers, speeding faster than any radio report. Leila put it to her, but Rivka refused to believe. Not the work of Jewish boys, of that she was certain. No, it was rumors, exaggerations, fabrications to cause enmity between the populations.

"Look to your own family," Leila said. "Look to them."

-417-

Rivka cornered Yudi and Tali. Possession of al-Qastal, she said, still hung in the balance when some toughs from the Irgun and Lehi—and, for all she knew, the Haganah as well—took it into their foolish heads to storm Deir Yassin. They'd pounced on it, won it. And then murdered the bulk of its villagers—who were just fellaheen trying to scrape out a living in an ever-more-troubled place to live. To make matters worse, they took whatever prisoners were left alive and paraded them through the streets of Jewish Jerusalem. It was disgusting, it was madness, a senseless bloodbath. Tell her they hadn't been part of it.

They assured her they knew nothing of Deir Yassin. "We were in Tel Aviv. I swear it," said Yudi.

"Then why do your looks keep shifting away from me?"

"I can prove we were nowhere near Jerusalem," said Tali.

A day later they brought her their proof. Two young beauties in Haganah uniforms testified that they'd all spent Friday—the Friday in question, yes—promenading together along the beachfront. The girls looked honest enough, so Rivka decided to believe them. But something was not right, and she dreaded getting to the bottom of it.

-418-

Leila's daughter Zeinab at Silwan...
with Assistant Inspector General Richard Catling
of the British Palestine Police
and Mr. Frederick Williamson of the Medical Service

The walls cannot hold in all the hubbub. Here in this room is wailing and shrieking, for we women of Deir Yassin don't know where our boys are.

Mr. Williamson, he says all he wants is the truth.

"Of course, the truth. But where is my boy, and when will I see him?"

"But the truth, please. Is it true you've been violated?"

"Yes, my boy has been taken." This is violation, is it not? So young a man, scarcely ten years of age, so straight and tall and proud.

"Best to tell right away what the Jewish soldiers did to you. Were you—um—handled in any way? Touched?"

"No, no. My in-laws—their house—was destroyed. Grenades. Are they dead?" May Allah grant they're not dead.

"Madam, please tell me. I can see your decency, your modesty. But it's best to say what's true, and no mistaking. You were raped, were you not? Other young women have told Mr. Catling...."

Told him what? That they were raped? Then the honor of their families is destroyed! Still, what good is truth or honor without my boy? "If I say so, will I get my boy back?"

"I won't reveal your name...um, Zeinab. It's just for statistics. You can tell me."

Tell him I've been raped? Now, I, in chorus with the others, shrieking, "What do you want from me?"

"Only the truth, madam."

"But tell me how to say it."

He shakes his head. "The words must come from you."

I turn tight-lipped away from him.

-419-

Reported in *The New York Times* April 10, 1948: *Irgun and Stern Groups Unite to Win Deir Yassin,* in house-to-house fighting [that] killed more than 200 Arabs, half of them women and children.

Reported in *The Palestine Post* April 11, 1948: *Arabs Charge Cruelty,* condemning the attack at Deir Yassin as a massacre of 254 innocent people.

-420-

From the Qu'ran, regarding the Jews:

Evil indeed are their actions. (5:62)

-421-

Deir Yassin. The more Rivka heard, the more frenzied she grew. Torture, to teach the desert rats a lesson. Atrocities, to let them know we Jews are as capable as the rest of humanity of acting subhuman. Among other things, a pregnant woman —God in heaven!—had been disemboweled. And these foul things had been accomplished by Jews! Then, to march the pitiful survivors as trophies through the streets of Jerusalem? Our brave boys.

Once she'd come to believe it, once she'd allowed herself to credit it, and when she thought she could utter the name without retching, she approached Avram. "Were you at Deir Yassin?"

His eyes flashed. "You tell me."

"WERE. YOU. THERE."

"I was not. I'd have stopped it. Brainless kids running riot through a village? And to no purpose at all."

She studied him, a few seconds too long.

He mimicked her, hands on hips. "What? What, Rivka?"

"They'll want revenge, you know."

"Yes, we're arming. Waiting for that shoe to drop."

-422-

The whole country waited. Who could not ponder the Arabs preparing their revenge, working out the where and the when? Not too soon—let the Jews gnaw their fingernails a while. Not too late—it must be seen as a direct and timely reprisal.

-423-

Shimshon brought Rivka a neck-wrung chicken and for Leila a pair of bangle earrings. Why Leila? As a youngster, it was true, he'd interchangeably called the two women "Ima." Still, the gift seemed freakish to Rivka. Like a taunt of sorts. Or an apology? He ducked her direct question, but seemed to imply that all of Deir Yassin might have spied him raping a young girl dolled up in those very earrings. Rivka steeled herself against showing her outrage, since he so transparently craved to shock and confound her. She said, "An ordinary Arab village, as ordinary as they come, except that it's near Jerusalem. Being sited on the outskirts of Jerusalem, this is a crime now?"

"If you could see what we found, Ima. The weapons, the ammo. They're no ordinary villagers."

"I do the same here in my house, sheltering you fighters and hiding arms among the oranges. Do I deserve to be pillaged, raped, murdered?"

"Ima, Deir Yassin has never been a nice little Arab village. In the riots of 1920, it was a hub for weapons trafficking. In the riots of 1929, its people attacked the Jews of Givat Shaul, Beit Hakerem and the Montefiore Quarter in Jerusalem. In 1936, again they went on the attack against Givat Shaul."

"Where do you come by this intelligence?"

His lips twisted. "Probably from you. Probably gathered by you with your friend Elli." He hadn't forgotten all those file cards he'd helped her collate and organize for the Jewish Agency.

"And that's how you *bulvans* use my demographic information? To kill whole families?"

"Me, I killed a man who was dressed as a woman. Underneath his skirt, he wore khaki pants tucked into his boots."

"And so?"

"He was Iraqi."

"You know this? You asked him?"

"He was dead. Wearing Iraqi uniform pants."

"Maybe he got the pants from someone else."

"Sure. Maybe by mistake he cut off his own trousers while

pruning his olive trees. Maybe The Prophet appeared before him with Iraqi surplus."

Outside, the crows set to cawing in raucous chorus. She went to the window and shooed them as best she could. Persistent pests, they were worse than the stray dogs, worse than abandoned cats and the dislocated farm animals that since the winter rains she'd spotted roaming untethered across the fields. "Leila's gone," she told Shimshon. "Because of Deir Yassin."

He picked up the earrings, put them back into his pocket. He said nothing.

"Two hundred and fifty-four people are dead. All of them were terrorists?"

"Nowhere near two hundred and fifty-four dead. Probably half that number, every one of them shooting at us."

"A hundred and twenty-seven? That makes it all right?"

"It's only the beginning, Ima. We're redeeming the land for the Jews."

"Mark my words, this is poison in the belly of our cause."

"Tastes good enough to me." Smacking his lips.

She advanced on him, crowding him, jabbing her forefinger into his chest. "I want you gone. Take your things and don't come back."

-424-

Avram went after the boy and found him combing the beach in Haifa, bunking at Ahuva's. He brought Shimshon back and set up camp for him in the tool shed. After a time, he forced Rivka to have a talk with them. She barely touched down on the edge of the seat he offered her.

Earnestly, Shimshon denied what had been in the news. He denied any looting, denied any rape, denied any butchery.

All the while, her foot snapped steadily against the floor.

"Why won't you believe me, Ima?"

As evidence against him there was the dead chicken and a pair of Arab earrings. There were the clots of panicked Arab families on the roads, their belongings piled atop their heads or bumping along in low-slung baby carriages. "What am I to think, when all the world tells a different story?"

"But I know what really happened. I was there," he said.

"More's the pity."

-425-

What really happened at Deir Yassin was less important in those crucial days than what could be done with it, what story could be told about it. Every side had reason to make an emblem of Deir Yassin: the Jews, to scare Palestine's Arabs into fleeing their villages; the Arabs, both to demonize the Jews and to oblige surrounding Arab countries to back them up; the British, to abandon Palestine; the press, to sell newspapers.

Shimshon was closer to the truth than Rivka—but years would pass before any semblance would emerge of what did and did not happen at Deir Yassin.

-426-

It may be that forty survivors, mainly women and children and the elderly, were loaded on trucks and transported to a nearby Arab section of Jerusalem, given food and water and later released. A small number of additional survivors were put on a truck and driven toward the Arab sector, passing through Jerusalem's downtown and Mea Shearim, the orthodox Jewish area. It's said that people there spat at the trucks—incensed not at the Arabs, but at the drivers for going through their neighborhood so close to the start of Shabbat.

It is certain that some fifty-three orphaned children were unceremoniously dumped near the Church of the Holy Sepulchre, barefoot in pajamas, exhausted and hungry— where they were happened on and rescued by Hind Husseini, a woman with the soul of an angel, who took them all home with her and started an orphanage cum school for them.

-427-

Zeinab's husband was killed at al-Qastal that same day. Her boy was taken prisoner from Deir Yassin, held for a year, and then released to her in Nablus, a different boy by then.

-428-

The staccato of gunfire resounded all through the country —at Mishmar ha-Emek, near Latrun, at Beersheba and Tiberias: twelve Jews killed here, seven Arabs there, dozens wounded daily. Each morning, Moshe and Elli sipped their coffee and shook their heads over their newspapers. Above all else, the Deir Yassin massacre undid them. They dreaded the inevitable Arab reply, which would spew venom whenever and wherever it came. Though what could the Arabs do, Moshe wondered, that would hurt more than the sore awakening that this fight for a homeland had sunk Jews to the level of barbarians? They agreed this had to be the work of mis-creants, dregs of the dregs—until a report trickled out that Palmachis, too, had shamed themselves on the people of Deir Yassin. Palmach, deemed the elite force of the Haganah! "Rivka's Avram is a Palmachi," Elli said with a huff.

Every detail appalled and sickened them both, yet they couldn't stop thinking about it, talking about it. Women molested, old men lined up and put to death; children, too, as young as three years of age. Like something the Arabs would do, but not us. Like something the British might do, but no, please not us. Like something the Nazis did. Here was a stark loss to the collective Jewish soul. What loss of a Jewish eye, or arm, even a life in Arab reprisal—could match this sadness?

-429-

After Deir Yassin, in Arab villages that the UN plan mapped as Jewish, or in strategic spots nearby, some Zionist with a friendly tie to the mukhtar would drop by and murmur, "There's word the Haganah is headed here. Best take your family and go. Shhhh, keep mum. It's between you and me."

All over Palestine, Arab families were leaving their villages, their lands, their homes, the graves of their ancestors. Some were frightened off by rumors, others driven out with guns. They fled with their house keys in their hands. Not long, they thought: another month, as soon as the British leave, we Arabs will join forces, the armies of seven countries will drive the Jews into the sea, and we'll return home with our heads held high.

-430-

[God] will certainly test you with a touch of fear and famine and loss of property, life and crops. Give good news to those who patiently endure—
—Qu'ran 1:155

-431-

Avram

And should we give them free sway, as in those years of restraint? If they do succeed in throwing us all into the sea, will the world tell them to back off? Two thousand years say no. But if they don't succeed, we should take pity on them? We should let them have their success anyway?

-432-

If you retaliate, then let it be equivalent to what you have suffered. But if you patiently endure, it is certainly best.

—Qu'ran 16:26

-433-

Rivka, though she didn't know it, had the last word on Deir Yassin. Madness, she'd termed it. Today, what's left of that once-lively village has become an actual madhouse. Well—an exaggeration: today it's a place for people suffering from mental illness. Oddly appropriate, though.

-434-

Elli didn't say she was going up to the hospital. She rarely ever went to the Mount Scopus campus—not many did if they didn't have to. The coiled road—a mile and a half of be-draggled Arab neighborhood—had become a practice range for snipers. They picked off cars, motorcycles, Jewish buses, pretty much anything Jewish that moved. Up at the top, seven hundred patients, plus staff of the hospital and the university, had become isolated. Food, supplies and personnel could only go in or out by that one long and perilous approach. She caught up with the convoy leaving at 9:15 that morning. In all, she counted ten vehicles: a Haganah escort in an armored Ford car took the lead, then two ambulances, three buses filled with medical staff, three trucks filled with provisions, and, in the rear, a second Haganah escort.

Magen David Adom's insignia on the vehicles should have protected them, but of course by April of 1948, all that had gone by the boards. It was now 9:45, and they'd just rounded Wushashibi Bend, when the gaudy blast of a buried mine in the road crippled the lead car. That blow released a torrent of bullets from Arabs lying in ambush behind thick scrub on both sides of the road. Elli made a dive under her bus seat. Up front, the disabled car's Haganah guards made a crouching, zigzagging run for the ambulances. The two rearmost supply trucks managed screeching u-turns and hightailed back toward base. The rest were stuck in the enfilade. Yet not without reasonable hope. A British light infantry station stood just a couple of hundred yards farther up the road. Only a dozen or so men, but still.... Where were they now, with their machine guns and bazookas and frayed—though still functioning—British authority? Nowhere in sight. Maybe soon.

Hunkered down with the doctor, her seatmate in the middle bus, Elli hung on through two salvo-laden hours from God-knows-how-many furious, revenge-taking, *"Minshan Deir Yassin"*-bellowing assailants. Brutal, frenzied, gory hours these were, in which the Haganah defenders fought full out against their Arab counterparts; and in which evidently the laggardly British major finally made up his mind to come calling. The shooting died down. He knocked at the door of Elli's bus. A nervous exchange with the Haganah spokesman and something encouraging, a hint of promise. But no, he couldn't negotiate a cease fire after all, though he tried his very best. And so he took his men and withdrew.

Then Molotov cocktails did their job, lurching underneath engines and smashing through splintered windows, setting all three buses aflame. No way out, bullets zinging, caroming every which way.

Five o'clock in the afternoon: at last the British open fire on what's left of the ambushing Arabs—and at long last they salvage the convoy's remnant. There are twenty-eight survivors in all. The seven hundred still sealed off up at the hospital will wait a few more days before the British evacuate them.

At about 4:30 that afternoon, Moshe was alerted that he might be needed later to consult on the victims' burns. He went home to rest. Elli wasn't there, but Marian was, and she was frantic. Where could Ima be? It was his first inkling that his wife might have ridden in the convoy. Neither of them knew for sure; neither judged it likely, though fear leapt ahead of judgment to the worst possible conclusion.

Within the hour, he was called back in to evaluate several patients. Their condition was dire, yet even so, he couldn't keep from putting the question to them. Had Elli been aboard? With the feeblest of wheezy grunts or fluttered eyelids or faint finger-waggles, each and every one managed to get across that they hadn't seen her. He could still hope.

Through the night they waited for word from Elli. Word never came, nor the next day, nor the one after. They drifted through the house like twin ghosts, unable to give solace to each other, but unwilling to separate. When Moshe went to see patients, he took Marian along with him. On the second night after the attack, they cooked dinner together. Neither of them ate, though each urged food upon the other, insisting it was what Ima would want.

"Would want," their language vaulting ahead of their acknowledgement of the truth. By such small steps they came to tell each other that Elli was never coming home again.

-435-

Seventy-eight Jews were killed in the reprisal for Deir Yassin, among them fifty-five men, and among those Elli's colleague Dr. Chaim Yassky, ophthalmologist and Director of the Hadassah Medical Organization. He'd done pioneering work on trachoma, with Elli working alongside him. Together, they'd saved the eyes of tens of thousands of Arabs.

Also among the men was Moshe's colleague Dr. Moshe Ben-David, slated to head up the new university medical school. That project would now have to be put on hold.

Twenty-three women perished in the attack on the convoy, among whom was the light of Moshe's life and the length of his days.

-436-

One British officer lost his life.

-437-

The number of Arab casualties is unknown.

-438-

Thirty-one bodies were given a proper burial. The rest, either too heavily burned or too completely torn to parts and shreds, were heaved into some sort of mass grave—this much Moshe and Marian were able to learn. Events quickly overtook everyone in these headlong, pivotal days, and there was no further information to be had. Forty-seven Jews disappeared from the face of the earth. One of them—one of them— inhabits the dreams of a father and his daughter.

-439-

It was the unbearable measure of the guilt Moshe carried

in his heart. If not for him, Elli would never have come to Palestine. She'd be alive still, maybe in Paris, maybe in Canada, maybe another somewhere entirely. But not here, not tending to business on Mount Scopus. Where Moshe had put her. His responsibility, just like the—well, the accident—back in England. A boy hidden away among the foliage in a tree, whom Moshe's novice driving had caused to tumble out and to hit the hard ground and to lose the use of his legs. So very long ago. But now, now this was the end-all, how could it not be? Because unlike that poor young stranger, Moshe loved Elli, loved her more than life itself. Because she'd left him a daughter, who kept him in life; a daughter whom he adored and resented bitterly, precisely because she kept him in life, when all he wanted was to be done with life and the illusion of hope and the assurance of guilt for his own unsoundness as a human being.

-440-

Rivka, devastated by Elli's death, searched high and low for Avram. Just when she needed his arms around her, that's when he held out against being found. For the second or third time, she approached his workshed, straining to hear him muttering within, to the dinking of metal against metal. Again no sound—but such a dark empty noiseless blankness of sound that it struck her he had to be in there listening to her moving about out here. Each one intensely aware of the other, and neither wanting the other to know. Rivka wavered. The plain wooden handle had given her a splinter once when it was new. Now it was smooth to her tentative touch. She eased her fingers around it, tightened them, and threw open the door. It squealed like a banshee, a dybbuk, a thing alive. There he was, crouched in the semi-darkness, his hair dust-covered, his cheeks streaked.

His red-rimmed eyes bored into her. She identified then what she'd already sensed without having given it a name. "How long?" she said.

He shrugged. "What does it matter?"

"How long?"

"A couple of years."

"Couple meaning two?"

"Two, maybe three."

"Maybe five?"

"Does it matter?"

"What did Elli give you that I couldn't?"

He squinted at his wife, a mountain of pain in his face. She longed to cradle him. She longed to throttle him. Between the two longings, she stood paralyzed in stiff grief.

"Was she good in bed? Better than me?" Rivka blurted. Not what she wanted to be able to fathom, but a practical substitute.

His grimy hands rubbed at his face. "She—said things."

"What things?"

"Names. She called it names."

No. Elli? No. "For heavens sake. Like Lady Chatterly? She didn't, she couldn't. What, like 'Ooooh, Abraham, father of nations?'"

"Rivka, please. Leave it be." He rose to full height, but Rivka, unmoving, filled the doorway. He sighed. He'd be forced to shove her aside to bring off any escape. He said, "Just ordinary names, slang terms. You know, like if I called yours pussy."

"Pussy?"

"Or cunt."

"And this you liked. For this you went to her."

"For friendship I went to her. For caring without owing

anything I went to her. For freedom, for fun. For I-don't-know-what. But I will miss her."

"Who else has there been?"

He looked every inch undone. He said no one, and she believed him. She wanted to ask if he loved her; she knew not to ask. "We both loved Elli," he said.

Tears filled her eyes. "If you hadn't made love to her, I would have. I'd have had the chance."

He never knew whether this was true, or just said to hurt him. Either way it hurt him.

In the night Avram held her as they both wept.

From somewhere in the distance came a faint rumble, distinctly an explosion. "I have to head north," he said.

"When?"

"Tomorrow."

"Is there no end to this endless fighting?" she implored.

He shifted onto his elbow. "This is only the beginning. It's the prelude."

She shuddered, as always when he made these somber pronouncements of his.

"But if we're lucky, it's the end of the beginning," he said.

-441-

Avram was gone in the morning. The prelude to war drummed on without pause: in Jerusalem, in Haifa, in Safed, in the Negev and all the way north near Lebanon. Everywhere the opponents put their hearts into the fight—the Jews to imbed themselves securely in the Land, the Arabs to uproot and strip them from it. That very night, April 15, Rivka had a ticket to the National Opera's first performance in Tel Aviv. They were doing Massenet's *Thais*—in Hebrew. God forbid the ticket should go to waste. She wouldn't go because of Elli, but sent Ahuva in her stead. Hard to say whether Ahuva enjoyed the music or not. Much of it she could barely hear over the screek and crackle coming from outside the hall. Tel Aviv's rowdy gunfire didn't impress her, she informed her mother. Even so, said her mother, Ben-Gurion was there in the audience, and didn't you get to see him up close?

-442-

British troops had been shipping out for home in their numbers. By April 21, the balance of the force was ordered to pull back to the port of Haifa. Until May 14, the Mandate announced, the High Commissioner, along with a small staff, would maintain a skeleton government in Jerusalem. At midnight of that date, its authority and responsibilities would end.

-443-

The Jewish holiday of Passover falls on the fifteenth of the Hebrew month of Nisan. As reckoned by the lunar calendar, this date usually coincides with the first full moon following the vernal equinox, when the sun on its trip north is directly above the equator. Passover in the year 1948 began at sundown on April 23. In the weeks leading up, observant Jews had been scouring their homes to make ready. All traces of leavened food were eliminated before the start of the holiday and would be shunned for its duration.

-444-

Ahuva 1
I suppose when you think of Arab Haifa you picture tin-

roofed shacks squeezed against each other; filthy streets full of groveling beggars and mangy animals; blind alleyways and seedy nightclubs where you smoke a water pipe while Latifah dances naked on a tabletop. All true enough, just not all that's true. I found another Arab Haifa after I moved here. I found a group of wealthy and cultured Arab merchants. Eventually, I was hired to look after their children. They led decent lives not very different from yours or mine. And I watched them all go. Over the past several months, between December and March, one after another picked their families up and deserted Arab Haifa, taking their businesses with them to Lebanon or Syria or wherever it's safe.

Did I want them gone? No, I tell you I did not.

-445-

Ahuva 2

Ha, ha! Don't you believe it. I did want them gone, every last one of them. We Jews need this city, need this country. Go ahead and sue us for being smarter, for being more adaptable, for working hard, for keeping our communities together in the worst of times and through centuries of troubles. After Hitler, with the world still shunting us off or outright killing us, are we Jews in a position to be tenderhearted and noble? Sometimes I listen to Arab radio. Well, I happen to like their music. I could do without their long-winded tirades against us. Why shouldn't we be suspicious of a people who my whole lifetime have been parading their spite in front of our faces? You want me to figure out who among Palestine's Arabs are innocent and who guilty? Have they asked the same question in their attacks and blockades on us? In starving our women and children?

-446-

Haifa's Arabs had always lived in the narrow maze of streets down by the harbor; Haifa's Jews had settled in the surrounding hills. In late April, the Haganah undertook two operations focused on the Arab sector. The first, Operation Scissors, was quickly and easily accomplished. Its mission, like a pair of scissors, was to cut off any possible aid coming to the Arabs from outside the city. With a nod toward Passover, the second was called, chillingly, Operation Cleansing the Leaven. It began with trucked loudspeakers urging Arab women and children to leave the city without delay. This advice did not go unchallenged. Haifa's mayor, Shabtai Levi, took to his own loudspeakers to encourage those same people to stay. He promised them no harm would come to them—but his voice was a chirp in what was becoming a howling wilderness.

Haganah's soldiers had their orders, which they doggedly set to carrying out: to force doors ajar—with hand grenades if necessary—to set fire to anything flammable, and to kill any Arab who might rear up against them. The air over the one-and-a-half-square kilometer area grew thick with smoke from gutted houses. The streets grew foul with a reek of death and decomposition. Is it any wonder that families deserted the bread and coffee laid out on their tables and fled in raw panic?

-447-

Fear and trembling invade me;
I am clothed with horror.

—Psalm 55

-448-

Before December 1947, Haifa's population included roughly seventy thousand Jews and an equal number of Arabs.

By late April, the Arab number had fallen to some forty thousand. Dawn of April 22 broke on most of those thousands jamming the streets to the port, carrying nothing with them but their terror. They heaved to and fro against one another in a clamor of sobs and curses and prayers and the wailing of frightened, half-smothered children. Above the din, what leaders they still had instructed them through loudspeakers to go to the old marketplace adjacent to the port, where an orderly evacuation would be arranged. Amid contradictory, alarming rumors, most of them were headed there. Then the unthinkable: Haganah mortars exploded into the eddying crowd in the market. Shrieks, and the now-crazed throng rushed the gates of the port. Its guards got muscled aside as the roiling, single-minded mob made for the handful of docked boats. In the frantic crush, parents lost hold of their sons' and daughters' hands. The old, the weak and the very young tripped or fainted and fell down—and were trampled. The stronger elbowed their way aboard vessels that were never meant to accommodate such a surge. The lighter craft quickly filled, overfilled and overturned. They sank, taking their doomed human cargo down with them.

-449-

Within a week, the Arab streets of Haifa were barren. The rich had already left the country; most of the surviving poor now sheltered in Acre. A small number did hunker down within the city, less than five thousand in all. They faced an even darker and more uncertain prospect than did the ones who'd taken flight. All-out war was just around the corner. Over the radio from Egypt, the Mufti kept pledging a massive Arab invasion that would once-and-for-all extinguish, wipe out and finish off the Jews. To the Jews, any Arab remaining in the Land was likely an anti-Jewish spotter and a spy. To Arabs looking forward to their inevitable victorious return, only a traitor would choose to stay and knuckle under the evil rule of Jews. From either side, the likely action toward those who remained behind would be a speedy arrest and a mindless execution.

-450-

Tali came home, something different about him. He strutted in and sank into the easy chair. His arms and legs splayed outward, claiming an excess of space. The sour stink of sweat and beer attended him. "Home is the hunter," he boomed, the announcement resounding off the walls of the room.

"Shh, I can hear you," Rivka said. "Your home is a what?"

"A poem I learned once in school. 'Home is the hunter from the hill.'" His eyes glittering.

"Where's your brother?"

"Where's yours?" he shot back. Then sniggered.

Her hands flew to her heart. "*Mischa?* Oh God, what are you telling me? What happened?"

"Nothing, Ima. Yudi's fine. Sleeping it off."

She moved toward the kitchen, grimly shaking her head. "Take a bath," she told him. "I'll fix you something to eat."

"Where's Abba?"

"Did you hear me?"

"Did you hear me?" he aped.

Shtarker! What made him think he could get smart with his own mother?

And still that odd gleam, like he harbored behind his teeth a first-class delicacy. "Your father has gone to Jerusalem to sit a while with Moshe. Your Aunt Elli was—" She swallowed, kept going. "Was killed. In the revenge raid. For Deir Yassin."

He stiffened. "Deir Yassin?"

Her throat swelling, she nodded.

"It had to be done, you see."

"*Vey iz mir.* You were there too?"

"No, unfortunately. That would've been the grandest moment of my life. No, Ima, I've been in Haifa cleansing the leaven."

Innocent blood was the morsel he'd been savoring. "Proud of yourself?"

"And the Lord said to me: do not say 'I am still a boy,' but go wherever I send you."

"Another poem you learned in school?"

"It's from the Bible, Jeremiah."

"You rebuke me with Jeremiah?"

"I tell you what I know."

"And what is that, my arrogant, foolish child—that the Lord speaks directly to you?"

"No, only that I do God's work when I stand up for Jews."

"Is that what you call it? Standing up?"

"Not just me, everyone. It's only you who's in love with the butchers that murdered Aunt Elli."

She blanched, her hand groping for a firmness to steady herself. He uttered an obscenity picked up from out of the gutter and got to his feet and marched away.

Tali mein tateleh.

-451-

Throughout Palestine, weary Arab families went without rest. Long, dusty queues of them choked the roads—women with wriggling children in their arms, girls balancing rotund bundles of clothing on their heads; men leading scrawny donkeys or pushing carts heaped up with household essentials. Some packed their belongings in trucks, some took only the shirts on their backs and the keys in their pockets. They crowded into the closest places of refuge—into Jericho, into Nablus, into Hebron, into Nazareth. From the ruined city of Safed they left for Lebanon, and—as word flew—from the villages of the Huleh Valley, as well. From Jaffa in their tens of thousands, they pressed south into Gaza. From the Galilee, thousands more fled to Transjordan. Some left by dint of Jewish threat and some by Jewish force. In this way the UN's crudely mapped Jewish borders were rejiggered. In this way— and minimally—the fetal Jewish state became viable.

-452-

May 1948 was ushered in by a new round of Arab attacks on the Etzion bloc. Since January, the four small settlements straddling the Hebron road had held out against all odds. Most of the women and children had been evacuated; the remaining handful of settlers had been strengthened by Haganah and Palmach reinforcements, who'd also contrived to fly in weapons and supplies by Piper Cub.

-453-

In Germany, a twenty-piece orchestra of survivors from Dachau played a concert conducted by Leonard Bernstein, who wept his heart out all the while.

-454-

Two weeks left of the Mandate and the time slipping by in a blur. So much going on, so many rumors flying. You can't go out early in a soft morning to see butterflies flitting and hear birds singing in the groves without exposing yourself to harsh tidings of strife close by. You can't travel any road and avoid facing down refugees on the move. Everyone is eager for the British to be gone, yet everyone leery of what will happen then. Up to the last hour, Jewish combatants are locking in the continuity of their territory, and Arab forces are thwarting them at every turn, crushing them at every opportunity.

From one end of the country to the other, Palestine drips blood. To stanch it, the United States now calls for a cease fire of three months. During that time, the UN would mediate a pact agreeable to both sides. Good luck with that! Three months? We've had three decades of mediation! Rivka holds onto the one good thing she can observe: unlike in Russia in 1917, none of the Jewish soldiers she sees are hungry, or ill-clad or grumbling. She hears nothing of desertion or of people going AWOL. On the contrary, morale is high.

"What will the Provisional Government do?" Rivka asks Avram, home for a few hours on a short leave before the expected long onslaught.

"You're asking me?"

"I want to know what you think. Are we better off accepting the cease fire?"

"If we do, we can't declare our own state. We could lose it all."

"And if we don't we could lose it all to the armies of Egypt, Syria, Lebanon, Jordan and Iraq." Counting the allied Arabs off on her fingers.

He shrugs. "So how will it help if we wait? What do we gain?"

"Avram, don't play with me. I'm asking you—will we win? Can we win?"

He takes her hand and holds it palm up. "Some say yes, and—" turning it palm down, "some say no." He waggles it, *comme ci comme ca.* "I say we have a fifty-fifty chance." And with a grin, "Such good odds we haven't had since the exodus from Egypt."

-455-

On May 12, the four settlements of the Etzion bloc were punished by a hellish Arab bombardment. Hollow-eyed men hunching in basements brooded—was this the rehearsal? Would the looming war inflict this nightmare on all of Jewish Palestine? Also on May 12, in the ongoing struggle for the Tel Aviv-Jerusalem road, the Haganah took the ancient hill fort of Gezer. The fort had been a wedding gift to King Solomon from the Egyptian Pharaoh. History, always history in this place, deep and abiding. And everyone now keenly aware that history would, within days, be of their own making. For on May 12, the Provisional Government of the Jews decided not to accept the cease fire.

-456-

May 13. Arab forces severed the Etzion settlements one from another. In armored cars they invaded the main settlement, Kfar Etzion. What happened next still hangs in doubt. That there was a massacre isn't disputed, but who, and why, and how many are matters for argument to this day. Most accounts agree that the Arabs ordered their captives—fifteen Etzion fighters—to stand in a line. Assembled as if for a group photograph, they were mowed down by a sub-machine gun. Hidden away in the cellar of the nearby Russian Orthodox monastery were an uncertain number of surviving Jewish noncombatants. They were ripped to pieces by a blitz of tossed grenades. According to one account, a local Arab family had stayed on, being friendly with the Jews. They, too, were murdered. Whether this grisly work was done by Arab Legion fighters, or by irregulars fighting with them, or by neighboring Arab villagers; and whether the killing was provoked in any way or inflicted willfully and without cause—in any case the name Etzion swiftly became a Jewish byword for courage, for perseverance, for unwavering allegiance.

The other three settlements in the bloc surrendered the following morning, the morning of May 14. Even their captors were stunned by the pathos of it: how the gaunt survivors hugged the earth, slinking ragged out of the ruins to be trucked to prison in Jordan.

One hundred fifty-seven men and women are known to have died in defense of the Etzion settlements. Fully a year and a half would pass before their unburied remains would be allowed to be gathered and then laid to rest on Mount Herzl.

-457-

By midnight on that same day, May fourteenth, the last British managers were slated to leave Palestine. The Mandate was at long last—and yet it seemed all of a sudden—at an end. In the morning, Rivka washed and dressed and pulled on her hob-nailed work boots. She filled a canteen with water and walked toward Leila's village. She came over the rise— Zarnuqua was gone! A void, just piles of rubble and the outlines of streets. Not a goat, not a chicken, not even a stray cat. In her distraction, had she come the wrong way? She swung completely around. No, here was the place, but the place had disappeared. Been erased.

-458-

She stumbled her way back home, not even trying not to let herself picture what had happened. Had there been mortars? Yes, now she recalled hearing them. And then the hand grenades. Where had the men gone—Syrians or irregulars or whatever—who'd infiltrated the village and sent Leila and the other women away to Yibna? Did they defend the villagers, or did they melt away when the shelling started? Was anyone left when the Jewish troops moved in? A few old men waving a dingy bedsheet? Or were there young men still, and some of their wives and children? They'd all be rounded up in the village center. There'd be an informer—you could count on the informers. From Nazareth to Afula, Avram had told her, large clans were collaborating with the Jews; why not from Gaza, as well? This collaborator would step forward, hooded to protect his identity while his rodlike finger pronounced judgment on them one by one—from a list, or out of his own animosities.

She imagined someone putting up a fuss. Someone like Leila's son Ibrahim, who'd always been rash. What would they do in the face of Ibrahim's protest, these brave Jewish troops? Shoot him on the spot? Or worse—humiliate him with a slap? Or worse—make him select some number of younger men, then have to watch them lined up against a wall, then the wall running with their blood? Or, worst of all, in his despair making him pull the trigger on the pistol they held tight against his own skull?

No doubt they'd marched the remaining few to the edge of the village and ordered them to run. Oh, run they would, with the soldiers shooting over their heads! A common practice, according to Avram. Scare them half to death, raze their homes, leave them with nothing.

-459-

And Leila? When they'd met many years before, Leila was

a young wife in the bloom of her first pregnancy. She'd called out from the head of the path to Rivka's kitchen, offering a tray of fresh strawberries for sale. Rivka liked the calm of her, not to mention the gloss of the produce at its peak of sweetness. Over cups of mint tea, it turned out that both women had, as girls, been dealt the chore of raising vegetables. Both came to prefer the romance of fruit. Out of such small likenesses a friendship was ignited. Where could Leila be now, and when would they see each other again?

-460-

Leila made a stay near Jerusalem, in Abu Dis, with her daughter Zeinab amid a cramped jumble of other relatives. Zeinab had walked there from Silwan, her mother all the way from Yibna. Leila became bent and hollow reaching Abu Dis. Her hair had streaks of gray. Never again in her life would she speak to Rivka.

-461-

At 4 p.m. in Rehovot, Rivka sat alone at the table in her kitchen, steam rising from the glass of tea in her hand. The radio broadcast from the main hall of the Tel Aviv Museum commenced with the orchestra playing "Hatikvah," The Hope. Its strains brought her to her feet. She took her glass to the window, rested her elbow on the sill and stared out. "Our Land," she murmured, "as long as we can hold it."

She hadn't the least notion what to expect from the Provisional Government. What could one find to say at this crux, this hinge, in time? Where find the words equal to a birth, a national letter aleph? Even so, moment by moment, each word that's said strikes her as the best and only thing to say. A Declaration of Independence for the State of Israel. She

chews on those words: declaration, independence, State of
Israel.

Perhaps you think the name Israel was preordained, and
also the flag, with its suggestion of both the *tallit*—the prayer
shawl in which Jews wrap themselves—and the six-pointed
shield of David. But there were other designs. There were
discussions, arguments and then a vote. The name might
easily have been Zion, Ziona, Judaea, Ivriya, Herzlia. Who
would go for any of those? And yet the choice became
irresistible only after it was made.

The world doesn't know this name until Ben-Gurion reads
out the Declaration of Independence over the airwaves. If you
look up this document, if you read it, imagine what it meant
to be standing at the kitchen window gazing over her groves
at the Jewish Land, and remembering all the years that had
brought her people to this place and time. What an honor to
be alive, to be at home, finally, in her Jewish homeland after
all those years of wandering and strife and hardship; yes, and
of joys—sunny joys, rare and sublime, although never
unsullied or uncomplicated, not even at this hour, by sorrow
and dread.

-462-

Shout, O heavens, and rejoice, O earth!
Break into shouting, O hills!

—Isaiah 49:13

-463-

After all those years the Jews had proclaimed a state—but
would they know how to govern it? I'll tell you how Rivka saw
they'd be all right, and perhaps you'll laugh. Not because of
Ben-Gurion, their able prime minister and minister of defense;

not because of the exiles, who could now be ingathered and settled in Eretz Yisrael according to no one's say-so but their own; not because they had their own orchestra playing "Hatikvah" at the ceremonies; not even because the new state was officially recognized by America in the eleventh minute of its existence. No, it was the littlest detail that showed Rivka they'd be all right. Ever after, in her pocket she kept a small glassine envelope. In that envelope was a postage stamp marked *Dor Ivri*, Hebrew mail. It had the minimal value: a three-mil yellow stamp with the image of an ancient coin showing a palm tree. That's how prepared her government had been. Not just with guns and bullets hidden away, but with postage stamps printed up in advance of the day.

Epilogue
1998

All at once they wanted to hear from her what she had to say. Like she was an oracle and would predict the country's next fifty years based on its first fifty. Like they couldn't get through their thick skulls that she didn't have to care what they wanted. She wished them no harm, but some of them behaved as if she owed them her time, her attention to their questions—their endless questions all so much the same. They were young, with the sharp logic of youth, and its foolishness. What was there to say? At twenty she'd been just as foolish, grown wise at sixty. But now? Now her reachable answers were too complex, except when they were too coherent. She felt sure if she could figure it all out, it would simultaneously morph into something else. Explain that, why don't you, to people who don't know you the way the old ones did. Or didn't.

The dead gathered round her at odd moments, sometimes mocking her, sometimes enfolding her in their ghostly arms. She had old scores to settle with many of them, was frightened of the rest. But still on the whole she understood them better than all the living: the woman who lived upstairs with six cats, the aide who visited five mornings a week, her almost-niece once a week on the phone from Seattle, even her daughter-in-law, Ivy, who twined herself around but never squeezed.

The boy had simmering eyes that were small and dark, overhung by slashes of straight black eyebrows. 'Boy,' she thought him, though he was already well into his twenties from the look of him and from the ease with which he wheedled his way in. They all looked like boys and girls from the viewpoint of two years short of a hundred years old. If their skin doesn't wrinkle and sag, if their bones haven't begun aching....

They treated her like it was an accomplishment to be born at the birth of the twentieth century and to be here still, like she'd set out to do life with a plan. What's your secret, they wanted to know, just as if she hadn't blundered into it. The only reason she agreed to talk to this young fellow is he didn't beg for her formula. His eyes didn't regard her wolfishly, like they envied and would snatch away her longevity at the first opportunity. She'd gladly give it away, if she could, even recognizing that she was bound to be relieved of it soon enough.

She'd refused him an interview over the phone. Twice. "You want my story? Where would you like me to start? At the beginning? When is that? The Babylonian exile? The Bar Kokhba rebellion? At what point was my fate—and yours—sealed? The Spanish Inquisition? The Kishinev Massacre? You see, one story leads seamlessly into the next. I should start with Adam, and maybe you wouldn't hang on."

"Isn't that what you want?" he said, just before she hung up the phone.

Then he showed up at her door. She quietly apprised him of her every right to call the police on him. For harassing her, for stalking her. Or whatever, he was a nuisance.

"I was born a month late," he said.

Something kept him fixed there—something kept her fixed there. What was it? He struck her as an ordinary *yidele*, straight dark hair, a long curve of Semitic nose, a clear complexion and full lips and white teeth and strong neck and wide shoulders and narrow hips—all the trappings of youth and health. No doubt he took them for granted and wasted his self-respect fretting over a mole on his back or the way his ears curled out from his skull.

He claimed he wasn't a reporter and had no interest in any old postage stamps she'd carried around for fifty years. Why should she believe him? And yet she invited him in. Well, she got tired on her feet and needed to sit down. He helped her to a chair without making her feel a thousand and ninety-eight years old, aged and frail and infirm—more like a suitor of hers escorting her after a turn around the dance floor.

"I saw your name in the newspaper," he said.

"I've never been in the newspaper."

His eyebrows rose. He shook his head.

"What newspaper? When?"

"*Ha'aretz.* A few months ago."

"No. Not possible."

"You were talking about your farm in Rehovot. 'Before Rehovot went upscale,' you said."

Had she? "So maybe I did give them an interview. I'm done with that, though. Tell your editor I said no." Her story wasn't for him. It was how she made sense of what happened. If she told him anything, he'd only find the meaning he wanted, which might have something to do with her, but not much.

She watched the fine hair rise and fall as he shook his head again. Already he was losing it in front. By age thirty, he'd be combing over.

"What paper did you say you're from?" she asked him.

He told her once again, as he'd said on the phone and at the door, that he wasn't a reporter, and this visit was strictly personal.

"Personal? How personal? You don't know me, I don't know you."

"I recognized your name in that article in the newspaper. It was the same name on some papers my parents left behind when they went back."

So this was the story he was making for himself. "Back?"

"My mother and father came here in 1978. I was a year old. They'd wanted desperately to be out of the Soviet Union. My mother's father—my grandfather—was a dissident, so they hadn't much of a chance there. They pulled some strings, I guess, and we came here. But they never really liked Eretz Israel, either. They hated the climate, hated the landscape, had trouble learning Hebrew. They thought the people were—"

"Were what?"

"Well, brash."

"I don't know what that means."

There was an awkward pause, during which the boy examined the pattern on her linoleum floor.

"But you didn't go back with them," she said finally.

"I'm an Israeli."

"You could have ducked army service."

"I like it here."

"You like the climate?"

"Yes."

"You like the landscape?"

"Yes."

"You like speaking Hebrew?"

"Of course. Although if you would, I'd prefer Yiddish."

"You like me?"

"Yes."

She'd have respected him more if he'd said no, or I don't know yet. People coddled you when you were old. They said what they thought you wanted: pap. Pap to hear, pap to eat, pap to see, pap for your spirit to gum on. But just you mutter one curse word the way the younger ones do all day—fuck me, suck you, shit on him—and they call you a nasty old witch. Say it a second time, and they decide you're well on your way to dementia, which only makes them sweeter and sappier still. She said, "You like me even though I'm brash?"

"I like you because you're brash."

She'd given him a second chance to lay off the pap. This was the result. She said, "Why do you want Yiddish?"

"It's the language my mother and father spoke to me. Now I don't hear it anymore."

Yiddish. Mischa died still ranking it as the mother tongue, Hebrew as the holy tongue—while in Palestine, we embraced Hebrew as our national tongue and would have nothing to do with Yiddish, it being the tongue of our wandering, our subjection and our ignorance. Only now, when Yiddish is close to vanishing from the Land, does she feel the want of its richness. When people argue their different points of view, you think you must choose, must take a stand. Maybe so, but never forget that whatever the issue, it's temporary, and in the end all sides may turn out to have had a piece of the truth. She said, "What's the Yiddish word for brash?"

"Oy, there must be a hundred of them. I think—yes, *chutzpadik.*"

In Yiddish, she said, "You must miss them, your family."

"Must I? Do you miss yours?"

Every hour she spent missing them. It was amazing how you could go on day after day like that, and how the days turned into weeks and then months. Soon it was year after year of missing them, and one part of her wondered how that could be, while another part understood completely, for though they were gone, they were more real to her than this impudent boy. So she just went on in the same old way, missing them, knowing that if she ever saw them again she'd break down and cry a hundred years. "I can bear it," was all she said.

He said, "They thought I'd be a simpleton, so late a birth.

They kept looking for something to crop up, something wrong with me. Finally they found it: I liked living here. I wanted nothing to do with Moscow. Not even to have a look."

"What do your parents miss about the Land?"

"I don't know. If it were me—"

"Yes?"

"I'd miss the butterflies. So many of them and so beautiful."

It occurred to her that of all the insects Shimshon had brought home not a single one was a butterfly. She said, "Every time a butterfly twitches its wing, something big happens somewhere in the world."

"I don't think so," he said.

"It's true. There's a name for it."

"There's a name for unicorns, too. And chimeras."

"The butterfly effect it's called."

"For me, it's enough that whenever I see a butterfly twitching its wing, something big happens inside my heart."

He brought her a honey cake the next time he showed up.

"You should have called to say you were coming."

"I was afraid you wouldn't see me."

He held up to her view something else he'd brought—the scrap of paper with her name on it. Her maiden name, Rivka Lefkovits, and in a different hand, her married name, Ben-Yohanan. She studied the writing, studied the paper, studied his face. "Who are your parents? How do they know me?"

He gave her their names and an address in Tel Aviv. It rang no bells. "Maybe through business? I ran a very prosperous citrus business, you know. I built it myself, ran it myself." The children—none of them wanted it. For a while she'd had hopes for Yudi. He'd watch the skies just like any farmer. It turned out that growing things had no allure for him. Weather, that was his interest.

"My parents weren't merchants or traders. They had nothing to do with the citrus trade. My father's an accountant. My mother had a job with *Keren Kayemet*."

"She managed land?"

"She was a clerk. Anyway, I think it was my grandfather who knew you. Or knew of you."

"I doubt it. I was barely seventeen when I left Russia. Unless—where was he from?"

"Originally Volhynia, I think."

She shook her head. "No—unless maybe they knew my brother? Mischa? Mikhael Mendelevich Lepkin I believe he called himself." Here, he'd have been Moshe ben Menachem Mendel.

"My grandpa's name was Yankel. I was named for him. Yankel Korngold. Somehow, he was related to you. A cousin?"

"No. No Korngolds that I know of. Just Schneiders, Rabinovitches, a few Tarnopols. Anyway, the ones Hitler didn't get, died in Stalin's Ukrainian famine." She alone remembered them.

"Is there someone else who would help you recall? A family member?"

So now he thought her senile. "No one," she said. In the years and wars since May of '48 she'd lost her family one by one. Her Ahuva only a five months later in the War of Independence.

Abruptly, she pulled herself up out of her chair, went to the sideboard and rummaged in the top drawer for a snapshot. After the '56 war she'd found it in one of Avram's pockets—the twins and Shimshon, hilly desert behind them, their arms about each others' shoulders. She supposed they'd all met up somewhere at the battlefield or in a rest area or on the way home. She never asked. Avram was different by then. He'd closed himself off, crying in his sleep, unwilling to talk about any of it. Now she tapped at the photo, Shimshon's puffed-out chest. "This one became a great warrior, serving the State of Israel well—quote unquote his obituary. Obits only got written for soldiers of particular courage, or daring, or those willing to do the ugliest jobs of murder. So that was my Shimshon."

"Handsome man," he said, a bit of flattery that set the pap meter buzzing in her head.

"Not my doing," she snapped. "He was adopted." When there was nothing to say, she preferred people say nothing.

Shimshon she lost in the '67 war, along with Yudi. Two children gone in six days only. The Yom Kippur war took Tali's life. Tali left behind a wife and a son. The son was killed by Palestinian guerrillas out of Lebanon while hiking near Mount Hebron in 1982. All the children gone, and she and Avram rattling around the big old house. Avram, who spent his entire life at war, died at home, a massive coronary while watching the news on tv, in 1985.

She toyed with her slice of honey cake. He was using the pad of his forefinger to lift the crumbs from his plate to his mouth. "You could take another piece," she said. He grinned, and his dimples were irresistible. "Now tell me, please, how did your parents have my name?"

"I don't know."

His gaze shifted from the photograph to the paper he'd brought and back again. Was he avoiding her eyes? She said, "It was barbaric, what we did then."

"It was necessary?"

"It made a Jewish state, which we desperately needed. It

piled up anguish, which we still suffer, along with millions of Palestinians."

He said, "I wish you'd tell me about those years."

She heaved a sigh. Now it was her eyes avoiding his. Finally she said, "There was a time we thought the Mandate would never end; and yet every year we expected the next one to bring something good to untangle our lives. Our sages taught us about the time when God entered history, and our scientists taught us about how time could bend. We believed the time had come when God would bend it to our will." She offered a sodden smile. "Were we right?"

He began singing the opening lines of 'BaShana HaBa'a,' and then hummed the merry chorus that predicts sardonically how good things will be next year.

"You have a nice voice," she said. It was full of sweetness and longing.

The fine hair rose and fell as he shook his head, saying nothing. She stood. "You'll find out why your parents have my name. You hear me? You'll find out, and you'll tell me, and you won't come back until you can."

A full week went by. She had the aide do some marketing and spent an afternoon baking rugelach for him. In the second week she made blintzes. This was something she hadn't done in years. She found she hadn't lost the knack of spooning the eggy liquid into the hot pan, swirling it to a thinness, then knocking the pan against her breadboard to release the fine skin. Later, she folded a dollop of sweetened farmer cheese into the cooled wrappers, making plump little envelopes. Now they huddled together in rows in the freezer and waited for his return. Perhaps they also feared he'd never come back again.

Old photographs now were strewn across her table. She spent her idle hours poring over them. Sometimes, she found herself talking to the boy who wasn't there, telling him each picture's story. Here was the only shot of Avram, and here one of the two of them together on their wedding day. "I suppose I never truly understood Avram, though we lived together sixty years and more. He was all Israeli, but he seemed to hold it lightly at the very times I held it seriously, and vice versa. He married one kind of girl, who turned into another kind of woman. Our thinking just got farther and farther apart, and I guess he missed his buddy." It wasn't until Elli's death and then Moshe almost succumbing in the blockade that she was ready to take up arms again. By then, she considered herself an old woman. Forty-seven years old: it's all in your perspective.

Somewhere she had a photo of Moshe and a few of Ellie. Where would she have put them? "They said Moshe died of a broken heart. If that's true, what does it mean about me?" Her heart had splintered many times over, but here she was, still breathing. Moshe, he never looked the type to last. After Elli died, he had a look of ill health. Paunched and bloated, he threw himself into his work. Plenty to do, with the war on for independence. He healed Arabs and Jews equally, and Marian was hurt by that. "Marian I lost touch with for a while. She married, had kids, moved to America. Then she got in touch with me from Seattle. Her husband's an archeologist of some sort, or maybe in forestry. Anyway, something outdoorsy. She became a teacher. Getting on in years herself now. Retired, waiting for grandchildren."

In the middle of the third week, he called. "Come tomorrow," she told him. "One o'clock. Don't have lunch."

He showed up ten minutes early and fumbled the jar of blueberry preserves he'd brought for her. "Perfect," she said. "How did you guess?" The frayed ghost of a smile was all she got from him. She spooned the fruit into a cut-glass bowl, sat him down at the table with its fresh cloth of embroidered whitework, served him the blintzes and sour cream, and after the briefest of suitable intervals inquired, "*Nu?* What did they say?"

"Who?"

"What do you mean who? Moishe Rabbenu and his 613 cousins is who. Or else you think maybe I mean your parents? What did they say to you?"

"I'm telling you, that's what they said. I gave them your name, and they said, 'Who?' So I mentioned the papers they'd left and the note I found...."

"And?"

"And they bawled me out. What was I doing going through those old records? Don't I know they're worthless and can only cause trouble?"

"Uh-huh. Just like you—worthless and troublesome, born a month late."

"Exactly like me. And also I should have known to throw out all that stuff. I had no business prying into their affairs."

Her fingers traced the embroidered patterns and twiddled beside her plate. "What if I get in touch with them?"

He blanched. "No. No, that would be worse. Them drumming me, 'Who is this woman and what does she want from you? What do you know about her? Nothing.' My mother says the note must be from Grandpa, and she has no idea how it came to be mixed up in their effects. 'Effects,' like the two of them are dead here. You see, they still think like Soviets."

"I understand."

"They're not like you and me," he added. She felt herself flush. He said, "Am I being presumptuous?"

She made him wait a good long time. At last, "Presumptuous?" she echoed. "Maybe not. I'd call you...brash."

He no longer looked glum. Must be the food.

"I'm sorry," he said later. "I did what I could to find the connection for you. I guess I should have looked into it before I ever contacted you."

"You did enough," she said. "Now it's my turn. What do you want to know about the old days? I'll do my best to tell you."

He had questions, a load of them, and for the most part she had her answers. It wasn't primarily the wars he wanted explained, though he did wonder how the Jews became good fighters. "Believe me, when you have to, you learn fast. Besides, we had the British, who in both world wars and in the Arab revolt, used us as fighters. They trained us how to attack, they taught us how to cow a crowd and stymie a prisoner, how to subdue a population. So well did they teach us that we ended up suppressing them. But of course, they had somewhere else to go. We did not."

She discoursed a full half hour on the various Jewish political factions in the Mandate and what she thought they stood for. He wanted to know how she viewed them now, after all this time. "You know, it's easier to have an opinion when you're young," she said. "When you get older, you've seen too much. What I think is that all of us were necessary—the ones who restrained and the ones who did not, the Zionists and the not-so-Zionist, the radical left and the revisionist right, Ben-Gurion and Jabotinsky, the Yishuv and the Diaspora supporting us. All of it necessary, all doing their part. Not a very satisfying answer, I suppose."

"All is for the best in the best of all possible worlds? Thank you, Professor Pangloss."

"What's that?"

A shake of his head, a wave of his arm. "Never mind."

But she did mind. "All I meant is that you can't say any one person or party did it all. In the end, even the ones I despised may have gotten us our country."

The gorilla in the room was *al Nakba*, the Palestinian catastrophe. When finally he broached it, she described Leila and Leila's family and the other Arabs she'd known. How they expected to come back, how they thought their Arab allies would make short work of the Jews. "It's no wonder they were angry later when Israel destroyed their villages and refused them return." The way her Avram looked at it, the Jews coming in had suffered at least as much as the Arabs leaving— and the Jews had nowhere else to go. At least the Arabs did. More than six hundred thousand Arabs fled Palestine; their places were taken by around the same number of Jews who left or were forced out of the Arab and Muslim lands of North Africa, the Arabian Peninsula, Syria and Lebanon. "The true Nakba, according to my husband, was the way the Arab world conspired to keep them refugees by refusing to absorb them."

The boy said, "You could say the same about all the Jews through history and all the lands they went to, while still dreaming of this Land."

"Not the same at all, since they weren't going to Jewish lands. The Palestinians could have been settled into other Arab lands." Avram used to pace back and forth, braying that it wasn't his fault the Arab nations kept the refugees poor and landless and helpless. They could have taken in those people, as we did the Jews who were mistreated and sometimes expelled from everywhere across North Africa in the late forties.

The boy didn't know Avram and didn't give a hoot about her husband's opinions. He cared about her, he said, about what she thought. He could read the history. God knew there were plenty of books to study, and he'd done some of that. What he wanted was her own idiosyncratic, personal, one-of-a-kind sense of things.

"Just because I've lived to see the year 1998 doesn't make me important or knowledgeable."

"But you are to me, Mrs. Ben-Yohanan."

"You're crazy."

"We've established that. Worthless and troublesome, too. Still, I'm a good listener." He grinned, and again she was charmed by his dimpled cheeks.

"Look, Yankel," she said. "Somehow we're at fault in the world because we did our homework. We built organizations. We worked every angle, yes we did. We accepted everything offered us, no matter how meager. We worked with anyone of good will and many who were not of good will. So because the Arabs didn't, we're at fault? We did this because we had nowhere else to go. We were a traumatized people, and this Land was our last hope. Were we ruthless? Yes. Were they? Yes. And if they could have pushed us back into the sea, they would have—making no distinction between Zionists and non-Zionists. Do I wish it could have been different? You know I do. Do I think it could have been? I did once. Now, I don't see how."

"You have no regrets, then."

"Of course I have regrets! How could I not?"

"It was awful."

"It was, yes. Still is." How we herded them and curbed in their lives, how every one of them still was a suspect. How our suspicion ate up our own souls. "Not a very happy ending, I'm afraid."

"But you would do it again?"

Would she? All those Palestinian refugees were our problem. Not the Arab world's, not the whole world's. Ours. And how badly we were handling it. She sighed, "Thank God it's not up to me." How tired she was.

The clock was rounding toward six. They'd been at it all afternoon. "You'll come again. We'll talk more if you want."

"Thank you. I want."

"It's good, I know how good, to slip into somebody else's world for a change and prowl around a bit with no responsibility for making up anything. But you'll have to make up your own story, you know, sooner or later. That's what this Land has always been about. The stories we make, those we tell each other and those we tell ourselves."

"Lies?"

"Well, sometimes lies. And by the way, stop calling me Mrs. Ben-Yohanan. I'm Rivka."

He said with a grin, "I'll call you Rivka if you'll call me by the name my parents use."

"I'm not interested in your parents. Your name is Yankel, after your grandfather. That's what you told me. Though if you're staying in Israel, maybe you'll think of something more up-to-date. Avner is a nice name."

"Actually, I'm thinking of Dov. You like Dov?"

"I do," she said, frowning.

"But that's not the name you'll use, Rivka. The name you'll use is Dudie."

She startled, as at a streak of lightning. "Dudie, they call you? No. Also after your grandfather?"

"Yes, after my grandfather."

She could barely breathe. "My little boy?" She scrutinized his face, explored every feature, gazing and gazing until finally he blurted, "What?" She explained then how she'd cared for a child in Russia and loved him from his bris at eight days old until he'd been torn from her two years later. She'd called him Dudie. "He remembered my name for him? He only knew a handful of words. How could he remember?"

"My mother once told me Grandpa didn't know himself why he insisted on the name Dudie, but all his life he wouldn't answer to anything else."

"How did he have my name?"

"I guess he could have heard it from my great-grandfather. I guess he could have learned his history and tried to trace you. I don't know. It's a mystery."

Dudie, her first child, had become a father and a grandfather. Not biologically her child, yet he was the one she'd given herself to whole-heartedly, as she'd never been able to again after she'd lost him. Now here, in proxy, he stood before her, another dissident with the same dark eyes, the same dark hair.

But still she wasn't satisfied. With trembling hands she started gathering the dishes. He got up to help. She caught his wrist. "Dudie died in bed?" she said.

"He died in bed."

"You know this for a fact?"

"He died in bed, in their house. A month later, I was born, and they named me Yankel Dovid after him, and I slept in his room. At night I watched the shadows moving in the corner and thought they were his ghost whispering to me. 'Find her.

Find her. I won't rest until you do.'"

"Now you're giving me a story. A ghost? Who do you think you are, Shakespeare?"

He shook his head, the hair rising and falling maybe a little bit like her Dudie's. He said, "More like Sholem Aleichem."

About the Author

Marilyn Oser lives in the Hudson Valley and on Long Island. *This Promised Land* is the third in a "loose trilogy" including *Rivka's War* and *November to July*. She is the author, as well, of the novel *Even You* and the blog *Streets of Israel*. An earlier novel, *Playing for Keeps,* was published under the pseudonym Jack Kendall.

www.marilynoser.com

Made in the USA
Columbia, SC
16 September 2022